THE KNOWLEDGE DANCE

As I sat there, the wall danced with reverberating light, as Khi-Rehm, Khi-Sang, and Khi-Lohm placed themselves at either side of me and behind me. The pulsing of their glow became rhythmic, making a pattern of flashes flicker through the walls like visible echoes. The light became hypnotic. I entered a half-waking trance, storing the knowledge that began to come to me in both my conscious and subconscious layers of being . . .

Ace Science Fiction Books by Ardath Mayhar

GOLDEN DREAM: A FUZZY ODYSSEY (trade edition)
HOW THE GODS WOVE IN KYRANNON
KHI TO FREEDOM

ARDATH MAYHAR

KHI TO FREEDOM

ACE SCIENCE FICTION BOOKS
NEW YORK

KHI TO FREEDOM

An Ace Science Fiction Book/published by arrangement with the author

PRINTING HISTORY
Ace edition/May 1983

ISBN: 0-441-43726-5

Ace Science Fiction Books are published by Charter Communications, Inc.
200 Madison Avenue, New York, New York 10016
PRINTED IN THE UNITED STATES OF AMERICA

To Beth Meacham,
who showed me what needed to be done

KHI TO FREEDOM

Hale Enbo

There's nothing in the universe as bored as an off-duty Scout. To be stuck on a vessel full of Ginli with nothing to do but devour the library or stare at the wall is a thing that brings out the worst in me. Always has. Even back on Big Sandy, when I was a boy, my folks found out early that they had to keep me busy. Idle hands and all that, you know.

We had been in orbit around a middle-sized planet for entirely too long. The Ginli techs were scanning the place with unusual care, and I'd been wondering if it would be my good luck to be assigned to go down there and accumulate the usual assortment of specimens and geological readings. I hoped so, but I doubted it. They had had me boning up on wet-planet techniques again, though after some of the assignments I'd had anyone but a Ginli would have taken it for granted that I knew how to handle myself on such a world. Otherwise I'd be long dead and forgotten. The planet below seemed, when I could sneak a peep through a scanner, to be a goodly mix of land-mass and small-sized seas.

The ship-days were long and full of nothing much. My stints of studying were skimpy, I'll admit, but perusing something you know as well as your own name is deadly. So I managed to poke around into places I hadn't had a chance to see before.

That ship was big. It wasn't, you understand, of Ginli design or make. The Ginli wouldn't admit that, but all intelligent beings know that the Ginli are technologically deficient. Mentally, too, I had found out the hard way, but nobody would believe me even if I ever had a chance to tell them. I never did, having worked alone and lived mostly to myself even on shipboard since I was eighteen and got roped into a Ginli contract. My employers didn't approve of Scouts getting too friendly with their peers, either. And as it was necessary to be a loner in order to make a good Scout, that didn't bother any of us as much as you'd think.

So I spent a lot of time slipping along the dim corridors in my best silent-woodsman style, having a great time startling Ginli by touching them on the shoulders and asking abstruse questions that I knew they couldn't answer but would be flattered to be asked.

That palled after three days. I had never before been stuck for so long without anything to do; usually between assignments they put us into hypno-sleep. It's a great time-waster but better than this boredom. And my real life was conducted on wild green worlds teeming with all kinds of creatures, both intelligent and not. That was where I really felt at home and comfortable, even if I had to spend all my time fending off affectionate furry worms or paddling through endless knee-deep swamps. That, in fact, was where I formed my attachments with others. Note that I didn't say other people. Just others.

I'd better make it clear that the Ginli were not looking for other intelligent life in this galaxy. On the contrary, they were looking as hard as they (and we) could manage for evidence that only Primates, in all the worlds and all the galaxies, are truly and basically rational, thinking creatures. And as we Scouts constantly run across highly developed civilizations on worlds tenanted by ursinoids, felines, and even reptiles, that makes our job harder than necessary. We've learned, every Scout among us, to delete evidence that goes counter to Ginli goals, no matter how important our discoveries may seem to us. Better that than brain-train, believe me.

Anyway, I found myself entirely too antsy to do any of the normal things one does when bored stiff, so I waited my chance and slid through one of the irising portals that separates the living and working portion of the ship from the labs and specimen-pens. I'd wanted to get in there since my first Scout. The Ginli had kept me too busy to do anything about it, until now. That was a major error on their part, as it turned out.

I'd followed a gray uniform (they wore that shade to match their skins) to the portal, then melted into the wall and waited. Ginli are not a noticing people, among many other flaws of physique and character, and poor Twenty-Six (they think names are effete frills) never realized that passageway walls don't have mansized lumps in them. He turned, when the hissing of the opening began, and I was right up against his back when he stepped through. Even then I almost got caught in the closing petals.

It looked just like the rest of the ship, gray corridors with dim light-strips set so far apart that the light was no brighter than a planetary twilight. The Ginli are famous for their thrift. Round-topped hatchways lined both sides of the way, all closed except one. As Twenty-Six went into that one, I padded on down the passage, trying pressure-locks on my right. I figured that I'd catch those on my left as I returned. My plan went slightly astray, though, when the portal at the other end of the section began to hiss. Somebody was coming through from that end, and it would be a big-wig for sure. Only they had access to the area beyond that point, as I knew from my researches into the ship's plans in the library.

I then had one of my most inspired ideas. That end of the corridor was even dimmer than the rest of it, for the light-strip had burned out and hadn't yet been replaced. I rushed to the wall beside the closure and flattened myself against it, as I'd done before.

Just in time. Six, the commander of this vessel, stepped through. Just behind him was Ten, who was in charge of all the specimens. He was saying something to Six, very urgently, but I was so intent on getting through that opening without being seen that I paid no attention to his words. And I did get through, scooting between him and the iris with exquisite timing.

This was just another Ginli corridor, and I had begun moving along it, trying pressure-locks, when the hissing behind me told me that either Six or Ten was returning. And at the same moment a lock responded to my touch, opening into the kind of small space that should have been a storage-room. I went through like a greased eel and pulled the door to behind me. My heart was thumping uncomfortably, and I sat down on something to catch my breath. A Scout, who has made his solitary way through the most perilous of places, shouldn't be so shaken by the chance of being caught doing something forbidden by the Ginli.

Still, I had always had a creepy feeling about my employers, though they had always been impeccably correct in their dealings with me. There was something behind those colorless eyes that hinted at things I didn't want to see at closer range. They were heartless bastards, the Ginli, and nothing in the literature ever tried to say anything different.

As I sat there, almost panting in the total darkness of the little room, I found myself running my hand along the wall a foot from my right side. There was a switch there, and I flipped it with enthusiasm. A little light would help a lot.

There was light, all right, but not in the room with me. The wall wasn't that at all, but opaqued glass that was cleared at once by the action of the switch. I found myself looking into a white space filled with instruments. There was Ten, in his lab coat, saying something inaudible to Number Forty, the surgical tech who was seldom seen anywhere in the rest of the ship. It looked like . . . and it was, I realized . . . an operating room. On the small table that rose between them was a limp shape. It took me a moment to recognize it. It was a Fleer!

That brought me up short. I had brought the three specimens of Fleer to the ship. Theirs had been the last world I had examined for the Ginli. And according to universal law, they had no business poking around with one of the little beings unless it was ill. The law was quite specific about examination of specimens. Dissection was a vile memory among all the rational races we knew, since scanning-machines could give us far better rundowns on the physical and mental attributes of any living thing than carving up a dead one ever could.

Ten nodded. Forty picked up a scalpel and ran it along the underside of the creature's arm, deftly avoiding the limp hand with its six slender fingers. Bile rose into my throat. I remembered the lovely sculptures that such hands had carved into the rabbit-like creatures' warrens. I'd been allowed to crawl, snakewise, into one complex to see. The Ginli, of course, hadn't been told that the Fleer were intelligent beings, but I couldn't see that that made any difference. The law made none.

The Fleer's narrow mouth opened. I couldn't hear its scream, but cold sweat popped out all over me. It wasn't even sedated, and they were skinning it!

I looked about the room in which I sat. A blocky chair sat beside the one I had taken. I lifted it and swung it at the glass with all my strength. Glass exploded into the dissecting-room, shards nicking the two Ginli and glittering all over the floor and the little Fleer. I was in my regular Scout garb, complete with innumerable pockets and attachments. I had my tranquilizer gun in my hand when I followed the glass into the room. A second later, both Ginli were down, sleeping the sleep of the just, though neither could claim that title.

The little Fleer looked at me, its eyes glittering in the harsh light. Its lips moved, and I knew what it was saying when I got a look at its lower body. They had already partially eviscerated it. I blinked back the tears in my eyes and broke its neck with one short chop of my hand. If I had had one suspicion that the Ginli were breaking every article and intent of the investigation laws, I would never have put one single creature, large or small, rational or not, into their dirty hands.

I paused for a long moment, getting myself in hand. I'd done it now. There was no way the Ginli could or would let me go free to spread this unpalatable truth. They were very careful of their reputation among the other varieties of Primate that tenanted the worlds. And besides, if the truth were known, they would be confined to their own planet. Nobody would be allowed to lease or sell them a ship or to carry them as passengers until they were found to have brought themselves into a more civilized state.

I had to run for it and hope I'd be luckier than I deserved to be. I closed my eyes and pictured the schematics of the ship. Lifeboat stations aft—ahh. There should be a life-bay at the end of this segment of corridor. If there were no Ginli in the passage, and if I managed to open the hatchway leading into the bay, and if I could boot it loose from the ship before the alarm sealed the outer hatches, I might just make it.

I bent over Ten and felt up and down his coverall. And there it was—the master key that all the Brass used. I unzipped the pocket and took the thing out, then went to the door and palmed the lock. The door slipped aside into the wall, and I burst out at full gallop. At this point, caution made no sense at all. Only speed could help me now.

I bowled over a small-sized Ginli who was carrying a covered tray along the corridor. Before he hit the wall, I was at the hatch of the life-bay. The master was in my hand, and I was through faster than it takes to tell it. With much relief I heard the hatch slide shut behind me. At least I'd be uninterrupted while I figured out the procedure.

It was simple, after all. If, that is, you read Ginli, which was a thing strictly forbidden to all non-Ginli personnel. But, none of the Enbos ever took kindly to rules, and old Hale less than most. I'd learned to speak and to read Ginli while being educated for my work as a Scout, and none of my employers had suspected it. So a lever marked, "Outer Hatch" invited pushing, and one that announced, "Emergency Drive" insisted on being moved along its slot. I could hear the connections with the ship being broken. The light wavered as onboard generators took over.

Light poured in from the outer hatchway, which was wide open in an instant. I hit the drive, and power pulsed through the little craft and the seat of my pants. We were off!

It took seconds for the drive to overcome inertia. We moved, but too slowly. I could see the wide sky, an orange sun. Then I felt a jarring, ripping, screeching of metal in the aft section of the lifeboat. I held my breath, but there was air. No hissing announced a breach in the cabin compartment. I took it that I had lost something back there, but it was too late to worry about it. I shoved the power lever all the way up. The lifeboat shuddered. Then it took off like a Varlian through treetops.

The Ginli ship came into view through a side port. Uh-oh! The rear steering-vanes that allowed the boat to land on a world with fair gravity were sticking out of the now-closed hatch like mouse-legs from the mouth of a smug cat. That blew it.

But there was a world rocketing toward me with terrifying speed. I was reading monitors, checking readouts on the survival-scopes, and hoping. Then we hit, that sturdy little boat and I, and it wasn't a clean landing at all.

II.

The Hril Who Watches

Amid the long work of watching physical suns and planets, energies and material things, living and almost-living things, there came a spark of unusual interest. I focused my thought upon that phase of time and space and held myself ready. The one we waited for was moving within his own skein of time toward the point at which we must take part in his life and education.

Some among the Hril have asked why we trouble ourselves concerning the happenings among those who are, after all, only figments of our thoughts. That is not asked by those of us who watch, for we can see the shadow of ourselves in these creatures we have made. They, too, in their small ways, are groping toward enlightenment. Only the fact that we have been far longer upon the road has given us the power to make and unmake their kind.

And we know dangers. Such a peril is there, in its spot in the weft of time that is in the future of this one for whom we wait. We, in our present forms, would be unable to control it and to return it to its own place. It would devour us and our nearest servants, for we are, as it is, energies focused into purposes.

Nearer at hand there is the problem of the Ginli. One who had not scanned that physical future carefully enough conceived of them. Now all must quease at their doings among their fellows in that small corner of all that is. They must be taught or unmade. There is no third alternative. This task, too, awaits our pupil.

Outside time, we can see all possibilities. If this one who

even now approaches Khi-Ash is able enough, strong enough, he may make the correct decisions at the proper times. We do not—perhaps cannot—compel him or any of our creations along the ways we would have them go. Chance and individual choice seem inextricably woven into the weft of all that is. As we grow nearer and nearer to the Total Enlightenment, we see even more clearly that only through free choice is any good thing made or done.

That has been made clear to us, with many other matters that were obscure, by those who instructed us upon our way. For we are not the last nor the ultimate dwellers along the interdimensional layering.

Beyond us, there are still greater Others.

III.

Hale Enbo

The bushes were thick and springy, covered with leaves that blazed with fantastic color. Peering cautiously through that autumnal foliage, I could see the beach clearly, a strand of white sand that curved gently inward, just here, and was lapped by purplish waves. That lapping effectively screened any footfall that might have moved behind me in the forest. I scuttered backward as silently as possible to find a safer place to wait. The Ginli were looking for me, I was certain, and my tranquilizer gun, my only weapon while aboard ship, had been smashed in the crash of the lifeboat.

The forest was quiet. Too quiet for a world that had evidenced the many lifeforms the scanners had indicated. Perhaps my presence—or that of the Ginli—had hushed the native beasts. With that in mind, I looked about for a tall and climbable tree. Though I invariably mock the Ginli, that is little more than a matter of whistling in the dark. They are dreadful people. If they catch me, I will spend eternity in a jar—my brain, which is the only important part of me—as a part of a guidance system. I do not intend to be caught alive, but I also do not intend to die unnecessarily.

A few rods into the wood, I found a thick-trunked grandsire of a tree, with low-growing limbs within springing distance. Like all its companions that I had seen, it was clad in leaves that merged from cream through golden amber to scarlet. The deepest tone was brown, and it would have been a wonderful forest for a wounded man to hide in. Blood wouldn't show at all. Luckily, my inept landing hadn't damaged me much.

As I settled into the thick branches halfway up the tree, I heard the vicious *zzzip!* of a Ginli scoutship. I crouched low as it slashed across the sky, but that reassured me, too. They probably weren't expecting to find me in one piece, after the job the hatch had done on the lifeboat. It was doubtful if any search parties had been sent down . . . at least, not as yet. And maybe, with luck, they would decide that nobody could have lived through the mess the landing had made of the lifeboat.

Nevertheless, I'm a great believer in the adage that it's better to be safe than sorry. I found a comfortably wide junction of fat limb with tremendous trunk and stretched out. From my lofty perch, I could see a fair distance across the forest. A maker of Persian rugs (the Ginli favored those priceless things) would have gone mad with joy, for this world was done in all those warm shades in which his kind delighted.

It puzzled me that none of the present generation of planet-grabbers had yet invaded this beautiful world, cut all the trees for shipment off-planet, and settled a bunch of swindled and enthusiastic colonists on what was left. Having grown up on just such a world, I knew their methods well. My trusting grandparents had found themselves settled on Big Sandy, where wind-driven sand bombarded everyone twenty-seven hours a day.

Another *zzzip!* announced the passage of another Ginli scoutship—or the same one. I didn't look up to see. I was becoming bored with the Ginli. Enbos don't like being terrified. They tend to turn it into amusement, if possible. And the Ginli had no sense of humor, which gave me a royal pain. They took themselves and their project so *seriously*. It is, as anyone knows, impossible to limit intellectual development to Primates, but this slight matter of the facts would never deter the Ginli for a moment.

If, of course, I'd known the sort of people they were, I'd never have contracted with them, even to learn a profession and to get away from Big Sandy. They were offering good terms, guaranteed by the Contract Commission of our sys-

tem, to youngsters of Primate descent. They offered a good
education, albeit strictly slanted toward their own purposes.
It had looked like a wonderful deal to a boy who had spent his
entire life battling the wind and the sand and the cantankerous
beasts we grow on my home planet.

After I'd gone through most of my training and had devoured their micro-library from end to end, I understood a lot
more than I had. But it was too late. I owed them the term of
my ten-year contract, and the only thing my prideful people
had given me was a stubborn insistence on paying my debts.
Only when I found them dissecting the Fleer did I decide to
jump, and that couldn't be called a rational decision. Just the
logical outgrowth of my instinctive reaction to their activities.

So here I sat in a tree, watching what could easily be my
last sunset. In a fairly peaceful state of mind, I might add.
Somewhere, away off in the increasingly dark sky, the Ginli
lab-ship waited for the scoutship to report me safely dead in
the wreckage of the lifeboat—or elsewhere.

That might come about by means other than Ginli, I
thought, scanning the dark distances. I'd learned to manage
on all sorts of strange worlds as I went about the Ginli's
business, but that didn't mean that I hadn't missed being
eaten or inhaled or otherwise ingested by local fauna (or
flora) by narrow margins. And that was on planets that had
been catalogued enough for me to study them in advance in
the library. This place wasn't even marked on the computer-
charts in the lifeboat. I had no way of guessing what it
held—besides, of course, Ginli.

It got darker. Reds faded into grays as the sun went down
beyond the reaches of forest. The stillness that had disturbed
me was now broken by rustlings, squeaks, hisses, and muffled roars. It was reassuring.

There was no hint of the terrible racket that accompanied
a Ginli expedition in wooded countryside. Their inflexible
method of progress was the exact reason they needed Scouts
from among the ''lesser'' Primates, who could not, of
course, be considered the equals of Ginli. Nothing alive that
had ears could be sighted, much less caught, by any band of

Ginli that ever had been sent out to hunt for specimens. In addition to a lack of humor, they lacked imagination. They did everything "by the book," and their book had been written by other Ginli. Adapting method to circumstance wasn't even a minor footnote. Still, if some accident or carelessness should betray me to them, I would be just as dead as if they improvised brilliantly, laughing all the while.

So I made myself comfortable in the tree, closed my eyes, and tried meditation to quiet my growling interior. At that instant I became aware of something inside my head that had never been there before. It was a sort of subliminal murmur . . . something like a radio transmission picked up so faintly that you could hear the voices but you couldn't make out the words, which seemed to be in a foreign language, anyway. There was no feeling of urgency or immediacy, though. In fact, I had the strong feeling that whatever it was didn't concern me at all. Whereupon I went peacefully to sleep.

I woke with the feeling that I was being watched. That being the last thing in anyone's world I wanted, I opened my eyes cautiously and slanted them as far as I could manage, back and forth without moving my head. I could see nothing but the browny-red bark of the tree and a fan of bright leaves. Well. I made a good show of waking up, sitting up and stretching as normally as I could manage. As I turned to hang my legs off the wide branch, I looked up into a pair of curious, dark-green eyes. They were set in a face covered with green fur, and that brought me up with a start.

My inadvertent motion startled the creature. It drew back into the branches, which were thick enough to hide even its obtrusive coloration. It had to be a Varlian. It was against all logic that a green-furred creature had evolved upon a planet with warm-colored foliage, and the readouts of the lifeboat had assured me that it was setting me down in a spot where it was midsummer. This was not autumnal foliage. So that must be a Varlian.

I sat still, waiting for the devouring curiosity of its kind to bring it back into view. They had been, I well knew from my training and library-absorbing, widely distributed on suitable planets by a race that my kind called the Ffryll. From the scanty information available when Man arrived in this galaxy we had learned that the Ffryll had been a fairly harmless, curious, spacefaring race with one trait that eventually proved fatal to them. They had an insatiable appetite for one small creature halfway between monkey and man. They planted it on planets with climates that let them thrive and multiply (first making certain that no intelligent inhabitants objected) and allowed them to breed. This had insured that their favorite delicacy would be available no matter what their comings and goings about the systems or how far they might wander from their home planet.

It hadn't worked all that well. A planetful of Varlian had contracted an internal parasite that did them no harm at all. It just killed off all the Ffryll. That much had been chronicled by a very ancient feline-descended race, the Fssa, who had been much amused by the mishap, as they preferred Varlian to Ffryll, anyway.

I had met Varlian on most of the planets the Ginli had investigated. I liked them, too. They were about the size of a ten-year-old human child, and their fur was almost the exact shade of the lime sherbet that my mother used to make once a year from expensive, imported limes, at Festival-time. Their faces were so nearly human that you forgot the long, brachiating arms, the prehensile toes, and the short, strong tails.

If this *was* a Varlian, and the species had survived here for so long, I knew that there could be no large arboreal predators on the planet. Or at least on this continent. That was a relief. It's hard to sleep with all your senses alert for surprise attack.

While I reviewed my Varlian lore, the creature crept back into view. I didn't move. Soon it edged nearer. After about a half-hour we were sitting within arm's-length of one another, looking eye into eye. Though I sat still, it slithered about, scratching a haunch or an ear, wriggling its nose. Now and again it risked laying a pink-palmed hand for an instant upon the toes of my boots or the sleeve of my overall. When it was confident enough to touch me on the knee and put its face close to mine, I knew it was safe to move again. I stretched a cramped leg and did a bit of scratching on my own.

There came another *zzzip* as a Ginli ship began its morning search. The Varlian looked up with a most humanly annoyed expression on its face. For a moment it stared after the now-receding craft. Then it tapped me on the knee, very deliberately, rose and descended the tree. As the Ginli emitted either a physical scent or a mental aura that repelled Varlian on every planet where I had found them, I felt certain that it would be safe to follow.

Standing at the foot of the tree, I looked up. Even concerned as I was with survival, I was held still for a moment, admiring the sunlight striking through the stained-glass foliage. Nothing I had seen on the many-dozen worlds my ship had set me onto had been comparable. When I looked down again at my companion, I found it studying me with something like a smile. At that moment, I realized that the murmur in my head had grown more defined, though it was neither distracting nor uncomfortable. It was like a purr from a satisfied cat, perhaps. Or the ripple of a small stream. And it was concerned, now, with me.

The Varlian chattered softly in its too-rapid-for-interpretation tongue and took me by the sleeve. As quietly as I could, I followed it through the forest. Never having been disrupted by the doings of a culture, the wood was clean of low-growing brush. Its roof of bright treetops let only an occasional sunbeam through to touch the soil, which was covered by a springy cushion of mulch that had accumulated for millennia. The going was easy and quiet. Once we heard a noisy bunch of Ginli thumping through the wood, and we made a wide arc around them and went on our way. But that gave me pause. Were they looking for me or for something else—something that had held them in orbit, scanning closely for all these weeks?

My companion looked back, when we were well out of their path, and made a gesture toward their position that looked to me as if it were mightily insulting. Then it laughed, a real rolling-on-the-ground, tear-making laugh. I began to chuckle.

When you really thought about them, the Ginli were, among all their other attributes, extremely funny. When, of course, you were *not* in their hands.

IV.

L'K'K'T, the Varlian (Called Lime)

Matters had been strange in our forest for many weeks. Things that were not birds had been seen in the sky, and there were moving lights in the night that were not consistent as are the paths of the stars. Worse, pale-skinned creatures had been walking through our trees, tearing and breaking the bushes and vines.

The Elders had sent me to consult with the Khi, and I had made the trip to their valley and was returning when there was a terrible noise overhead. It was late afternoon, and the red sunlight caught something smooth and bright as it went across the sky. Not flying. Falling. It was very obvious that the thing was wounded . . . even dying, perhaps.

If the Khi had been more reassuring, I might have followed the path of the thing even through the dark hours. But they had been full of warnings.

"Do not approach those pale people in the wood. Stay hidden from them and from any of their ships that come low over your village," they had said. "You are able to deal with them when you are awake, but they do not live by honorable rules, and they might attack your villages while all are asleep."

I had been hard put to believe this, but the Khi speak only the truth, and I knew that it must be so. Therefore I oriented myself to the path of that falling thing, followed it as long as there was light, then went high and slept until dawn.

I woke early, though the horizon was beginning to show pale in the east. Impatient to be done with this, I began slipping through the treetops toward the place where the thing

16

must have gone down. Halfway down the first long branch leading into the next tree, I heard something crashing through the forest. I hurried into the highest, thickest part of the new treetop and curled into a ball—the color of our fur is not easy to hide among the bright shades of the leaves. Below, a group of those creatures went thumping past. If they were looking for the wounded thing, they were going in the opposite direction, which pleased me.

As soon as they were out of my hearing, I went forward, more cautiously this time. The sun was well up when I swung into a particularly large nut-tree and came to a sudden stop. In the crotch formed by its lower branches lay something unusual. It looked something like those I had just seen in the forest, yet there were differences. It was quiet, for one thing. Though it was many times my size, still it looked vulnerable in some odd way. Besides that, it was a strange color—rich brown like the veinings of the *krr* leaves. It was, of course, asleep, and I felt that it was probably hiding from those others.

While it slept, I went forward to find the spot where the hurt thing had fallen. It was a tool, not a living being, and it was terribly smashed. The track of the sleeping creature in the tree led from that place, so I knew that he had been with it when it came down. Strange—was it a thing he rode? That would be interesting to learn from him.

When I came back to the tree I sat on a high limb and felt for the Khi within my mind. The hum was there, filled with approbation. This, then, was not one of those they had warned me against. Should I help him? The hum grew stronger. And that was good, for my own instinct told me that that was the thing I should do.

It was in my mind that my young would find delight in him. There was something about him that I felt would respond to children. Too, the Elders should see this new kind and assess it for our records. We have studied all the creatures of our part of this world, with the help of the Khi, and we learn much from them to enrich our own lives. Such an alien being as this should have valuable things to add to our store.

I knew when it slipped out of sleep. It knew that it was being watched. I saw its muscles tense very slightly, then relax again. Very wise, under the circumstances. It made a show of awakening, then turned to look at me directly. It jumped a bit, and that startled me so that I, too, jerked back into the leaves. Then I recalled myself. The Khi hum rose in my head purposefully, and I moved forward again, very slowly so as not to startle the being.

Very quietly, I touched its arm and said, "Come. I will take you to the Khi. You mustn't stay in the forest alone, for those stupid creatures will surely find you if you remain so low in the branches."

It didn't understand my words, of course, but it was evidently an intelligent being and it came without protest. As it was obviously not made for traveling through the treetops, I descended to the ground and started out toward the Home. My mate waited and would be beginning to worry; and I wanted one night of rest in my own hammock before I started the long journey back to the valley of the Khi with this rather awkward and ignorant creature.

It traveled well aground, I had to admit. Its long thick legs out-stepped mine in distance, though with effort I managed to stay ahead. Ground travel is, however, a thing that my kind does seldom. Though I knew the rules and the dangers of such a course, I had grown careless. Only a warning from my companion gave me time to leap clear . . . one of those miserable serpents that the Khi brought into our world for its strange coloration almost fanged me as I crossed a stream. That serpent gives a messy death.

We had been lucky to avoid predators thus far. As I focused the will of the Khi upon the snake, I realized that we must take to the trees, awkward as that would be for this creature.

And it was terribly awkward. My youngest at one year of age was infinitely more skilled at getting about the treetops. The being's furless skin oozed moisture as it struggled through the branches, slipped upon brown-mossy bark, tried to follow me hand-over-hand in the crossovers.

From time to time it would call to me in its deep, booming voice, and I would come back and sit beside it as it panted and rested. I could understand something of its problem. Its far greater weight must put terrible strain on its arms as it swung across the gaps. Its hands had not the unbreakable grip that is built into mine. Its feet were worse than useless—even when he removed the coverings from them, the toes proved to be short and without any capability of grasping.

Worst of all was its lack of path-sense. I had taken for granted all my life that any sentient creature could measure ahead of itself a sure route through the branches. This one was obviously bright, the effort it was putting forth was easy to see, but it had no eye for sound growth, no instinct for dead-end ways. Time after time I had to rescue it from dilemmas and lead it back to the good ways that I could see without thinking about them. At last I realized that I must act as a guide for him, giving him a way to follow.

It took him a time or two of getting off the track and being scolded before he understood that I had taken on the services of guide. Then he did make better time. I could, of course, have come and gone four times while he was making the distance once, but it was not too bad considering his inability.

The People did take to him. My own young adopted him as one of them, though he was so huge and so brown and so clumsy. The Elders, too, were well impressed with his bearing and his manner. They were not at all surprised to learn that the Khi wanted him to come to them, though they were most amused when I told them how he had been induced to go into the treetops—did I mention that one of our larger beasts darted from its burrow and almost had us both for breakfast? Even a Varlian never went into a tree more quickly than this newcomer did when faced with those big teeth.

The Elders did not, of course, require that I take this one to the Khi. Our society is not organized in that way. Each does the thing that he does well and happily, which makes for both harmony and good workmanship. My roving nature makes me something of a messenger and scout, and I enjoy moving about the forest, even with those grublike creatures hacking and smashing their way around it. I volunteered to go with our guest, and Owl, my mate's sister, said that she would accompany us.

So it was that I set out for the valley of the Khi for the second time in a very short span. This time I was burdened with this large brown Hale Enbo, but Owl took the most onerous duties upon herself, leaving me free to scout through the wood, to watch for the Ginli (Enbo's term for them, which is more respectable than ours), and to rest while waiting for my companions to make their laborious way to me so that we might go on together.

It was a strange thing. The longer that I remained in the company of this oversized, ill-smelling creature, the fonder I grew of him. There was something about him—a childlike good will and interest in everything that made me think of him as one of the young. Willful, at times, and not always wise, but worth the effort of guiding and protecting.

V.

Hale Enbo

We traveled at what seemed to me to be a good pace, though I could tell that the Varlian was frustrated at being unable to go skiting through the trees as he was used to doing. He kept looking up longingly, then gazing sidewise at my obviously inadequate arms. I noticed, as he trudged along, that he was getting a bit footsore, too. It still seemed fast to me.

While I trusted the Varlian (I'd never known one that wasn't straight), I did keep a cautious eye peeled for anything that looked dangerous. No Scout can move through strange country without doing that as a matter of habit. And I knew that the fact that there were no arboreal predators didn't mean that plenty didn't wander down here on the ground. It was just as well I kept lookout . . . as we crossed a shallow stream, I saw something blue (it stood out like a spotlight because of its color) sliding from beneath a rock.

The Varlian was standing on that very rock, getting ready to step into the water. I grunted and pointed. He jumped like a monkey, clearing the rest of the distance to the bank, and I was right behind him. That snake looked poisonous, flat-headed, wide at the jawline where venom sacs would be.

Once we were well up the bank, the Varlian stopped and looked back at it. He seemed to go out of himself for a minute, and while that was happening the babble in my head rose to a higher pitch. Concentrated, in some way. And aimed at the blue snake, which promptly curled itself into a circle, straightened with a flick, and lit out like a whipped puppy.

"Did you do that?" I asked the Varlian, though I knew he

couldn't understand me. To my astonishment, he looked me in the eye, grinned, and pointed in the direction in which we were headed. Then he moved his hands, forming a shape between them.

It was identical to that one used by a spaceport drunk to describe the girl that got away . . . or didn't, depending on how drunk he is. There was a burst of Varlian-talk, but I had no recorder to catch it with, then rerun it at quarter-speed to find out what he'd said. I remembered quite a lot of Varlian, having met them on many worlds.

Anyway, I nodded, and we started off again. This time the green creature watched as closely as I did. I suspected that a lifetime of travel above the ground had made him a bit careless.

So we both saw the big red-brown beast as it rose out of a hole beneath the roots of a giant tree. It came quietly, speedily, but we weren't there. As if I had reverted to some long-forgotten Primate ancestor, I leaped for an overhanging limb nearly as fast and as high as my companion did. We swarmed up adjacent trees, my guide skipped over into mine, and we both crouched there, taking wicked delight in throwing twigs and the heavy oblong nuts down into the face of the four-legged creature below. It had a mane like a lion, but its conformation was something that was not quite dog. The muzzle was too short and broad to be akin to the canine, but the teeth were those deadly white fangs that human instinct recognizes from the aboriginal wolf.

As we straightened our backs, the thing gave a frustrated grunt—or roar. It wasn't quite either, and I thought what a short way I had come, evolution-wise, from my apelike ancestors. Throwing nuts, indeed!

Lime (I'd decided that I had to call him something) had come to the conclusion that even limited as I was, we simply must take to the trees. He made this clear with sign-language and gave me a short lesson in swinging from limb to limb, with a short aside on how to tell a sound branch from a rotten one.

Given the choice between breaking my neck cleanly and being chewed on by the set of teeth below, I was an attentive student. As the maned creature pawed the treetrunk and grunted, I removed my boots, tied them onto the back of my tunic with the straps, and stepped gingerly out onto the long thin limb that Lime had crossed in one easy bound.

It was an unsteady journey, for the branch bobbed with my weight. I finally sat and inched my way along it until I reached the point at which there was a stout limb overhead, to which I gladly transferred myself. Lime had watched anxiously, his hands twitching like those of a mother who wants desperately to take some new task from the inept hands of her child and do it herself. I fervently wished that he could . . . but I made it safely and scrambled across a webwork of heavy branches to a trunk. When I stopped and looked back, it was a surprising distance from the tree up which I had originally scrambled.

The animal was still grumphing and prowling about the tree. I thanked every power I knew that he wasn't as bright as a leoric or a venn. As I started to climb down the far side of the present tree, Lime came skittering back from the top and caught me sternly by the arm. Pointing up and over, he tugged me to another cross-limb and urged me across it. This branch was wider than the first, with a definite upward slant. I found that I could go up it more easily, bent over at an angle and steadying myself with my hands. As we went forward, it got easier.

Though I found it all but impossible to negotiate the hand-to-hand transfers from one branch to another, Lime went ahead of me, finding paths through the treetops that I would be able to manage. While ours couldn't be called speedy progress, we did move through the forest, leaving the red-brown carnivore far behind.

I had thought myself a strong and athletic man, though I've never been very tall nor any sort of heavyweight. But as I went high and low, zig-zagging to follow my green guide, I realized that I had met more than my match. The Varlian might not be a Primate of the sort the Ginli respect, but he was brighter than any Ginli I'd ever met and ten times more helpful. Anybody laughing at the Varlian after this would find himself counting his teeth.

It was after midday when Lime motioned for me to pause where I was, in the midst of a giant beech-like tree. He sped to the top of the neighboring tree, raised his cupped hands to his mouth, and gave a long, quavering call that echoed through the surrounding wood so eerily that my neck-hair crawled. For a short while we waited. Then an answering cry rang faintly in the distance. With his lines of communication established, the Varlian proceeded to give a sort of oration from the treetop. The surprising thing was that it wasn't framed in Varlian but in a code-like arrangement of short and long whoops, mixed with spans of tremolo quavers.

When he was done, he again took up the way through the upper forest. I was hard put to follow, for he moved more quickly than before. The floor of the forest below us disappeared from my consciousness, as I struggled along swaying branches and swung painfully hand-over-hand through mazes of small growth. When my guide stopped, at last, I heaved myself onto a wide limb and looked up at an amazing sight.

There was a natural glade in the forest. In its center stood a group of lofty and wide-spreading nut-trees. The lower branches were trimmed up the boles so that their lowest sweep was a stiff Varlian-jump from the ground. In the tops, a connected network of vine linked an aerial community of woven and nestlike shelters. Among and about the "town", as well as in the glade, were numbers of Varlian. More than I had ever seen in one grouping. That, more than anything, told me that this had proven to be a hospitable planet for the green people. On more hostile worlds their numbers in one place seldom reach more than a dozen or so.

There must have been nearly three hundred at home when we emerged from the forest. They came to meet us without surprise. I surmised that Lime had told them, via the whooping-code, all about me. We walked across the belt of grass toward the grove, and as I exchanged shy pats and stares with the beings, I began to wonder if I would be able to make it into the branches. Without, that is, the impetus lent by the white-fanged beast that had sent me into the trees to begin with.

I need not have worried. As we approached a ladder-like tangle of living vine was lowered for my use. The pint-sized young ones sprinkled among the group about me scampered up it gleefully, and I realized that the very young and the very old must use this way habitually. With a grin at Lime, I accepted the helpful vine and made my way up the swaying mass, being careful not to dislodge any of my fellow travelers by awkwardness. Lime flowed up the nearest tree and waited for me about two-thirds of the way between ground and treetops.

Emerging onto the branch beside him, I found that I could now see for miles across the forest. Though I hadn't realized it, we must have climbed slightly but steadily all the way we had come. Now we stood in a tall tree on a ridge of land that overlooked a vista of many miles to east and south and north, as well as a shorter distance toward the west. I could see, glimmering on the edge of vision, the arm of the large lake or small sea that I had seen the day I arrived. Those eastward reaches were now striped with purple shadow. I could define clearly the rolls of land that we had crossed, unknowingly, in the treetops. As we gazed backward along our trail, a Ginli scoutship shot across the sky, a glint of silver against the deepening blue.

I pointed along its trail. Lime grunted. He made a gesture with his green-furred paw that was so accurate and insulting a caricature of the Ginli that I choked with laughter. Then and there I knew that, even if they *had* been the meat-animals of the Ffryll, the Varlian were as human as I. Only fully rational people with a sound sense of the ridiculous could have summed up the Ginli with a single sweep of the hand.

But now Lime was tugging at my sleeve and gesturing toward one of the dwellings hanging just above the spot where we stood. I nodded and followed him to an opening. There a lightly smaller Varlian, whom I took to be Mrs. Lime, met us and asked me in with great courtesy and no words. But entering proved to be impossible. I'm no giant, but a house hung like an oriole-nest with a set-in solid floor and already containing Lime, Mrs. Lime, and three little Limes was pretty fully occupied. There just wasn't room, even if the hole that was the doorway hadn't been six sizes too small.

This caused some consternation among my new friends and would-be hosts. They retired to a huddle to discuss ways and means. As bursts of machine-gun Varlian flew past my ears, I found myself able to sort out a word, here and there. I felt that practice might well return to me some command of the language. With a bit of slowing down, I just might eventually be able to converse with Lime and his people.

After a bit the huddle broke up. Lime and his wife, with apologetic gestures, scurried away across the trees, while the young ones retired into the house. There their frantic activity made the whole structure bulge and swing in an intoxicated fashion. As I watched, I saw a hole appear in one side of the wall. Dexterous paws rapidly enlarged the opening, weaving back into the wall any loose ends of vine and grass.

Before I could get my wits together, I found myself faced with a door large enough to admit me. When I looked around, Lime and Mrs. Lime were hurrying up with armfuls of grass and vine that they had obviously scrounged from friends and relatives. Before slow-witted human beings could have made up their minds that there really *was* a problem, the Varlian had knitted onto their home a spacious chamber for me.

Midsummer though it was, a chill was creeping through the wood on the heels of the waning sunlight. I was glad to know that I wouldn't have to spend another night crouched in a tree on a bare limb. I slipped through my oversized door into the new room, then through the enlarged door into the main house. Aside from piles of mosses for beds, there was no furniture to speak of. There were, however, stacks of bowls cut and polished from the tough husks of the nuts, in a sort of pouch let into one wall. As I moved back into my own room, Mrs. Lime entered her domain and caught up a batch of the bowls, together with spoonlike utensils. She hurried out onto the branch that was her doorstep, arranged the bowls in line, and squatted to wait.

After a bit, a large Varlian came chattering and chuckling through the treetops. He carried a skin bag that sloshed to his motions and a basket that bulged with something lumpy.

Spying our waiting crew, he hurried over, tilted his bag, and poured into the bowls a neat stream of broth. Then from his bag he counted out enough brown pods for two each. There was a cheerful crackle of Varlian as I patted him on the shoulder. Then he was off to fill the supper dishes of the next family in line.

The broth was good. There was no meat in it (I could see that these people had good reason for being vegetarians), but a mixture of vegetables and nuts made it thick and tasty. The pods gave me a bit of trouble until Lime seized one in his paws, gave it a sharp twist, and cracked it open. Whereupon I saw that it was filled with a creamy-white "inside" that tasted much like bread. All in all, it was a filling meal, made delicious by the fact that I had had nothing to eat for over two days.

When we were done, the youngsters were sent, protesting, to clean the bowls in a sand-pit at the foot of the tree. Lime and his wife and I reclined on the branch. I could see that my friend was waiting for something. The sun was well down, the sky filled with painfully bright stars. There was no moon here, according to my computer's sketchy information. I was just as well pleased, for I had known the Ginli to use a moonlit night for their own purposes. Still, the starlight was bright enough for desultory sign language, as we waited.

A whisper of motion in the branches announced the arrival of someone—several someones, as it turned out. In the dim light I could see five Varlian step onto our branch, nod to Lime and Mrs. Lime, and arrange themselves in a convenient semicircle around us.

There ensued a rather complicated dialogue, the gist of which seemed to be that I (the gesture for me, while funny, was friendly. They indicated one of the big brown pods, sketching it effortlessly on the air, and adding to its upper end two arcs that could only be my somewhat prominent ears . . . and I had to agree that the shade of the pods almost exactly matched that of my skin) was to accompany Lime and another, smaller, Varlian westward. To meet someone. Again I encountered the curvaceous shape that Lime had sketched before.

Now the Varlian, intelligent and helpful though they were, were definitely not shaped like Homo Sapiens. Their females were, except for their size, identical to the males, at least to my unpracticed eye. So the shape they caressed onto the cool air of evening was that of some being other than a super-Varlian.

Try as I might, I could catch only a chance word here and there. My attempts at Varlian elicited polite attention and some well-concealed amusement, but it didn't further our mutual understanding. So when the delegation stood and completed their business with a manglingly complex hand-shake, I was still in the dark.

VI.

Hale Enbo

I was awakened the next morning by a soft babble of voices. Sitting up, I looked into three small, green-furred faces peering around my door. The moment they saw I was awake the younglings bounced into my room and onto my chest. In some way during the span of a night I had become, to their young minds, a part of the family. We indulged in an all-out game of tussle and tickle. It was brought to a halt only when Mrs. Lime appeared at the door-hole and scolded the four of us impartially.

Breakfast was a melon with deep red meat, two of the bread-pods, and a bowl of sweet, milky fluid. As with the meal the night before, I found it filling, tasty, and satisfying. Never in any of my spans of eating with the Varlian did I suffer any problem with their foodstuffs, reinforcing my belief that their metabolisms were all but identical with ours.

The delivery of meals by our jolly bagman fascinated me, and in the dawnlight I followed him about his round and back to his source of supply. This was a neat "kitchen" located in a rock formation hidden among the trees. By sign and hint, I gathered that the best cooks among all the Varlian did their cooking for the entire tribe and were honored as particularly valuable citizens. I thought that an excellent arrangement.

Still, I hadn't much time for poking into the domestic affairs of my hosts. Before the sun was above the trees to the east, Lime found me and pointed westward. I climbed back to the nest for my boots and a fond goodbye to the rest of the Limes. Then Lime and the other Varlian who was to share our

journey gathered up packs of webbing and strapped them to
their backs, and we were off.

Our new companion was, I believe, a female. She had
circles of creamy fur around each eye, which gave her such a
wise and owlish look that I named her Owl forthwith. She
seemed completely easy with me and my peculiar problems
with treetop travel. She set herself to find easy routes that I
could negotiate. As neither Varlian would consider traveling
aground again, I was glad of her help and her patience.

Lime concerned himself, this time, with scouting ahead
and behind and to both sides, all of which my slowness gave
him ample time to do. We had gone half the morning without
incident when he returned from a foray and gestured us into
a particularly thick treetop. I went up obediently . . . and
far more easily than I'd ever have dreamed of being able to
do.

We had time to find comfortable spots to hide and get
bored in. Then I heard the unmistakable sound of a Ginli
party moving in the forest. Owl was stretched beside me on a
thick branch that was screened so heavily from the ground
that we couldn't see. I wriggled silently up to a crotch where
the limb branched into three segments and peeped through.
Sure enough, there was a tiny space of leaf-strewn soil in
view. I lay there watching it.

The ungodly clamor of Ginli in forest drew nearer. I found
myself wondering what they found to slash and crush and
hack in so clear-floored a wood. Their manual had been
written, evidently, by some Ginli who had had his experience
of exploration in a jungle setting. He had stated explicitly that
all vegetation along the line of march must be cut by those
who marched before, so as to implement the movement of
those coming behind. He had not envisioned a forest without
undergrowth, and no Ginli of wider experience had ever seen
fit to amend the manual. So I watched as a broad, booted foot
stepped into my patch of ground, paused a moment, then
demolished a small cluster of brown grass. I wondered if the
Ginli attached noise-makers to their implements—there was
certainly nothing there to account for the vicious "crusssh!"
that accompanied the action.

There was commotion in the wood for quite a while, and I guessed that some dozen must be strung out in a long line. What concerned me was the fact that, as nearly as I could estimate, they were headed for the Varlian village. When they had stamped off into the distance, I touched Owl's arm and pointed back along the way we had come. She chattered something, gave an impatient gesture, and called to Lime.

He appeared so silently that I started when his green face came through the leaves above me. He sat patiently while Owl explained my question to him. Then he chuckled that indubitably human chuckle that had endeared his kind to me. Calling me to attention, he stood on the limb and gestured toward the village. He mimed so well that I could all but see the grove and the hanging nests and the busy inhabitants.

He sketched in the Ginli, stamping and hacking through clear forest. The Ginli spied the village and stood for a short time, evidently planning what they would do. Then Lime became the council of elders . . . each one came into being for a fleeting moment as he adopted his or her gestures and posture. The elders reached out and folded something . . . very carefully, very painstakingly, as though it were of the utmost importance.

There followed a demonstration that I couldn't follow, try as I might. Lime erased the Ginli gesture and seemed to indicate that the aliens were not where they had been, but the connection and the method of their removal escaped me. At last the Varlian sighed and made the curving sign, pointed westward. We took up the trek again, and I followed Owl with a head full of unanswerable questions.

For two days we traveled, without any frantic haste but with all convenient speed. Ginli ships zipped over at intervals, but the road we took was invisible to them. Below our lofty way, however, I noticed that there were many trails and paths and the beginnings of a fairly well-worn track that spoke of some sort of organized foot-travel. When I pointed such matters out to my companions they nodded cheerfully and pointed in the direction in which we were going.

Sure now that we were going to meet another race of intelligent people, I redoubled my efforts and added some-

thing to my speed above-ground. The danger the Ginli posed,
not only to me but to any intelligence living on the planet, was
a constant worry. I am a man of affection, and the Varlian had
helped me, taken me in, and made me feel welcome. I didn't
want any harm to come to them, and theirs was the greatest
danger. It was standard practice among Scouts to conceal the
presence of the green people on any planet we investigated
for the Ginli. Our employers considered the Varlian to be a
sort of cosmic insult. Primate yet not humanoid, intelligent
yet more like beasts than men in some ways, they didn't fit
into the Ginli calculations. They eliminated them entirely
whenever they felt they could get away with it.

Those other beings to westward would probably be in
danger, too. From all I could gather, they must be even more
advanced than my green-furred friends. And unless they
were white-skinned, humanoid Primates, they would be in
trouble when the Ginli found them. It seemed impossible for
me to convey to the Varlian the peril the Ginli posed for their
kind. I only hoped that the ones to whom we were hurrying
would be better able to understand me.

At the end of the third day, Lime, who had ranged far
ahead, paused to let us catch up. Then he went into a treetop
and cried a code of whoops and quavers into the sunset. No
sound answered him, but the odd hum inside my head, which
had become so familiar that I had forgotten it, intensified. It
sang along a sort of vector, making a directional signal like
those on which ships home to planets. Though I still needed
Owl to find my way through the trees, I could, if on the
ground, have walked straight toward the source of that signal.

Before nightfall we emerged from the fringes of the russet
forestlands onto the brim of an immense cupped valley. Its
grasses were dimmed by the shadows of evening, but I could
see by those about my feet that they would have shouted in
triumphant oranges, if the sun had still been high. On the
western side of the valley, a series of ridges rose, and beyond
them again I could see distant serrations that might be mountains.

Except for the grasses, occasional groupings of strangely

ornamental trees and shrubs, and outcroppings of stone so aggressively natural that I felt they must be the result of art, the valley was empty. No city stood there. Not even a village of huts nestled into any of the groves. Yet I could feel the presence of activity. A bustle like that of a city street was occurring before my eyes, but I couldn't see anything at all except the motions of wind-stirred grasses and the lengthening of shadows.

Lime paused for only a moment on the edge of the valley. He looked out across it with a contented expression on his furry face; then he motioned for Owl and me to follow him down. But just as we set our feet in the wide smooth trail, the Varlian paused again and looked back toward the east. I turned, too, trying to see what had distracted him, but there was nothing except the towering verge of that tremendous wood to be seen.

Owl and Lime stood as if frozen, their attention seemingly turned inward. Thinking back, it occurred to me that the Ginli could possibly have missed the village on their outward sweep and might even now be finding it. I shuddered, thinking of that busy and happy community burned from its trees by the weapons with which I was too familiar. But neither of my guides seemed distressed. Indeed, both had an amused expression, as if watching something truly funny.

I looked into the sky. As I gazed, it . . . wrinkled . . . for a split instant. The forest-edge seemed to shimmer its graying reaches, a quiver so swift that I doubted that it had really taken place. The two Varlian nodded slowly, chattered a burst of talk at each other, and turned again into the now-dark valley. They took a hand on either side of me and tugged me along between them.

The guide in my head now dimmed to a comfortable purr, as if we had all but arrived at our destination. But unless our would-be hosts had learned to build invisibly, no roof or doorway awaited us. Still, the green people walked confidently down the track, passing trees that were now dark shapes against a slightly paler sky. At the bottommost curve of the cup, they turned aside and made for one of the sculptured piles of stones. As we approached, a golden light began to glow, lighting the entire thing with a dim and firefly brilliance.

In the midst of that tenuous light, there was a shape standing, waiting. Into my mind came a deliberate flow of nicely-paced Varlian, formed by no lips and tongue but by a shaping thought.

"Welcome to our place, Hale Enbo. Well it is that you have spoken with the Varlian of other worlds, for it gives us a way in which to greet you. The shaping of forms and actions in the mind of an alien being is no easy matter, if communication is to be thorough. Come, now, with your companions into the place of the Khi. Know that few of your kind have ever encountered us and none have come here before."

Gaping with astonishment, I looked down at that shape. It was golden, like the light. I felt, after a moment, that the light had come from it. The being was small, though not so small as the Varlian. It came to my collarbone, though for some reason when I looked down at it I had the feeling that I was actually looking upward. It was shaped in pleasing curves above and below a small neat waist, though those curves were in no way those which decorate a human woman. They were, instead, continuous and regular as though metallic golden flesh had been turned on a lathe, shaping a somewhat human-like form. The legs and arms were slim and finely shaped . . . and when I glanced at its feet I was puzzled to notice that the grasses on which they rested were standing upright as though nothing weighed upon them. All in all, I realized that none of the unusual or exotic beings I had encountered in the past had approached the degree of strangeness the Khi possessed.

As if amused by my reaction, the creature glowed more brightly and said, "Truly, we of the Khi are unlike—most unlike—those who now walk in flesh upon the worlds. Ages upon ages ago, we roamed the vastnesses, looking with childish eyes upon their wonders, grasping with infant greed those things that glittered most brightly. Now we are content to dream upon one world, when we must incarnate, looking afar only at need."

It moved one shining hand. A buttress of stone shimmered

away, showing a passage that led downward. The Varlian stepped forward and disappeared into that downward curve. I followed my golden guide into the place, holding my innate caution in control with difficulty. But there was no feel of threat in that smoothly cut and polished tunnel. Light glowed within the walls at elbow height, and the floor glittered like black marble. When we reached a level place, the tunnel ran straight, the ribbon of·light reflected in the dark floor as far as I could see. My days of unaccustomed and muscle-straining travel seemed to fall upon me all at once. I sighed as I went forward.

"You are weary," said the golden Khi. "It is not far, truly. We need not travel the length of this corridor, only a short way more. Then you may rest and find nourishment. I, Khi-Sang, assure you of that. Even now we are approaching the doorway."

Though I looked closely at the shining walls I could see no opening, not even a hairline crack that might mark one. Lime and Owl had stopped ahead of us. When we drew even with them, Khi-Sang lifted her (its?) hand again. A segment of the tunnel fogged to nothingness. An oval of light appeared, and at that point a side passage opened to the left. It was very short, and at its end was a round chamber that seemed cut from topaz, its faceted walls multiplying the golden light that seemed to emanate from the air of the room.

A pair of Khi waited beside a circular table on which was a display of foodstuffs that caught my always-hungry attention immediately. Even the strangely lovely shapes of the Khi who rose to greet us hardly distracted me.

When I had satisfied my hunger and had time to look at the Khi carefully I found them to be even more unorthodox than I had thought. No life-form in any of the Ginli tapes mentioned anything like them, either in physical form (and I had an odd feeling that that form wasn't as substantial as it seemed) or in ability for telepathic communication. Beautiful they were, without doubt. The "feel" I got from them was altogether good.

When they were sure that we were sufficiently rested and fed, they sat down with us at the cleared table and proceeded to attune the Varlian and me into the network of minds that was their system of communication. Surprisingly quickly, because of my knowledge of the Varlian language, they were able to key themselves into my own native tongue, which was not the Terranglo that was the common tongue of space but my own people's polyglot, which had grown from roots in one of Terra's now-extinct languages. With the aid of technical terms from other languages, the illustrations for which they picked effortlessly from my mind as I pictured processes and equipment and even illustrations from filmed books, they were soon able to feel at ease inside my mind.

But when I tried at last to warn them of their deadly danger from the Ginli, I met a stone wall. In no way could I convince them to take the Ginli seriously. When I pictured scenes from my own memory (the fate of the Fleer was topmost among them, not to mention cultures that I had seen subtly warped and torn apart by Ginli machinations) they understood, but such things caused no concern among them. I pictured my own fate, if I were caught alive. The thought of all those trapped brains, doomed forever to do the Ginli's work, seemed to sadden but not to frighten the Khi.

At last Khi-Sang said to me, ''We are not strangers to the Ginli, Hale Enbo. But you must realize that this little people cannot endanger us. We will fold them away, if there is threat from them. Even the Varlian have learned this from us . . . why do your people not use the technique?''

''I've never heard of it,'' I answered. ''We only know the ways to kill our enemies, when they threaten us. Nothing that I ever read mentioned folding away inconvenient citizens. How do you do that?''

I felt a concentration of energies inside my head. Then it withdrew, and Khi-Sang said regretfully, ''The parts of your mind that can manage such techniques are unused. Reflecting, no doubt, the distrust your kind feels for non-physical things. It requires much exercise, much practice, great flexibility, to learn the non-material ways. We will teach you, in time. That is the reason for your presence on this world at this time. Yet at the moment you are incapable of learning or understanding or using the things that you must know.''

''The reason why . . . I'm here because of a series of random happenings!'' I interjected. ''There's no way in which I could have been finagled into being here.''

Khi-Sang glimmered softly, and I thought that she was laughing. Khi-Lohm raised a hand. The lights dimmed.

Khi-Rehm said, ''We have accomplished much in a short time. Now you must rest. Sleep is a need of both your kinds, and we must look afar. Through the diamond wall. Into the affairs of others greater than we.''

With gestures of agreement, the two Varlian looked about for someplace to rest. I felt terribly sleepy, too, and we all welcomed the sudden appearance from thin air of cushioned couches along the side wall.

I was asleep before the Khi had left the chamber.

VII.

Khi-Sang

It has been long since the Hril have used us as their instruments. Even to those who, as do we, exist outside the ordinary spaces and carnate delusions of time, it has been long. It delights us that they still have need of our abilities. But, indeed, in no other way might they achieve the education of this being whom they have brought into our hands. They would be totally beyond his unaided perceptions.

We find it disturbing, however, that the Hril have encountered a thing that they cannot master unaided. When those who are the authors of our being are outmatched, we who are the children of their thought are made to feel impotent, indeed. The notion that one who is still confined in flesh must be the ultimate instrument against that remote yet very real enemy fills us with unease.

He, however, is delightful. Unlike many of his kind whom we have observed from a distance, he has the straightforward and unselfconscious honesty of a child . . . that wedded to an excellent mind that has experienced much, studied much, and made good use of all. And his pure joy in such matters as eating well and sleeping soundly and looking about at the beauties of the world remind us of our own remote past, when we, too, were bound into three dimensions.

We have thought much about the best way in which to teach this large brown man the things he must know if he is to save the Ginli from their own folly and to save our known cosmos from that terrible thing that the Hril see and fear. It will not be an easy thing, for he has been taught to scorn non-material matters. As with a child, he must learn step by step, lesson by lesson. But he is more than able.

VIII.

Hale Enbo

I woke the next morning to a soft buzzing inside my head. I assumed that the Varlian were experiencing the same effect, for they rose with me, their expressions as abstracted as I felt mine to be. We were shown to a small room that held ewers of steaming water and basins into which to pour it, as well as more earthy facilities. Everything was well-designed, even beautiful, but I had the feeling that all such matters were solely for the benefit of infrequent guests who possessed solid bodies. The Khi, more and more, seemed as if they must exist on a plane at at least one remove from that which I inhabited.

We were served a light but tasty meal. Then we were asked to accompany Khi-Lohm and Khi-Rehm and Khi-Sang back up the tunnel to the surface of the valley. We had talked long into the night, and the Khi had left us to sleep late, so we emerged into a flood of brilliant sunlight that warmed the basin to almost Big Sandy temperatures. The grass, which I had judged would be orange, ranged in shades from palest tan to deep red-orange, making a fantastic carpet of the meadow. The trees, with impeccable taste, lacked the varied coloration of those in the forest. They were chastely clad in clouds of creamy leaves that made a nice contrast with the bright leafage below them. If Khi-Ash had a fault in color-scheme, it was in the lack of cool colors to balance the clamor of reds and ochres and golds. I would have given much to spy a blue flower or a green bush.

Khi-Lohm, beside me, turned his/her head toward me, and I was almost able to distinguish features behind the golden

shimmer of light that the being emitted. The purr of approval
I had felt when I stopped to admire the coloration of a tree,
days before, vibrated in my head.

"You are correct," said a voice inside my mind. "We
allowed Khi-Ash to develop without our attention for too
long. It went its own wayward path, and when we matured
enough to appreciate nuances of shading and contrast, it was
too late to correct things here. For that reason, among others,
we allowed the Ffryll to plant the Varlian among us—though
neither race suspected our existence then. Their cheerful
green enlivens our forests, and we find enjoyment in their
pursuits."

The golden glance turned from me, up the track toward the
east. "Watch!" came the whisper in my mind. "The Ginli
come!"

At the edge of the wood, small with distance, I saw a
gray-clad group moving along the trail. Without looking
about at the scene about and before them, they tramped along
with the bone-jarring stride they are so proud of inventing.
From the grass beside the tracks swirls of bright-winged
insects fluttered and crackled and flicked away. Amid that
throng, I seemed to see small bits of celestial blue . . . I
turned to Khi-Rehm, on my other side.

"Did I see blue butterflies?"

The Khi nodded. "We found them in our travels about the
dimensions and we brought back a few to seed our world.
You can see that we are working to make it aesthetically
pleasing." A feeling that closely resembled a chuckle ema-
nated from him, her, or it. I could never be quite certain,
though I always get a strong feeling of the feminine from the
Khi.

But Khi-Lohm interrupted with a sharp gesture. I focused
upon the Ginli and noted with dismay that one of them was
approaching a tree that drooped gracefully above the trail. He
had his flameblade in his hand and destruction written all
over him. His companions stamped along after him with
uninterrupted zeal.

"Oh, no!" I gasped. The removal of any part of the

valley's components would make a subtle wrongness in the landscape. But Khi-Lohm touched my elbow and gestured toward Lime and Owl, who seemed to be engaged in some weird pattern of ritual gestures.

They stood together a little apart from the stone formation, facing toward the Ginli. They seemed to be *folding* something, very slowly and precisely. Something that was either invisible or nonexistent. They worked in unison, bringing together opposite corners of whatever it was, making partial rolls, then doing the entire thing—or non-thing—into a small parcel that brought their hands close together.

I glanced back at the Ginli, as the Varlian finished their activity. The sky quivered, the bright scene winked briefly. And the Ginli were no longer there. The tree arched over the road, the sunlight brought the grass to fiery brilliance, but there were no Ginli there at all.

"What happened to them?" I asked Khi-Sang. "Are they dead? How did the Varlian *do* that?"

"They folded them away," said her voice in my head. "That is how it was done. Turn, now, and look toward the western ridges."

I gazed across the wide valley that rose in a smooth curve toward the hills. Light and color danced together so as to dazzle the eye, but I shaded my gaze with both hands and stared along the full length of the track that crossed the valley and zigzagged threadwise up the distant ridges. Halfway up the slope I could see motion, and it worked itself out into a somewhat disorganized group of gray-clad dots. Their proud and stamping gait had degenerated into milling. Those in front seemed to be turning in their tracks, while those behind seemed uncertain whether to walk over their leaders or to stop where they were. The sun glinted on flameblades held at all angles, instead of at the regulation slant over the right shoulder.

I looked around. Lime and Owl were watching the confusion with excessively smug looks on their green-furred faces. The Khi were glimmering visibly, even in the glare of sunlight that bathed us all. It occurred to me that one sort of light-emission might well stand in for what would be a chuckle in my kind.

"They folded them away," repeated Khi-Sang. I began, dimly, to understand. Away meant *away*, in a literal, physical sense. But how in tunket was the folding done? I'd never dreamed that such things were anything except superstition.

The Khi were turning again toward their doorway, and we were led back into the darkly polished tunnel. Without a sound, the stone reformed behind us, shutting out the sunlight. We went, this time, much farther down the tunnel than we had before, turning aside at last into a different chamber.

This was a larger room by far than that in which we had spent the night. It was cut, seemingly, from diamond-like stuff that sent brilliant refractions dancing across our faces and into faceted walls and roof in a mad exchange. The movement of light, as the glowing Khi entered, made me dizzy, and I clung to Lime for balance. He chattered uneasily to Owl, and both took up a rapid-fire dialogue with Khi-Sang. The Khi gestured them to silence at last and motioned into being a line of stools, upon which we were wordlessly asked to sit.

Lime and Owl took their places on either side of me. They took my hands in their own . . . protectively? It certainly felt that way. Their furry faces turned from Khi-Sang to me and back again, then to the glittering wall before us. Then, between one heartbeat and the next, I woke from the confident dream that had seemingly wrapped me about since the moment I had looked through the bushes at the purple sea and the white beach.

Fear thumped through me. I would have started up from my place, but for the firm grips of the Varlian on my hands. Khi-Sang's glowing face turned toward me, the features lost in a haze of gold. She was totally alien. The purpose that radiated from her was none that I recognized, but it froze me where I sat. The hum that had purred inside my head for so long was quenched, leaving me alone and full of terror.

The wall behind Khi-Sang glowed suddenly with shafts of light sinking into bright distances. At the deepest point, just beyond my vision, something moved, shattering the beams into a confusion of motes, ripples, and shards. I heard voices that were not made of sound-waves. I felt thoughts that were shaped in minds far more remote than those of the Khi. A maelstrom of activity was taking place in the spaces windowed by that wall, but what it might be was incomprehensible.

I moved my hands, pulling free so that I might cover my eyes. The Varlian loosed them and huddled close to me, crooning as if I were one of their own young. Their furry warmth comforted me only slightly for I sensed the inexorable presence of Khi-Sang. She did not move, but I knew that she was engaged in . . . folding. And I greatly feared that this time it was I who was being folded away.

The shining wall wavered before my eyes. The hands of the Varlian pulsed on my knees. A black wall came down behind my eyelids, inking out the room, the Khi, the Varlian. There was a long moment of disorientation. Vertigo seized me, whirled me madly for an incalculable time, loosed me abruptly.

Then I lost my hold upon both the world and myself and spun down a long tunnel, far blacker than that which had led me here.

IX.

Khi-Sang

It was a painful thing to do, and all of us felt keenly the distress of our pupil. Still, he had looked through the diamond wall into the world of the Hril. That alone imprints upon the mind matters that cannot be transmitted otherwise.

His terror beat upon all our spirits, and the Varlian were filled with anger at what seemed to be a betrayal of the things they had tried to tell their guest about us. It took a great while to calm them, for they could not really comprehend our explanations. How could they, when even we find the reasons of the Hril almost incredible?

Yet we sent Hale Enbo back across the miles. And as he went, he moved within a field of thought so strong as to force into his mind many things that it would have rejected under less stressful conditions.

He will be frightened and disoriented for a time, we have no doubt. But we all feel certain that he contains the potential to be what the Hril would make of him. How many of his kind are chosen to save a universe?

X.

Hale Enbo

The bushes were thick and springy, covered with leaves that blazed with fantastic—and somehow familiar—color. Peering cautiously through that autumnal foliage, I could see the beach clearly, a strand of white sand that curved gently inward at this point, bringing pale amethyst waters near enough so that I could hear their lazy lapping on the shiny stones at their edge.

I blinked hard, fighting simultaneous dizziness and déjà-vu. I had crouched here days ago, peering through this self-same bush at those very waters. The Varlian, the Khi, had I dreamed them all? Yet now it was not late afternoon, as it had been before. The sun blazed almost at zenith. There was a difference in the feel of the day, which held a hint of humidity that told me of impending rain.

Still, those lapping wavelets masked any quiet motion behind me, so I turned once more to find a hiding place in the wood. A red-brown beast stood twenty paces to my rear, effectively barring my way into the forest. I remembered very well the speed it had attained when first I met one. It would intercept any dash past at an angle.

With a desperate bound, I leaped over the bush and dashed for the water. I could hear the breathing of the creature behind me. It was coming faster than I was going. Praying desperately to all the gods that spacers laugh at but call on at a pinch, I made a long, shallow dive into the unknown waters, hoping they were deeper than they looked. As I hit, I cut at a long angle into a respectable depth of water, feeling behind me with a trailing foot the worn-away ledge that must have been

46

just below the edge of the beach. I pushed away with frantic strength and shot into the totally unknown lake or sea.

I felt certain that it held perils at least as great as the beast that was bellowing on the beach behind me. When I surfaced and turned, I saw the thing had waded to its waist into the water and was watching me with hungry intensity. Treading water, I studied my alternatives, one by one.

I was halfway across a narrow neck extending from what looked to be a small sea. The forest on my right I suspected to harbor the kin of the beast that had driven me out of the forest on the left. If I could get safely ashore . . . and if I could find my former hiding place . . . and if I could track Lime and me, both afoot and in the trees, I might possibly survive to find the Varlian again. IF.

And they would probably take me off westward to see the Khi again. And the Khi seemed to have rejected me out of hand.

I was getting weary of forests, anyway. The few dangerous denizens I had met so far were avoidable by the wary, but the Ginli were also there. Without Lime and Owl to guide and to scout, I might be unlucky enough to run afoul of them. I knew that a simple death wouldn't be my fate. They'd have my brain in pickle, hooked up to some of their fancy equipment, and I'd spend eternity working for them. That was an intolerable thought.

I turned totally about and looked out into the sea. To westward I could see a promontory projecting into the purple haze. To the west. Where the Khi were. I listened to the inside of my head, discounting the strange pops and crickles that belonged there when I had water in my ears. There was no hum, no purr nor anything else. So they (assuming I hadn't dreamed them) weren't monitoring me. If they were ignoring me, maybe I could sneak up on them.

A long time later I asked myself what I thought I could possibly accomplish by sneaking up on the Khi. I had no answer. But my brain, never what I'd call a first-class bit of equipment, had had too many shocks too fast. It needed a purpose. It was in no condition for careful ratiocination. It said, "Go westward, Hale Enbo, and find out what those inscrutable Khi are up to." So I went.

My first task was to find flotation. I was a fair swimmer, though it had been something of a problem for any native of Big Sandy to contaminate large containers of water with his body. Only when the Ginli had landed me on my first water-world had I felt free to practice the art. I'd learned pretty well, but that knob of land was much too far away to reach unaided, even if I had been twice the swimmer I am.

I went under, just enough to hide my destination from the waiting beast, and headed for the other side of the neck of water, where a stream ran down to join the sea. At its outlet I could see a tangle of deadfall. Keeping a very low profile, I surfaced and eased along a few yards from the beach, working my way around the tangle that was my goal. When I got there the jumble of roots and branches hid me from my would-be consumer.

It was like some frustrating game that grownups foist on children to get something usable out of that witch's nest. If someone had tried deliberately to knit and wrap and tangle and twist that glob of dead vegetation together in the most inextricable way possible, it couldn't have been done more thoroughly. I found that branches were wrapped lovingly about one another; vines laced the whole mess together and anchored it to two terrific treetrunks that were half in and half out of the water. Dripping with a mixture of sweat and sea water, I labored to free a fair-sized log that I had spotted in the midst of the tangle. Quietly. Now and again I cautiously peered through a cranny in the bush and checked on the whereabouts of the beast on the shore. He was always there, looking hopefully toward the place where I had submerged.

At last I realized that I must work myself upstream and begin freeing bits and pieces of brush from that end, for the current kept bringing down new problems to cover what I had done. I ducked under and swam around the end of the dead-fall, then drew myself up into the stream by hauling upon exposed roots that projected into the water. Luckily, the shore was thick with undergrowth, just there, and it hid me from the beach that I had left.

It was easier to work in the shallow water. I didn't have to anchor myself to keep from floating away from my task. The current helped instead of hindering. I was worrying at a length of vine that was almost the last impediment to my objective when something made me look up. At eye-level, about two arm-lengths away, a blue serpent was coiled. Its head was swaying with my motions, and its slitted eyes looked entirely confident.

I had surprised myself several times, since landing on Khi-Ash. Now I did something that I would have sworn was impossible. I slid from beneath the strike, as the snake lunged, and shot downstream, taking my log with me. The fangs missed my arm by a fraction of a hair's breadth. If the serpent followed, I was too busy trying to master the art of climbing onto a floating log to see or to know.

A considerable current moved into the sea with the stream. I found myself rolling over and over, first on the log, then under it, for a good distance. At last I got the end of the log turned to move along the current, and the rolling stopped. Then I rested, holding onto branch stubs, and considered the problem. Had I been Khi—or Varlian—I'd have just folded myself onto the log. Or wherever I wanted to go, for that matter. Being myself, I had to find a way to mount it.

Unless you have tried the stunt, you wouldn't believe how difficult it is. This log, being quite dry, floated high. It bobbed a good bit, which at last gave me a useful idea. I drifted back along its length to the smaller end. It sank under the weight of my hand, causing the butt end to rise. With a heave, I pushed it under water and drew myself, lengthwise, along it as far as I could. When it bobbed back, it was beneath me. Though it took a bit of work to make my way up to a point at which I was clear of the water and riding steadily, it wasn't impossible.

The current from the inflow waned quickly as we reached deep water. I found myself drifting idly on a calm sea. The promontory was now easily visible, but it was by no means near. And, I recalled, there would be no tide to help me move, for Khi-Ash had no moons. With a sigh, I dipped my shriveled hands into the water and began to paddle, doing my best to steer the log by shifting my weight.

By now it was well on toward sunset. I hated the thought of trying to spend the night out there with who-knew-what lurking in the deeps below. I had made a bit of headway with my paddling, but the strain on the shoulders was comparable to that of swinging from branch to branch. I drew my miserable hands from the water and laid them on the log.

They glinted strangely in the reddish sunlight. I held my right hand up. To my horror, I saw a thin, colorless shape, something like an attenuated fish hanging from my skin. It was translucent, and as I watched I saw it begin to fill with red. I knew that it was my own blood lending it that color, but remembering the various blood-suckers I had encountered before that, I didn't pull it off. I did touch it with my left hand . . . two of the things were hanging from *it*.

I had nothing with which to make heat, though I knew that to be the best way of removing such things. But I could *not* sit there and watch them fatten on my blood! The chafing of the log's bark against my legs gave me an idea. I dangled the flimsy creatures above the roughest spot I could find and began dragging them back and forth, giving that almost-invisible skin the roughest treatment I could manage. They were stubborn, I'll give them that. It took a long time, and driplets of my blood were beginning to leak from scratches on them before they gave up and unclamped their suckers from my skin.

That was that, with hand-paddling. I couldn't spare the blood, for one thing. I had had no food since the Khi fed us breakfast that morning—that morning? Grace to the gods! It felt like a year! And I didn't have any idea when I'd be aground again to find more. The promontory wasn't getting any nearer, the sun was all but set, my hands were oozing blood slowly—it didn't seem to be clotting—and there wouldn't be any tide. Ever.

The Varlian, while lovely people, were not, I knew, the equals of *Homo sapiens* in either intelligence or creativity. But they could fold things away. The Khi had taught them how. If I could fold things away, I'd fold away this expanse of sea and slap myself right up against that knob of land that seemed so far away. I looked in the heaving water, which was now the color of that "wine-dark sea" that I had painfully read about in ancient Greek, back on Big Sandy, where they believed in that very old-fashioned style of education once called "classical," even in the teeth of starvation and drought.

Closing my eyes, I painfully visualized the sea as a two-dimensional thing. I folded it crosswise, then crosswise again. I opened my eyes. Nothing. Deflated, I laid my head on my arm and looked hopelessly across the distance. A triangular fin cut across my line of vision. Oh, great! Khi-Ash *would* be possessed of a shark-analog.

A bump at the more deeply sunken end of my log interrupted my musings. A whole clump of fins had gathered back there, almost invisible against the dark water. The next bump was sharp enough to make me hold on tightly to branch-stubs and to curse in every tongue I could recall.

They were smart, those creatures. A bunch of them moved around to the side and began trying to roll the log over. It was all I could do to counterbalance their shoves with weight-shifts. And it was now as dark as it could manage to get with a skyful of stars overhead. I found that I was becoming disoriented, what with the rolling and the darkness and the dizziness that lack of food always gives me. As the creatures gave a determined heave at the log, I reached with all my being for the now-invisible knob of land that had been my goal.

The dizzy fall down the tunnel was just more of the same. It was a while before I realized that there was no slop-slop of water just below me, no heaving and bumping at the log. No motion at all. Reaching down cautiously, I set my hand on firm soil, still faintly warm from the sun. I had done it! I might not be on the promontory, but, by all the gods of space, I was on dry ground. And at the moment, I didn't care where.

XI.

The Watching Hril

We find that we have an apt pupil. Many kinds of rational creatures cannot cope with such stresses as we arranged for Hale Enbo. We felt sad that he must be subjected to such successive shocks, yet there is great need . . . he must learn with all possible speed.

Even the Khi did not know what we had planned for their guest. They found affection for him, even in so short a time, and they would have objected strenuously had we indicated our purpose to them. They are our best achievement, so far, yet even they lack the objectivity that is necessary for managing worlds and dimensions.

This new one whom we have taken into our attention . . . he has great abilities. He will be, I predict, the instrument suited to our long-term need. All have bent their thoughts toward achieving this end, to be sure. He, in and of himself, contains things that he has not dreamed of.

XII.

Hale Enbo

The sun woke me. I lay where I had fallen after rolling off the log, and I don't think I'd stirred all night.

The morning light turned the purple sea into amethyst, but the growling of my interior didn't allow me to enjoy it. Sitting up with proper concern for my stiff joints and sore muscles, I looked carefully toward the trees crowning the knoll. There was the tall one with the double top that I had taken for my marker. I had hit the promontory dead on, which I thought wasn't too bad for somebody who didn't know what he was doing.

I followed my shadow into the trees, looking with all my attention for signs of any carnivore of the sort that had put me into this predicament. The trees here were spaced widely. A profusion of bushes of every hue from palest golden to deepest ochre grew about their roots and in the open spaces between. As I worked my way into the tangle, I saw something familiar growing on a rather tall spindly shrub that sported palest tan leaves. Unless I was badly mistaken, those were the bread-pods that I had eaten in the Varlian village.

Naturally, that particular bush was growing in the midst of a thorny mass, and I got well and truly scratched while working my way over to it. But it was worth it. Twisting one of the pods, I heard the distinctive "crack" with which it split and knew that I was right. I stood there amid the thick growth and ate six of them, one after the other. Then, with my stomach purring like a well-fed kitten, I looked about at the thicket in which I stood. On the thorny bushes grew tiny scarlet fruit that might have been miniature apples. On the tall orange-leaved plant behind me were globules that gave off a strong lemony scent. Caution dictated that I ignore them both, but I have never liked being dictated to, so I gathered some of them both into my tunic-tail, together with a lot of the bread-pods. Then I made my way further into the trees, which now were growing more and more densely, becoming a forest. I found a spreading, wide-limbed tree, tucked my loot into a convenient crotch, and climbed up to try my luck with a gamble.

I'd spent a lot of time on a lot of planets. Sometimes the Ginli had supplied me well and checked on my welfare at regular intervals. Much more often, they got busy with their own pursuits and forgot about the poor Scout they'd planeted. This was by no means the first time I had been faced with the choice of hunger or alien fruits. With my appetite, I had become a pretty fair judge of what was edible and what was dangerous. I was still walking around, too, which had to prove something.

I broke one of the little apples and sniffed. It smelled somewhat apple-ish, at that. I sat there, letting the scent roam around inside me, testing and tasting every nuance. There was a hint, way at the back of my palate, of something acrid. I would have bet my socks (they weren't worth much by now) that the fruit would have tasted lovely—and would have made me sick as a first-jump spacehand before nightfall. I chucked the apples down and tore open one of the bright orange almost-lemons.

Now *there* was a scent. Rich, lemon-orangey, sweet with just the right suggestion of tartness. I examined it with my usual attention, stretching out comfortably along one of the broad limbs, touching my tongue to the juice of the fruit. There being no adverse reaction to either taste or smell, I proceeded to eat a bit, then to wait for the verdict of my interior.

It was warm now, even shaded as my perch was, and I found myself dropping into a doze. Shaking my head, I sat erect and looked into the forest around me. Once again I found myself looking into interested eyes. These were large, round-pupilled, and brown as the bark of the tree in which I sat. The owner of the eyes was standing, evidently, on the ground below me, looking upward through a chink in the foliage. I could see nothing except those eyes, a bit of pale oval face and a hint of short nose, for the leaves blocked out everything else.

I have no idea how long we assessed one another. That this was another creature possessing intelligence I didn't doubt for a moment. Those eyes were shrewdly summing me up. After what seemed hours, I took one of the fruits I hadn't yet touched and stretched downward to hand it to the watcher below. A slender arm the color of antique ivory (I'd seen ivory among the Ginli collections of artifacts) came up cautiously and took the thing from my hand. I noted that the fingers were long and flexible . . . and that there were six of them, counting the opposable thumb.

I settled down a bit, leaning back to ease my position. In one motion the creature was sitting on the limb that diverged at an angle from my own. She was almost human. Mammalian—oh yes, indeed! Pale-skinned and covered only with a light goldeny down. But her face was feline in many respects. Except for those round-pupiled eyes, she might have been related to the Fssa.

She might almost have *been* Fssa, except for, as I said, her eyes and the lack of thick fur. She had the same effortless ease of movement I had admired in the cat-people, as well as the blazing intelligence that was obvious to any except a fool or a Ginli. Studying her, I came to the conclusion that only curiosity had brought her up into the tree. No help-a-fellow-intelligent-being-in-distress feeling seemed to motivate her, as it had done the Varlian.

With little hope of success, I tried her with some Varlian, but she hissed disdainfully and swept a hand crosswise before her. I took that to mean no. Then I made the shape of the Khi, as Lime had done, with my two hands and pretended to fold an invisible napkin.

Her eyes narrowed. A stream of soft hisses and sibilants issued from her almost-lipless mouth. I didn't know whether to be encouraged or the reverse, but I persisted, gesturing toward the west and indicating by walking my fingers down the branch that I wanted to go there. She barred my way with her hand, then crept, with her other hand, toward my fingers, pounced on them, and proceeded to give a good imitation of rending them apart and chewing them up. Then she sat back, leaned against the bole of the tree, and meditatively ate the fruit I had given her.

Well, she couldn't tell me much about red-brown animals with sharp white teeth. But then she might have been describing something else entirely. I shrugged, leaned myself back, and began to stow my cargo of pods and fruit in the various pockets and pouches the Ginli build into their Scout uniforms. Much as I had grumbled at the lumps and bulges they caused in my usually svelte outline, I was glad of them now. I would eat along the way . . . at least until something ate me.

With a nod to the lady in the tree, I removed my boots, fastened them securely to the straps on the back of my tunic, and crawled along the branch that seemed most accessible. With my usual lack of finesse, more slowly than I had done when I had someone to search out a route for me, I moved through the trees, westward.

The sun moved higher, and I sweated along, cursing my ill-suited arms as I rubbed cramps out of the muscles at intervals. The lemony fruit saved me, for they quenched my thirst on frequent halts to rest, saving me laborious trips down to ground-level to search for springs.

As I back-tracked for the umpteenth time from a route that proved to be impossible, I saw motion in the tree I had just left. Arriving at a secure sitting-spot, I stopped and found myself looking into the face of the cat-woman. She had on her face an expression of amused amazement. In a fiber-mat pouch she held a nice selection of edibles, including a new supply of lemons. With the air of one rewarding a clever animal—or a small child—for a trick well done, she handed me a long, gray-mauve fruit that peeled easily and tasted like pudding.

I'm not stiff-necked. Not when it comes to food. I accepted her offering with gratitude and ate it with relish. Then I put the new supply into my pockets and pouches and accepted her offer of her own carrier. She gave a Lady Bountiful gesture.

In a leisurely manner, she wafted down the tree and disappeared into the forest. I watched until she was no longer to be seen, then I sighed, stretched and took up my frustrating way again. I couldn't expect, I felt sure, to have the luck to find another Lime. Once had been a fluke. Twice would be some sort of miracle.

The afternoon went by. Clouds began to gather, confirming yesterday's hint of rain. I toiled through the wood, doing my best to check my direction by infrequent glimpses of the sun. The sky got darker and thicker, until the clouds seemed to be hanging at treetop level. Fearing that I might lose my bearings entirely, I decided to find shelter for the night and pack it in. It was just as well that I did.

I found a thick-boled tree that lay at a long slant. Evidently, from the misshapen area on the topside of the tree, another tree had fallen across it when it was young and bendable, and deflected its growth to a forty-five degree angle. It had put out the typical broad limbs parallel to the ground, but above them, on the underside, the great width of the trunk made a porchlike roof. Though I had passed better spots on my journey, I had no intention of retracing my painful efforts. I scrambled down from the tree I sat in and gathered up branches heavy with leaves to shut out any rain.

Using the deadfall, I made a rough windbreak, for I knew from long experience that no matter how balmy the weather, how warm the climate in sunny weather, it was more than likely that rain would bring a certain chill. What with the circumstances of my escape from the Ginli, I had brought no personal items with me, and I had been forced to leave the lifeboat so hurriedly that I had had no chance to rob its stores. I knew that any help I could give myself would be all to the good.

When I was satisfied with my temporary haven, I burrowed into it and closed my eyes. I was even too weary to eat. Though my muscles were twitching with exhaustion, it didn't take me long to fall into a doze. I sank into sleep, and some time long after dark I woke to the drumming of rain on leaves. A light mist of spray wafted into my lair, now and again, but my efforts with the branches served me well. I was dry and reasonably warm, though I could tell that if I had been exposed to the wind and the wet I would have been thoroughly miserable.

When I emerged from the shelter into newly-washed sunshine, the next morning, I found someone waiting for me. Not the cat woman, I knew immediately, but surely one of her kin. Much smaller, much younger, and male. The original cat-person had been tall—even taller than I—and possessed of an assurance that only comes with maturity. This one was about my height, well-furred, and awkward with the unsureness of youth. He was waiting for me, and that led me to wonder if he hadn't watched me from a distance the day before, as I labored through the trees.

He accepted my offer of fruit and bread pods, but he sat well away from me in the tree I had chosen to breakfast in. When I gathered fruit rinds and pod hulls neatly into a heap and proceeded to bury them at the foot of the tree, he emitted something like a deep purr. He evidently approved of my habits.

When I was ready to move again, he climbed ahead of me, surveyed the sprangle of branches ahead, and gestured toward a projecting limb that connected, high up, with the branches of the next tree.

I had a guide again, grace to the gods!

XIII.

Hsssch, Called Purrl

I had not intended to catch the eye of the Lady Clan-Mother. Not that I dislike her—she is, after all, the one who guides our clan in all things. But she always has tasks for us who are young and without families. Not always pleasant ones, and sometimes very ugly ones, indeed. I had been sent upon one of those in recent days, tracking ill-looking Primates about the forest and seeing that they found no over-young kit or helpless beast in their path. We had seen what happened to such when they found them. Our clan had not lost a kit to them and did not intend to.

My stint over, I had intended to slip away into the trees for a bit of bird-stalking. Not that we are allowed to kill and eat them, any more, but simply for the practice of going silently through the high ways. Sometimes, however, I regret that our kind has embraced the civilized ways so well. We might as well be taught by the Khi! We are losing the earthier ways of our ancestors rapidly, according to the tales of the Old-Fathers. If ways must change, then I cannot see why we can't learn really interesting and useful things, as the Varlian learn from the Khi.

I was almost out of sight amid the tawny foliage when I heard that distinctive hiss and stopped where I was. The Clan-Mother stood below, one hand crooked to call me back. I said a few choice things under my breath, but I went to her, for she is like that.

"There is one in the forest!" she said, fixing me with her compelling eyes.

"I know that," I answered shortly. "I've been tracking them for days now."

One clawed hand descended upon my shoulder, and I felt the slightest possible touch of her killing-claws. "Do not be impertinent!" she snapped. "I did not say many, I said one. A single being, unlike those pale ones who destroy things in their way. This one is . . . different. There is a feel about him . . . he goes to the Khi. I am sure of that."

I stared at her. "What concern is that of ours? It was the ruling of all the Clan-Mothers, generations past, that we would go our own ways and leave the Khi to teach those who wanted their help. Why should we send one to them, whatever the reason?"

She looked at me with such disgust that I remembered quite suddenly that she was my mother's mother, with family rights as well as clan rights. But I still didn't understand. And I am stubborn. "Well?" I asked her.

"You are still a kit!" she hissed with disgust. "Do you understand nothing of what is spoken in the Clan-meets? We are not enemies of the Khi, even though we rejected their ancient offer to civilize us. Those of our descent are not easily molded into any pattern except their own. Yet we are not thereby rendered crude, uncivilized, or stupid. You have watched those alien beings in the forest. They are dangerous to all they meet—that is obvious even to the youngest. This one, so like and yet so unlike, must be linked with them in some way. If he were of their mind-shape, he would know nothing of the Khi. He would want to go anyplace else but to their valley. Therefore he must be against them. Use your mind, Child!"

Well, it made sense, as she put it. I admit that I am not one of those who find their keenest joy in thinking about complicated matters. To stalk a bird or to bring down game for the table are the things I find to my liking.

"You want me to take him to the valley?" I asked her, though I felt sure that was what she meant.

Her lip curled delicately, and I could see the pale gleam of one fang. Another touch of claws into my shoulder told me that I had pushed my good fortune as far as it was safe to go.

"I will go and find him and take him there!" I assured her. "Where did you see him?"

Her instructions were brief and accurate. I found him within minutes, for he was near the Clan-place.

This was a really strange creature. He was, as she had indicated, different from those others who were making chaos of the wood. He was clumsy, dark of skin, and what fur he possessed, which was all on the top of his skull, was also dark. But there was a good feeling about him . . . something within him reached out to me and made me feel almost a kinship with him.

It was not hard to find a way to make myself understood. He, in turn, seemed to be skilled at sign language, for once we got into the trees we were able to communicate with fair ease. But he was so awkward aloft!

He had traveled with Varlian—that much was clear. He used their methods, and although those are different from the ways of the Ssseelt, they are effective for traveling the high roads. He made great efforts, and I saw quite soon that my main task would be finding him a road through the branches that would hold his great weight and give him the many hand and footholds that he needed.

It was not exactly interesting, but I grew to like the big creature. I had something of the feeling for him that I had for my siblings in the family. I never thought that he might be of help to me, but I was soon taught otherwise.

We had returned to the ground to seek water and fruit. While he filled a bag with the one, I went to a nearby stream, where my family kept containers for water. On the path I stepped upon something that came rushing up beneath me. In one breath I was swung high in a treetop in a net not unlike those we use for catching fish in the streams. My killing-claws were useless against the tough stuff that formed the meshes.

I suspected that such an alien thing must have been set by those whom I had been watching. Certainly none of the normal tenants of our forests use such uncivilized equipment. As I pondered my dilemma, I looked into the trees along the streambank, and there was the brown face of my companion.

He gestured for me to be still. Finding nothing else to do, I did as he suggested, and after a time some of the pale people came and took me down, fastened me to a pole and carriéd me away along a path that they had made.

I knew that the brown person followed. I could not see him, but I could hear him moving behind us. My grub-white captors were no better at listening than they were at moving silently. I hoped that he was bright enough, stealthy enough to do a good job of my rescue, for I had no wish to find out what these gray-clad creatures did with their captives.

They had made an ugly scar in the forest, and inside walls were their mudlike houses. Everything was so hideous that it came to me that it must be deliberate. This gave me something to mull over while I waited for darkness to fall. I had never dreamed of a people so self-hating that they did not desire that things be beautiful. The Clan-Mother would be most interested when I told her of that—if I were ever to have the opportunity.

It grew dark, though to my eyes the night was not impenetrable. The ugly ones went into their houses, except for a few who seemed to be posted about the wall. After a long, quiet time, I heard leaves rustling. Against the sky, a tree beyond the wall was whipping back and forth in long arcs. Ah! Someone with Ssseelt skills was using it to get over the wall!

In another moment, I heard a whuff! of breath forced from lungs. It was accompanied by a soft thump, as a dark shape hurtled into the soft dirt where a bush or tree had been grubbed out. My strange friend had arrived, and in a manner that I would not have believed he could have known or devised. Surely, he was much more than he seemed, this dark-skinned seeker of the Khi!

Before there was time to think, we were beyond the gap in the wall, and behind us terrible sounds were shrieking at the sky. We went up high, and then we went very fast, though it isn't truly safe to take the high roads in the dark. By dawn we were far from the place I had been held captive. Then we went to cover in a hollow in one of the biggest of the trees.

All the while, I was thinking of the things I had learned in a short time. There were, I had found, ways totally unlike those of the Ssseelt. There were beings unlike any that had lived on our lands. Even one who had seemed helpless and stupid could do surprising things in surprising ways. The Ssseelt, I began to suspect, were not, after all, the only wise creatures, or the only effective ones.

Such musings occupied me all the way to the Khi's valley. When I motioned farewell to my new friend, it was with some regret. Yet he had given me much. I believe that from this point onward I will find joy in thinking.

XIV.

Hale Enbo

With the help of my new companion, whom I called Purrl, the journey sped up significantly. He wasn't quite as un-erring—or as patient—as Owl had been, but he was a great asset nevertheless. In addition, he knew where to find water all along our way. That was a blessing, for even with the help of the fruit I became very thirsty. Yet I hesitated to drink from puddles or catchments in the wood, as I had no idea what kinds of internal parasites I might pick up from them.

So we sped along, comparatively speaking, and when the sun set again I felt that we were well on our way toward the Khi. When I tried signing to Purrl, as I had with that other of his race, he looked away westward and laid his forefinger lightly against the branch between us. Three times he tapped, and I felt certain that in three days, barring accidents, I would look again into the valley of the Khi.

The second day was hot. Early in the morning we were already dripping with sweat. I speculated that the summer of Khi-Ash must be reaching its hottest point, and thirst was a problem. Even the fruit that Purrl gathered and brought aloft while I toiled along the ways he showed me did little to quench it.

Finally we descended, with one accord, to the ground and moved toward a deep ravine, from the bottom of which came an enticing gurgle of water. Along the lip of the bank grew a mass of bread-pod bushes. Into that tangle Purrl dived, emerging with a woven-bark basket and a large pottery jug. We had evidently arrived at an emergency stash of equipment maintained by his people. Handing me the basket, he took the jug and indicated that he would go down the overgrown and uncertain path to the water, while I filled the basket with pods and a large cream-colored fruit that was covered with scarlet dots.

I agreed and set to filling the container, as well as any pockets I might find that we had emptied. The fruit he showed me looked supicious, but he was eating one as he sauntered away. I ventured to taste, then I gorged. It was filled with a substance the consistency of thick cream, rather bland but with a nutty tang. In its center was a blob of deep red jelly-like stuff that, when mixed through the rest of the contents with finger or tongue, made a confection that would have made the fortune of any chef.

As I filled one end of the basket with this delight, I heard a strange sort of snap, then a whooshing sound of something flying through branches. I stood frozen for a moment. I recognized both sounds. What little specimen-collecting the Ginli did was done by means of a primitive but effective trap.

Setting the basket down so that it was hidden from any passer-by, I crept past the head of the dim path and moved down the edge of the ravine, keeping Purrl's original direction in mind. I watched both high and low, for I felt certain that Purrl was hanging in a net from some young and slender tree that had sprung back to its full height when he tripped the trigger that freed it. And he was. Almost at eye-level for me as I stood on the bank, he hung yards above the floor of the ravine.

I had opened my mouth to call to him when I heard, distant but distinct, the unmistakable sound of Ginli moving. I gave a low whistle, instead, and the young cat-man heard. He searched the growth until he saw me. Then he wriggled furiously. The net held fast, and I motioned for him to be still. Then I pointed toward the now nearby sound. I made the gesture that the Varlian used for Ginli. Purrl grew still. So . . . there *was* interaction between the two races!

Crawling into the thickest tangle I could find, I pulled vines and branches after me, closing the opening through which I had come. Then I lay low, waiting while the pale

Primates let down the net and secured my hapless friend. When they had trampled their way back up the path that now looked as if it had been used by generations of large-hoofed beasts, I was close behind them.

The Ginli who wrote the manual must have been an odd duck. It never occurred to him that an animal of only moderate intelligence might think to hide while the perfect file of mechanical Ginli that he envisioned stamped past, and then follow at a safe distance. If, of course, any intelligent animal was interested in their doings. I was. I had no intention of letting Purrl, who after all had been where he was only on my account, suffer from those immoderate people.

I didn't even drop back very far. I merely kept a screen of foliage around a bend between us . . . or at least a goodly distance so that I might jump for cover if the Ginli showed signs of turning around. There was really no point even in that. They never looked back, even when they halted for rest stops. I chuckled under my breath. They had always looked down on me because of my brown skin. Yet in every practical test, they scored well below infant Varlian and infinitely below a trained Scout such as I was.

Still there were a half-dozen of them and only one of me. I took no chances. In fact, I took the time to secure the jugful of water that Purrl had been interrupted in getting, as well as my basket of food. I knew beyond doubt that I could follow them, and it took little time to catch up to their file again. Though I was burdened considerably, I found it easy to keep track of them in their noisy progress through the wood.

They carried Purrl, still in the net, slung upside down under a carry-frame. I could imagine that the air around him was turning slightly blue. The language of the cat people was admirably suited to profanity. I had often envied his hissing and spitting expletives as he cussed out some obstacle or inconvenience. Now with a truly worthy object for his abilities, I felt certain that he was letting the Ginli have it, fore and aft.

The day had turned past noon, and it was still hot as Big Sandy in spring. The Ginli stopped for rest and refreshment more and more often, and I knew that they, with their cool-planet heritage, must be suffering. That pleased me no end. I was dripping with sweat, which meant that my breeze of passage cooled me by evaporation. The sun, which had begun to scorch fiercely through more and more numerous breaks in the foliage overhead, couldn't blister my dark skin. I could see, even from a distance, that some of those pale Ginli complexions were beginning to splotch with red.

It began to look as if I might just outlast them until they dropped with heat prostration, then pick Purrl out of his cocoon and take off at my leisure. No such luck . . . they arrived within hailing distance of their encampment. It was typical Ginli: they had felled every tree within leaping distance of their fence, scraped away every trace of vegetation, and put their beast-proof netting around the whole thing. Their ugly extruded-soil buildings centered the circle, and the effect was that of a pile of dung left on the site of some disaster. Which just about summed up my opinion of both place and inhabitants.

They trampled into their camp through a gap in the fence that had a force-guard across it. When the alarms began to hoot and scream they stopped and waited until someone inside the guard-post turned the noise off. Then they dumped their captive in the full glare of the sun. Typically, they neither fed nor watered their prisoner.

As there was no way in which I might enter that camp in full daylight, I withdrew into the forest, found a safe nook in a leafy treetop, and settled to rest. And of course to eat a bit. Though I was not easy about my chances of getting Purrl out of that camp, I managed to sleep the afternoon away, by fits and starts. I did interrupt my dozing periodically to check that they weren't doing anything to my friend that called for immediate action. Weaponless as I was, it was a relief that nothing of the sort happened, though another detachment of Ginli did leave camp for another stamp around the forest.

At nightfall I roused myself fully, checked my stores of food and water, and crept down through the forest as near as I could get to the fence. I was a short stone's throw from it, I

found, and just to my right was a tall thin tree, not too thick,
that looked as if it might have a good bit of spring in its trunk.
One of the valuable things I had learned from the Fssa, in my
infrequent but valuable encounters with that people, was the
astonishing use to which naturally growing vegetation could
be put. A grove or a wood could provide one of the felines
with a veritable arsenal of weapons and equipment.

Night fell, and except for the blaze of stars the darkness
was almost complete. Wishing for the easy grace of Purrl or
his kinsmen, I attacked the thin tree and made my way to the
top. It wasn't very easy to do it silently, but I managed well
enough. The Ginli ear (among other things) is not as well
developed as it might be.

A slight breeze was blowing up there, and it cooled my hot
cheeks as I sat in the treetop, nerving myself for my venture.
At last I gave myself a mental shake and said, "Hale Enbo,
sitting here isn't getting things done. Either go up and do
what you know is the correct things, or climb down and go
hide in a hole someplace." Then I began to sway the treetop
back and forth, shifting my weight to increase the motion.
When the tree had reached its maximum degree of whip, I set
myself, timed my jump, and found myself sailing over the
fence into the Ginli compound.

I alighted, strangely enough, in a pile of soft dirt that
limited the sound of my impact to a "whuff" of air expelled
from my lungs. Proving again, I suppose, that the gods take
care of fools and little children. Nevertheless, I scuttered to
one side and lay low against the wall of one of the buildings
until I was sure that no one was going to investigate the slight
sound. Then I rose to a crouch and tried to orient myself,
listening hard for any sound that might lead me to Purrl.

I could almost hear him listening to find out where I might
be. Those pointed, furry ears were as acute as any I had ever
found. Sure enough, as soon as he decided that the sound he
had heard was made by me, Purrl began muttering softly to
himself. Provided with this fix on his location, I stole across
the clearing and barked my shins on the carry-frame. My
pocket kit, which went where I went even when I was fleeing

for my life, provided a blade. I had Purrl out of the net very quickly.

He laid a hand on my shoulder, and I could fel his killing-claws flexing nervously, just beneath the skin of his palm. I took the hand, stood for a moment remembering the angle at which I had soared into the compound, the position of Purrl's net in relation to the gate, and every turn I had made during my stumblings-about in the enclosure. Unless I was far out in my calculations, we were facing the front (and only) gate.

There being no tree left inside the fence whereby we might spring out, I decided to go out through the gate. Taking the lightly furred hand firmly in mine, I led the cat-man through the darkness toward the spot where I hoped the opening might be.

Purrl, bright boy, divined my intention. With his superior night-vision, he guided me directly between the gateposts. As we moved through, I urged him into a mad leap for cover. We all but passed one another as we swarmed up a tree a short way into the wood. Then we looked back.

Our passage had set off the alarm system. As I knew well from my years with the Ginli, the field was set to prevent the entry of anything into the camp. It never occurred to any Ginli that anyone (or thing) might escape. While outgoing traffic also set off the alarms, it wasn't impeded in any way; and, the alarms being identical, there was no way the Ginli could tell in which direction one who set off the thing might be going.

Naturally, when they found their net empty they assumed that someone had just come in, freed the captive in a burst of superhuman speed, and gone into hiding somewhere nearby. They set guards at the gate and proceeded to search.

I sighed with relief. The Ginli who wrote the manual of search and seizure had never heard of an escapee with either brains or feet. I knew that they would be fully occupied until dawn—or later. By the time they decided that we *must* have gone outward, we would be well and untraceably on our way through the treetops.

Detouring to pick up our supplies, I led Purrl into the

brightest starlight I could find, made the sign for Khi, and
gestured again toward the west.

He put his face close to mine, looked closely, presumably
to make sure that I was in earnest, and gave what looked like a
shrug. He led the way back into the trees, and we moved
away together.

XV.

Hale Enbo

If it had been hard to move through the trees in full daylight, it was almost impossible to do it at night. But with the thought of the Ginli to spur me on, I managed better than I'd have believed possible. Purrl, too, was eager to put a lot of distance behind us, and he moved back and forth, ahead of me, determining by trial and error the best path for me to take. It wasn't easy—he had to move over some of the same ground three times.

Our rest stops were short, though they were considerably enhanced by our basket of fruit and the bottle of water. It was too dark to make satisfactory use of sign language, so we contented ourselves with talking back and forth in our own tongues. We didn't exactly communicate, but the sounds of our voices were a comfort to us both. In point of fact, I soon realized that this people must be some sort of kindred to the Fssa. I recognized several sound combinations that I remembered from my contact with the furred people on other planets. I had never learned Fssa well, but I could recognize it when I heard it.

Rummaging through my memory, as I carefully crawled, climbed, swung, slipped, and slithered through the tangle of treetops, I found at last the phrase that was the Fssa equivalent of, "What kind of being are you?" When we rested again, I threw my hard-won question at Purrl.

He hissed with pure astonishment. Then he spoke, very slowly, one word. It sounded like *Ssseelt*. Then he uttered one more word, "*Hsssch!*" Taking one of my hands, he laid it on his head.

I tried the first word. I felt his head nod against my hand.
Then I tackled the hissing, rasping purr of the second. It
wouldn't come right for my human throat and tongue. I felt
his head give a negative quiver, and his voice came again out
of the darkness. *"Purrl,"* it purred. I echoed it, glad to be
freed of the obligation to use the name his own people had
given him.

We traveled most of the night, halting only when
dawnlight made a band of pale color in the east. Even the best
tracker ever trained on Bahram, the planet of beast-hunters,
could never have traced us. We had left no track aground. But
I knew that the Ginli would have parties out in all directions,
as well as nasty little scoutships zipping through the sky in
search patterns. So Purrl made a careful scout, returning with
a pleased expression on his slanty-cheeked face.

He led me through a maze of branches into the top of one of
the tallest trees I had yet seen. Above a set of huge limbs that
grew spokewise from the tremendous bole, a bolt of lightning
had struck at some time long in the past. The killed wood had
rotted out under the attacks of weather and insects, and a hole
of ample dimensions had formed. Its floor was both springy
and uncertain to the foot, but we trampled it down until it lay
fairly smooth. Then we settled in for a long day of sleep and
hiding.

I woke in the early afternoon, though I had half-roused
several times earlier, when Ginli ships had gone over. From
the spot where I lay, I could see the branch that served as our
front porch. It was fully four feet wide and covered with deep
brown bark. In the crevices nuts had been caught upon falling
from higher in the tree. A small, busy creature was engaged
in harvesting this store, and I watched, fascinated, as it went
about its business.

It was about the size of a large cat or a small dog. Its fur
was a deep ruby color, which meant that it was fully camou-
flaged in the bright foliage worn by these forests. It had a
pouch beneath each arm in which it tucked away nuts until it
was comically lumpy. When fully loaded, it would scurry up
the treetrunk, and after a short absence it would return and
repeat the performance.

Though it seemed fully occupied with its task, any sound from below brought its short sharp ears flicking up until the noise was identified. As I watched, those ears came erect, stiffened, and didn't lie down again. Then I, too, heard the sound of Ginli. I lay back, as the little animal hurried away up the tree again.

Purrl's eyes were open, but he made no sound. I was glad to lie in silent security, letting them hammer through the wood below us. Even though they probably had life-detectors brought down from the lab-ship by now, I knew that on a world so teeming with animals of all sizes and kinds their chances of locating us at all was nonexistent. My principal worry was for the Varlian and the Ssseelt. Knowing the Ginli, I didn't doubt that they would either destroy or take away for dissection any of those people that they might find.

Cursing the limitations of sign-language, I tried to convey to Purrl the dangers of letting Ginli come upon any place where his people lived. I think he understood, for his eyes narrowed, and he hissed what sounded like a curse. I spoke the word that meant Varlian to the green-furred race, then I folded something invisible, gesturing away Ginli as I did so. Then I looked questioningly at Purrl.

He made that crosswise gesture that his kinswoman had used, days before. So the Ssseelt hadn't learned to fold away their enemies. I wondered why the Khi hadn't taught them that useful art. Then I remembered the distaste that both felines had shown when I made the sign for Khi. I wondered if there was enmity between the races.

Then, too, it might have been simply the fierce independence of the feline sort that kept them from accepting the Khi. Whatever the true state of affairs, Purrl was leading me to the Khi as swiftly as he could, though I could see by his actions that he wondered why anyone would seek them out.

Long after the Ginli had moved away, I waited with Purrl in the hollow, letting the sun go down. As twilight filled the forest, we could hear below us, in the leaf-molded aisles of the wood, the large predators beginning their nightly hunts. I sketched with my finger in the rubble on which we lay the outline of the red-brown beast. Purrl nodded, then with his

marvellously flexible hands he mimed such a creature hiding
in its burrow during the day. Those speaking hands told me
that it roused in daylight hours only when nearby motion
caught its ear. But at night such beasts roamed the forest
floor. That made our night-journey through the trees even
more sensible.

When it was fully dark, we set out again, and this time I
was able to travel with more speed and ease. The wood being
extremely dense and its trees giants, the road through the
branches was fairly easy to find. Indeed, I think that even
alone I might have found my way among those wide and
overlapping limbs. Still, I could never have held to my
direction in the dark, the stars hidden by roofing leaves.
Purrl, as well as being on his home planet, had the in-built
compass possessed by most animals with the exception of
Man.

This night saw more progress than the one before. Though
Purrl was neither as swift nor as agile in the trees as the
Varlian, this was irrelevant, as our pace was geared to my
own efforts. It seemed that I was becoming, by force of
circumstance, an arboreal creature. My arms, after giving me
fits with cramps, sore muscles, and general protests, seemed
to be hardening to their work. My feet, freed from boots,
were learning to grip with toes, to feel for sturdy holds, and to
steady me on perches that before this would have sent the
very toenails crawling back into my toes.

When dawn sent us to cover again, I felt that we were
coming near the valley of the Khi. I thought that Purrl agreed,
though the nearer we came to our goal the more reticent he
grew concerning the golden people.

This day we spent high in a tree that sent out nestlike
clumps of branches. We sprawled at ease in one of these,
shielded from below by the thick branches and leafage and
from above by the towering crown of the tree. This tree bore
no nuts, to my sorrow, though Purrl had refilled both basket
and jug before we took shelter. I had found that almost every
species of plant on Khi-Ash afforded some sort of edible
fruit, nut, or pod. It was a paradise for wildlife, not to
mention my own sort. I comforted myself with bread-pods

and the jelly-centered fruit. Then we dozed away the day,
rousing only to send insulting gestures after scoutships that
came ripping overhead. When we set out again with the
coming of darkness, I felt that we would be in the valley by
another dawn.

I wasn't far out in my calculations. The stars had wheeled
to their positions of predawn when Purrl drew me to a halt and
pointed outward with an all-but-invisible paw. I looked up
from my handholds to see a wide sweep of stars that was
unimpeded by treetops. We must have arrived at the edge of
the rim above the valley. I moved back along the branch on
which I perched and leaned against the treetrunk.

We waited for daylight. Now we must do down, and
neither of us relished ending the journey in the teeth of a
carnivore. It seemed a long time before the sun began to rise
behind us, sending light and color across the mountains that
lay across the western side of the valley. When the forest
floor was visible, we descended from our tree and I walked to
the edge of the cup and looked over.

Though it was still filled with the blue-purple of shadow,
light from the sky was bringing out the creamy foliage of the
trees and the warm colors of the grasses. The road down
which the Varlian had brought me lay at an angle to my
present position. I couldn't see, from where I stood, the
clump of stone from which Khi-Sang had greeted us.

I turned to Purrl and motioned for him to join me, but the
Ssseelt drew back into the forest. He made his crosswise
gesture, and I went back to try to persuade him to come. But
no, he would move no farther toward the west. I took his hand
and looked into his catlike face.

"My friend," I said, "you have helped me find my way. I
wouldn't have survived to do it alone. You and your people
have a claim upon me, always. Good luck to you."

He may not have understood my words, but he took my
meaning. He purred a long string of syllables. Then he made
a sign that meant "friend." With no more farewell, he
melted into the lower branches.

With a sigh, I began to walk southward along the rim.
Without the guide of the road I knew I would never be able to

find the stones that marked the Khi's doorway. I was quite a distance from the point at which Lime had led us from the forest, and by the time I found the track the sun was slanting down into the valley. Without stopping to wonder what I intended to do, I began my descent. I didn't even don my boots but enjoyed the feel of the warm dust between my toes. I hadn't done that since I was a boy on Big Sandy.

I came to the arching tree. Using that as a landmark, I decided upon the stone formation that must be the correct one. When I reached it I stood on the spot where the door had opened, but there was no trace of it now. For all I could tell, this had always been a simple pile of stone and nothing more.

There in the growing heat of sunlight, I felt desperate. Except for the Khi, I had no refuge, no hope of help on Khi-Ash. The thought of taking to the woods and living off the land, though I could have done both, left me cold. My people have always been achievers. Living the life of a carefree beast would be a kind of death for me. Only through this invisible doorway lay some chance of life and accomplishment. I laid my forehead against the warm rock. It was totally unyielding.

Then I envisioned the topaz chamber to which Khi-Sang had led us. Between this spot and that lay only . . . space. I seized that space in my two hands and, ignorant and desperate, I bent it to my will.

XVI.

Khi-Sang

We are filled with joy. Our pupil has found us again, through his own efforts. By his will, he has folded himself into our chamber once more, and there he rests.

We had doubts, at the first, when the Hril gave us this duty to perform. We should have known that those great beings know far more than do we and can judge the abilities of their thought-children far more accurately than any other might do.

Now the education of Hale Enbo will begin!

XVII.

Hale Enbo

This time there was no dizzy fall through the dark tunnels. Instead I seemed to be suspended, bodiless and without volition, in a blackness so intense that it was like a physical presence. My mind was caught in a wind that riffled every thought I had ever entertained, as if those thoughts were pages in a book. There was no time involved. So when I stood again in my own flesh and could see, I had no idea how long it had been since I had folded myself into the Khi's refuge.

I was in the topaz room. The light was dimmer than it had been, for no Khi stood within to cast its golden light. Still I could see that the furnishings that had been there for the use of the Varlian and me were now gone. The chamber was empty except for the table in the center. I swayed with weariness; then I sat in one of the places and laid my head on the table.

The past nights had been a strain and effort beyond any I had ever exerted. The energy required for the "folding" process was tremendous. I was exhausted and hungry. I had left my basket and the jug outside when I had attacked the doorway. Behind me, beside the curved wall opposite the door, I heard a soft sound. Sitting up, I turned to see a cushioned couch standing on low legs. Nothing had stood there before.

I had sneaked up on the Khi? Ha! But I was too tired to worry about it right now. I dropped onto the springy stuff of the couch, pulled up a downy cover, and fell into sleep.

That sleep was filled with vivid dreams, but when I woke none of them stayed with me. I sat up, dazed with drowsiness, and saw the rounded golden form of Khi-Sang standing beside the table. Don't ask how I knew that it was Khi-Sang. I can't tell you anything except that each of the Khi projected a different "feel." Even after being summarily folded away, I had no fear or suspicion of the Khi. I stood, tried to straighten my crumpled tunic, and waited for her to speak.

She didn't. Instead, she motioned for me to follow her to the washing room we had used before. I was more than glad to oblige, for it had been too long since I had a chance to take a real bath. Even hungry as I was, I didn't hurry over my ablutions. I soaked and scrubbed for a long time, and when I emerged from the bathpool a fresh tunic and trousers lay where mine had been. Either new ones had been made, lightning-fast, to the same pattern as the old, or the worn ones had been cleaned and repaired so that I could find no trace of wear or dirt.

When I came again into the dark marble tunnel, I was a new man. A hungry new man. Khi-Sang had been joined by Khi-Rehm and Khi-Lohm, and the three led me again to the topaz room and stood looking proudly at the table. I didn't stop to look; I just sat and began working my way through everything. Fruit and bread-pods had been good and sustaining, but I had no idea when I might sit again before a table of cooked food, with delicate meats and piquant sauces. While I suspected that no animal had died to provide the meat, and that no hand had moved to make the sauces, the fact that these were probably molecular constructs subtracted nothing from either flavor or, I was sure, nutrition.

At last I sat back, filled to the last chink for the first time in what seemed years. I smiled at the Khi, who glowed gently back at me.

"You have done well," Khi-Sang said, her precise Varlian sounding inside my head. "We were uncertain, limited as you have been by your training, that you could grasp the possibilities of the folding technique. Had we described to you the mathematical theories that were used to arrive at the method, you would have believed that you must attack it rationally. For us, with our long experience, this is the way.

For others it must be grasped emotionally. So with the Varlian. So it would have been for the Ssseelt, had they con-
sented to be our pupils.

"But those proud people live in their own way, making
their own arts and techniques, step by step, alone. We allow
and even encourage that, for it is in that manner that diversity
flowers. We are bored by too much sameness. There are on
Khi-Ash six races that are or will become rational. Four of
them are native to the world, including ourselves. The Varlian, as you know, were planted by those you call the Ffryll.
The Ssseelt we brought to Khi-Ash in the days of the youth of
our kind. When we, too, explored the worlds in this continuum."

"Ah!" I interjected. "I had wondered if they aren't related
to the Fssa. They are so similar."

"True," she answered. "The Ssseelt and the Fssa are
descendants of the same species. When we encountered that
race, full of the promise of intelligence and grace, we felt
both affection and admiration for its members. We brought
away with us enough to seed Khi-Ash."

Now Khi-Rehm interrupted. "We saw in your mind many
questions, as you moved through our dimension. Now that
we are existing for a time in yours, we wish to satisfy some of
your wonderings. We need, most of all, to teach you the ways
of folding space, however, for there is a task that only you
can perform."

I perked up my ears. I said before that I come of a family of
achievers. A new work, a unique task, a difficult challenge,
all those rouse an intense interest within me. I had hoped that
the work the Ginli offered would be such, but all they wanted
was the same sort of things done in precisely the same ways,
and only the same results were acceptable to them. Anything
the Khi had in mind would, I felt sure, be out of the ordinary.

Khi-Lohm took up the tale. "We made a pact, longer ago
than would be conceivable to your mind, that we would not
interfere directly with species that posed a danger to other
sorts of beings. Our reasons, at the time, seemed good, for
we had made a tragic error, as young ones will, in dealing
with one such race.

''This pact we might have rescinded, if it seemed good to us, except for the fact that it was made with beings as far removed from our actual physical selves as those selves are removed from yours. Those are the ones you saw as flickers of motion, deep in the wall of the diamond room. They are . . . wise, though that is a term that cannot begin to encompass the Hril. They maintain that the pact is still valid, still useful. They have chosen you as the one who must remove the danger posed by the Ginli to the peoples of Khi-Ash, and they hint that there is another, greater task waiting for you in your future. So we cannot protect our own world. We can only give you the training you will need and allow you to do that for us.''

Things were beginning to make a bit of sense. I have the sort of mind that rejects randomness, and the seeming senselessness of my career on Khi-Ash to this point had been bothering me all the way through. But if there was pattern and purpose . . .

I was thinking hard, now. The Varlian, I had seen, could protect themselves from the Ginli very handily—if they knew they were there. The Ssseelt possibly had ways of dealing with them, too, though I really doubted that. But the lesser races, just emerging into sapience, would be as helpless as infants faced with the Ginli. And I had been chosen to protect all these species? It seemed a tall order.

The Khi had been following my thought. They were all glowing when I looked up at them again, Khi-Sang said, ''This is the will of the Hril. You are well upon the path toward the skills that you will need, having learned to use your own fear and desperation to warp the fabric of space, which is, after all, a mere projection of the thoughts of those who live in this continuum. Now you must learn to use such knowledge with precision and accuracy. When you deal with incarnate beings there is no room for error. You have learned the practice, now you must learn the theory. When you have done that, you must work with it to achieve ease.''

We rose, then, with one accord, and went into the room with diamond walls. This time I faced another direction, looking into the curved wall instead of the flat one. The stool on which I sat, I understood now, had been formed by the thought of the Khi from the atoms of the air about us. It was a temporary arrangement only, and could be unthought as quickly as it came.

As I sat there the wall began to dance with reverberating light. Khi-Rehm, Khi-Sang, and Khi-Lohm placed themselves at either side of me and behind me. The pulsing of their glows now became rhythmic, making a pattern of sparkles flicker through the wall like visible echoes. The light became hypnotic. I entered a half-waking trance, and knowledge began pouring into me through both the conscious and the unconscious levels of my mind. At the same time, I seemed to move slightly apart from my physical self until I could see myself sitting on the stool, the room, the Khi, all from a different, higher angle. Around all those shapes I could see lines of energy or force or something else analogous to both. Everything was netted in this webbing. I began to understand, dimly, that I was seeing the fields emitted by every physical thing and, evidently, every non-physical but energy-emitting thing too.

The network pulsed as I watched it. The motion and its timing were also hypnotic. I felt as though I were being drawn along the lines into some dimension I had never suspected of existing. Though I felt some resistance to the notion, I quelled the feeling and moved with the pull into a shining space, shot through with glitters and beams and flashes that I was now able to recognize as Khi-Sang and her companions.

Though they had practically no physical appearance whatever, they were still uniquely recognizable as themselves. Language became unnecessary. Concepts and information flooded my mind. Though I knew my physical brain only existed in the dimension we had left, yet I still possessed my old sense of self. And whatever it was using in place of a brain was doing the job infinitely more efficiently than the flesh and blood computer that I had left behind.

It is difficult to convey this in words. To begin with, time did not exist, so that what sounds as if it took place in a very short span actually required both millennia and no time at all. There were no verbal processes. Gripped in what must have been the matrix that formed the universe, I saw/heard/felt/knew/understood the nature of all things, material and immaterial. The nature of space/time was made clear to me, and the correlations between space and matter, their interactions, their actual identity all took up residence within me.

The things that I had been taught as laws of physics and facts of nature were, in truth, agreements among the incomprehensible minds whose thought formed the Cosmos I knew. I found these agreements to be far more flexible than my kind believed. They were subject to change, at need, and the ways of making those changes, without endangering the fabric of all that is, were now becoming a part of me. I sat in that flow for a seeming eternity, absorbing everything.

Then there was a wrenching of the forces that held me. I was sitting on the stool, once more, with the Khi about me. I shook my head.

"The Hril . . . they *think* everything into being . . ." I mused.

Khi-Sang glowed, and the light quivered like laughter. "True. Though we and you and other rational beings—even the Ginli—contribute our small energies and our tiny and unconscious willings to the effort. The Khi are . . . between. Think of the dimensions of here and there, where you were, as two layers of fabric. Lie as closely as they may, still there will be a space between them. We exist in such spaces. We are between all dimensions, we and our kind, though we began as finite beings on this insignificant planet. The Hril are those who exist within, and between, and independent of, all dimensions. They are almost beyond our comprehension, even their most simple aspects. They exist in ways we cannot know, for purposes we have not been able to fathom or even discern."

I thought of those glints in the diamond wall and nodded. "What now?"

"Now," said Khi-Sang, and her voice, which was really no voice, managed to sound sad within my skull, "we must send you back, once more. For you must learn, surely and infallibly, to translate the things your greater self knows into actions that your lesser self is capable of performing.''

So I went whirling, once more, down that dark tunnel. This time there was neither fear nor bewilderment. Only anticipation.

XVIII.

Hale Enbo

Once again I was looking through thick springy bushes leaved in shades of gold and brown and red. The familiar purple sea washed the familiar shore where the pale beach was still shadowed by the trees from the glow of the morning sun. Behind me in the forest where I had met Lime I could hear the row that was Ginli moving through woodland. I sighed.

They were coming, from the sound of them, straight for me. I wondered, not for the first time since I reached Khi-Ash, if they were certain that I was still alive, or if they were after something entirely different. It may be that they had never planeted themselves on any world so thickly tenanted with life-forms. Their brainwave telltales must be going mad, back on the ship, with so many intelligent species registering . . . no wonder, I thought, that they hadn't managed to pinpoint me.

I hadn't time to think of that now, however, for they were getting close. I looked across the arm of the sea at the so-far-unexplored forest on its other side. Without thinking, I reached inside myself, took hold of the short space between there and here, and folded myself over into that thick wood. Then I realized what the Khi had meant about precision and accuracy. Not to mention "no room for error." Only luck kept me from folding myself *into* the tree on which I thumped my head so solidly.

As it was I stood for a bit with my head ringing like a carillon. Which gave the small but many-toothed black ani-

mal that had been going about its business a long arm's-
length away time to recover from its surprise. Before my
head had stopped ringing, it was on me. Small as it was it was
more than a handful. Those teeth were not terribly sharp, but
there were several rows of them, and when they clamped onto
my left arm there seemed no way to get them off. I battered
the beast against the treetrunk, but it only chomped harder. I
took its neck in my right hand and tried to choke it into letting
go. His windpipe must have been protected by thick shields
of muscle and bone, for I didn't even make him gasp.

I stood there with the creature hanging from my arm like
some oversized parasite. The time had come for thinking, I
decided. Blind reaction had done no good at all. The thing
had grabbed my left arm just above the elbow. My own arm
and shoulder got into my way when I tried to examine it
closely, so I raised my fist above my head, bringing the beast
up to eye-level.

The head was round. The body was furred with bristly
black hair that curled in much profusion. I couldn't even find
where the eyes might be. The nostrils were only evident
because the air the thing exhaled made the fur riffle gently
(only one riffle, which meant only one nostril). Its body was a
podgy oval, black on top with unexpected creamy bandings
on the underside. It had no tail that I might pinch until it
yelped. The feet (four of them, just like all the other animals I
had seen here so far) were thick-furred on top and horny-
leathered on the soles. No chink in the armor there. As I
looked at it in something like despair, the fur on what should
have been its brow wrinkled slightly. One dark, limpid,
soulful eye, peered out at me.

Something about that liquid gaze brought me to my senses.
I looked inside myself and found the store of knowledge the
Hril and the Khi had given me. There, in that other dimension
of myself, was the pattern of being and relationship that I can
only describe as a grid, though that does no justice to the
multi-dimensionality of the perception. Within that pattern
was, I now realized, every living thing on this world, from
tree to Khi.

Carefully, I grasped the space between my tree and the next but one. I folded gently, moving only that space in which I stood inside my skin and clothing. When the short spin was over, I was free of the beast, which was lying on the ground where I had been. It looked as confused as a round heap of fur can manage to look, and there were still a couple of its teeth in my arm. The bites weren't deep, and I figured that an animal with as many teeth as it had wouldn't suffer for want of two or three. Without waiting for it to decide to come after its property, I skinned up a tree and went a few miles through the treetops.

By now I was about as adept as one of my species can get at moving through treetops. I figured my route as I went along, avoiding many, if not most, of the dead ends I had formerly worked my way into. Being in no hurry, this time, I saw the country through which I was traveling, too.

On my journeys with Lime and with Purrl, I had been only faintly conscious of multitudes of moving creatures in the forest through which we went. Now, traveling slowly and alone, I would find myself sitting motionless in hidden spots, watching the beasts that swung and crawled and trotted and gamboled about the forests of Khi-Ash. There were more in the small space between the purple sea and the valley of the Khi than I had catalogued on some entire worlds for the Ginli.

There was a tiny scarlet monkey-like creature, distant kin to the Varlian and to me. (And to the Ginli, protest it as they would!) I realized that the trees through which we had moved before had almost certainly been thickly populated by these creatures. Yet they were so adept at dissolving into their bright-leaved aeries that I had caught no glimpse of them before. They were not alone in the high trails of the wood. I counted thirty sorts of small Primates, once I had learned how to spot them.

On the forest floor there were dozens of other kinds of beasts. The hooved and horned varieties that on other worlds grazed and browsed were here adapted to eating the fruits and pods and nuts that grew in such profusion. The only grass-eater I saw (though I actually saw only the result of its

grazing, not the creature itself) was a burrower that seized the
infrequent tuft of grass that found enough sunlight to grow
and pulled it neatly belowground. And at that it might have
used the grass for nests instead of for food.

There were more predators of the large sort than just the
red-brown beast that I now knew so well. They were limited,
in their hunting, to the ground. I saw no hunting cats . . .
indeed, no cats at all except for the Ssseelt. But there were
almost-wolves, pseudo-bears (totally carnivorous, unlike
many of the other ursine sorts I'd found elsewhere), and
creatures that seemed to have been shaped by a mind in the
throes of nightmare. None, however, were wanton killers.
All went about their business in the scheme of the ecology
with competence and enthusiasm but without real ferocity.
Even the red-brown beasts had only recognized me as meat.
It had been nothing personal.

As for insect and birdlife, I could have spent years at the
business of differentiating and cataloguing, though I was no
sort of entomologist or ornithologist. The Ginli, fearing no
competition from birds or bugs, weren't interested in finding
out about them. Still, I found myself so intrigued by them that
I wished for another education, along with an extra lifetime in
which to use it. Not to mention cameras and sketch-pads and
cataloguing forms. For the first time, I realized that I had
stumbled, with the Ginli, into the sort of work that I loved,
though I hadn't known that until I escaped from their rigid
specifications and requirements.

I don't have any idea how long I would have dawdled
through the wood, spending whole days in hiding as I
watched the interactions of the creatures about me. I was
celebrating the first high festival and holiday of my life, but I
was brought up short by two things.

The weather, which had been all but perfect, turned sear-
ingly dry and hot. Even in the deep shadow of the forest the
branches were hot enough to be uncomfortable. When I
ventured down to streams the stones in their beds could
blister unprotected skin. This caused a lethargy among the
creatures I had been watching, as they panted in dark nooks,
conserving their energies. The heat also affected the foliage.

The red and golden and garnet and umber leaves curled inward on their central stems, hoarding their moisture from the thirsty sun. This left me feeling unpleasantly exposed to the Ginli who came thumping along, now and then, still searching for me or for something else they seemed to want as much or more.

That would have been enough to send me folding, by degrees, toward·the Khi. Except for the other thing. Near noon one day, as I lay in the coolest spot I could find, I was called. Not by the Khi or the Varlian, I was certain. Most surely not by the Ssseelt, for they used no sort of mental contact. But something called to me, off to northward.

There were no words, no commands, yet I knew in that other sense that I now possessed that something terrible was about to happen . . . something that I could stop, if I hurried.

For the first time, I combined emotion with knowledge, feeling along the webbed forces that were the lives of the creatures of Khi-Ash. Spatial lines crossed and interlinked with those others, giving me an inner vision analogous to that of the orientation system of a spaceship, though mine seemed far more detailed and usable than any that engineers had ever described to me.

Using this grid, which was perfectly visible to my mind, I used the ''call'' as a vector, scanning the wedge of area that fanned out to northwest from the spot where I stood. Within that pie-shaped space there were several groups of lives that denoted villages or colonies of beings larger than the monkeys and other arboreal creatures of their size.

Refining my inner vision, I chose a spot near the first cluster of lives, making sure that I would be screened from it by a thick layer of trees. Then I delicately folded away the miles between, and I found myself surrounded by prickly bushes that had grown up beside the fallen trunk of a gigantic tree. It took a moment to orient myself. Then I crept through the growth, stopping for a number of reconnaissances of the surrounding area.

There were scurrying creatures of all sizes around me, but I could hear ahead the murmur of hissing voices. I knew

before I could see that I was approaching a Ssseelt village.
My curiosity was aroused, for I had wondered what form of
culture their race might have chosen. When I looked cautiously through the bushes that ringed their town, I saw a
pleasing group of stone houses, each of which was set about
with flowering bushes. They were built in a meandering
group that took best advantage of extremely tall specimens of
the ever-present nut tree. They were not the geometric
monstrosities we Primates feel obliged to erect: they were
free-flowing shapes of natural stone. They even had plots of
flowers and small blossoming plants set into the crannies of
their roofs.

I could see at once that this was an untroubled community,
for the Ssseelt were going about their daily routines in an easy
and unhurried way. Kits played among the tree-roots and hid
in the bushes. Adults gathered nuts and fruits, tidied homes
and paths, lounged in the shade, talking with their fellows. I
saw neither Purrl nor the lady who had first encountered me,
and I decided that they must belong to a different group.
Smiling, I felt beyond myself and folded gently northward.

There were three life-groupings in the next area, according
to the pattern inside my head. The first was Varlian, a village
arranged much as the home of Lime had been but considerably smaller. I inspected it from cover, not willing to spare
the time to make contact with them. There seemed to be no
problem there, everyone being busy and happy.

I crept through the treetops to the second group, for it was
too near to bother with folding. At first I wasn't certain that I
had found it, for it was like no community of intelligent
creatures I had ever seen. No dwelling was immediately
apparent, though several orange-furred creatures sat together
in a small clearing . . . and they were weaving. As I
watched, two of them rose from their hunkered positions and
moved backward to accommodate the lengthening fabric
they were making. Then I saw that these beings, registered
upon my inward chart as intelligences, were truly new to me.
They were arachnids.

Their eight arms were unequal in length and strength, as in
the lesser kinds of spider I had found elsewhere, but the limbs

were more mobile and half of them ended in definite hands.
Four were set in a swiveling double socket at a spot analogous
to my shoulders. Two were set to fore and two to aft at the
lower end of the long, cylindrical body, making a very stable
walking apparatus. An anthropomorphic head rose above the
shoulders, and faceted eyes sparkled in the afternoon sunlight
that was filtering through the trees.

I closed my own eyes and "looked" all around the peaceful spot. There was no trace of any other large, inimical
being, though the wood teemed with smaller creatures,
whose minds were limited to thoughts of food and sleep and
mating.

When I looked again at the orange beings, one had left the
group and was in the process of disappearing into an opening
that had magically appeared in the forest floor. The others
were folding up their handiwork, which one of them bundled
off into another burrow while a third and its smaller companion moved toward the wood where I was hiding. I moved
higher, very quickly, and they went below me, talking in
sputters and wobbling squeaks and clickings.

Intrigued, I slid over to the other side of the tree in order to
watch them further. They didn't go far—and when they
stopped I found another reason to travel through the high
places. Across a narrow gap in the undergrowth that marked
an animal trail they had strung a web. The strands were thick
enough to resist the struggles of a really big animal, and in it
was caught one of the black beasts of many teeth.

Chattering their Morse-like lingo, the two dampened their
"hands" with a secretion from their chests and proceeded to
free their captive. They evidently knew its kind well, for they
left a mat of webbing over its mouth and forepaws while
bundling it into a basket that expanded magically from a
tight-folded little package. Then they retraced their steps
while I moved to watch them.

In the time they had been gone, the other pair of creatures
had built a fire in the center of the space in which they had
worked. It seemed to be held in a wide, flat bowl of some
kind, and it blazed more hotly than its size would have
seemed to warrant. While I watched, the "trappers" moved

into view with their prey. In a very short time they had
skinned and gutted it and had it impaled on a rod that two of
them turned between forked sticks bracketing the fire-bowl.

I would have watched until they finished their feast, for
many more of the creatures were joining them, but I felt again
the compulsion to find the source of that call. With some
reluctance I left them about the cookfire, the flames lighting
their bright, hairy bodies until the entire group seemed to be
blazing.

As I puzzled, I went through the now-thinning trees. My
inner compass held me to my direction without effort, a
change that I found wonderful in my new state. Yet I was
filled with concern. Somewhere very near to me, lives were
endangered. And Ginli were there. Their strange mind-
patterns were coming through strongly on my guiding grid.

XIX.

Hale Enbo

The sun was down. Even the traces of red light had died from the west. The darkness slowed me to a crawl, though urgency thrilled through my bones. The meager starlight barely allowed me to move at all, yet I hesitated to take to the lower ways for fear of beasts and webs. Caught between problems, I paused in a crotch of a tree, high in the night, to think what might be best to do.

There was again that hum inside my mind that told me of the attention of the Khi. No word, no hint of suggestion came with it, but the hum itself directed my attention inward. Feeling dislocated, even disoriented, with my recently-acquired store of knowledge still not integrated into my here-and-now self, I settled myself, grudging the time, to sort out what I might use.

First I centered within myself, feeling the energies out, examining the network of impulses that was I. Slowly I moved my perceptions outward, extending the pattern now accessible to me to cover the area nearby. I found that even the slow, deliberate life of the trees could be detected as a multitude of silvery-faint lines. Reaching out more, I encompassed by degrees the entire space between myself and the group of lives toward which I was moving.

They were Varlian. In the forest just north of them were Ginli. Though I thought that waking Varlian could handle any number of Ginli without trouble, sleeping Varlian were another story.

Gauging the positions of the two groups to a nicety, I folded myself carefully through the forest, making certain of the locations both of trees and large life-forms. I missed everything handily. The Khi, I decided, would be proud of me.

But when I reached a point at which I could differentiate finely between Ginli and Varlian, I was stunned to find that several Varlian had already been captured and were mixed in with the pale people so that folding them away would take the Varlian, too. I moved carefully along the ground, feeling with one part of my senses for any dangerous presence. With the rest of me, I busily sorted through the group I was making for.

I was too preoccupied to recall the fate of Purrl, all those days ago. With a sickening swish, a net rose beneath my feet and whipped me into a bundle, high in the night-cool air. As I went up, I thought bitterly that the Ginli *would* have to throw away their old trapping manual just when they were after me. All these generations they've bumbled along, having to use others for getting specimens. Why had they just now thrown their old tactics out the window and begun to use common sense?

Swinging there in the treetop, I had a sudden thought. The Khi would know why. They might even know how. If they could hum around inside my head, they could do the same to the Ginli. And the Ginli, being who they are, would never understand or admit that the sudden bursts of brilliant insight weren't their own.

I could have folded myself safely away. Yet I *knew* that wasn't the right thing. Not at this juncture. So I watched with my new negative-image inner sight while the Ginli grouped their prisoners in a huddle and set up their flamers to focus on the sleeping village.

Usually, I had heard, they used flamers only for serious matters like burning out the plague-spot on Osis. Their use was forbidden by System Law for something like this. I could only surmise that the presence of so many groups of Varlian, as well as the matter of being folded away by Lime and Owl, must have set their teeth on edge. I would have bet my boots that they intended depopulating the planet of Varlian.

The germ of a plan was working inside me. I didn't really want to remove the Ginli . . . I wanted to move the Varlian to a safer spot, nests and all. It would be a shock to them, not to mention an inconvenience, but not so much as waking to fire and death. I thought back along my path. There had been a large clearing not too far from the Ssseelt village. It would accommodate, as far as I could tell, the trees, the Varlian in their nests, and a sufficiently deep layer of soil to hold the trees upright. Their tenants might choose to stabilize them or to find others, but at least they would be alive. That decided, I measured the pattern of the village against the pattern of the spot I had chosen.

So much tap root would be needed to sustain the lives of the trees. I knew that as if I *were* a tree, though I had never before considered the matter. So much area on either side of the grove was needed to hold the clump stable. Each problem raised itself and solved itself inside that inner system that I was now learning to use as the Khi had insisted I must. When all was settled to the satisfaction of whatever it was that now lived in my head with me, I closed my eyes, saw the entire area that I must fold away, and moved it as gently as possible. I found that I could look, by extending my grid, into that now-occupied clearing. It had become a grove, though one that thrust itself higher than the surrounding forest.

I was brought back to myself by the noisy surprise of the Ginli. They were standing in their strategically planned position, flamers planted for burning out the village. The spot that had been a dark tangle against the starry sky was now a pit of darkness. The sky blazed down, untroubled by leaf or branch. Ginli were scrambling over to peer into the pit by the light of their helmet-lanterns.

I grinned into the night and settled back. If they remembered their trap, after this unexpected setback, they would come to check it. I had nothing to worry about until then, so I found the most comfortable position I could and dozed off.

I woke to sunlight glaring into my eyes through the tree-tops to the east. I had slept long past daylight, though I'd intended to wake early and think about those Varlian still held

captive. I might have slept longer still, but the Ginli trapping
party woke me with their progress toward my net. I set myself
to play the terrified and helpless prisoner.

There was a babble of guttural Ginli from below, as they
found the trap sprung. The tree shook, and I was hauled down
by the trip-rope. I went limp and looked scared.

A familiar face peered down at me as I was disentangled.
"Ho, Brown Man, we have caught you at last!" Number
Forty grunted in the guttural Terranglo the Ginli used with
Scouts. "This *errhampfet* world had hidden you from our
scanners with its many inferior minds, but we have you at
last. Proof it is that we of the Ginli cannot be long befooled
by lesser beings." He chuckled. I grinned at him, remembered almost too late that I was terrified, and turned it into
what I hoped was a grimace of despair. Inside, I was roaring
with laughter.

They fastened me to a steel pole, strung together with three
Varlian and a Ssseelt. We were shackled, hands and feet,
with light chains, too short-coupled to allow a long step or
wide reach. Rings set into the chains were looped around the
pole. We all went along like a string of beads. The Varlian
and the Ssseelt were doped with animal-tranquilizers. They
could walk, but that was all.

After an attempt to whisper to the Varlian in front of me, I
gave it up. It was just staggering along, and the Ssseelt
behind me was groggy, too, He stepped on my heel more than
once, and that was totally un-Ssseelt-like. Twice he slumped
against my back, almost out on his feet.

I could have removed us all from the spot, leaving the Ginli
with pole, empty shackles, and a conundrum to last their
lifetimes. Again, I hesitated to do that. Something told me to
follow along, just short of letting the others be vivisected or
my own brain be removed for pickling.

We plugged along for miles, seeing no living thing, though
I knew that beasts were thick about us. The racket the Ginli
made was explanation enough. Only by use of the ship's
scanners did they know what hordes of living things teemed
on Khi-Ash. I wondered, as I walked, what sort of signal was
given off by the Khi . . . or did they register at all? It might

well be that their physical brains, if any, existed outside this
dimension entirely.

As I mused, we neared a compound. It might have been the
same from which I had rescued Purrl, or any other they'd ever
set up. All Ginli camps look alike. We were marched in, and
the pole to which we were fixed was snapped into slots in two
posts set deep in the ground. Locks snicked over the slots,
and we were secured to Ginli satisfaction. We could sit on the
ground or, by shifting the rings along the pole, we could lie
flat with our hands hanging from the chains.

It was past noon. We'd walked all morning without rest or
water, and the sun was now doing its best to melt us into the
shadeless dirt of the compound. I gave up my imitation of a
rabbit and stood up.

"You, Forty!" I yelled. "If you must have specimens to
torture and a Primate brain to pickle, you'd better get us some
water, some food, and some shelter from the sun. You're
going to end up with five stinking corpses, otherwise.
Number Ten won't like that at all."

Forty emerged from one of the dunghills and looked across
the glare of the compound. "You dare to *demand?*"

"Picked it up from you bastards," I replied.

He growled a stream of Ginli that sounded (and was)
profane. But he stalked across and looked down at my now-
unconscious companions.

"They passed out as soon as they stopped," I said. "If
somebody doesn't get some shade over them and rouse them
enough to drink some water, you're not going to have anything but carrion to show for your night's work. And how are
you going to explain to Ten that the village you were about to
obliterate vanished before your eyes? You'd better have
something to distract him from that."

Though he didn't like it, Forty knew I was right. He saw
that a shelter of leafy boughs was put up, oversaw the water-
ing of his captives, and had a tray of the flat-tasting bread that
is staple Ginli fare set before us. Then he went back to his
dunghill. I paid no attention, but set to and ate all I could
hold, regardless of flavor. I had no idea when I'd eat again,
and I intended to be fortified for all eventualities.

The sun went down. It would be tomorrow before we were sent to the labship, I knew. My companions were sleeping, naturally now, after their unappetizing rations. I waited until it was quite dark. Then I folded the sleeping Varlian and the Ssseelt away into the wood to a spot we had passed as we came. Their shackles jangled softly as they fell, empty, the lengths of the chains.

I lay back in the sun-warmed dust and let my hands dangle above my head. I closed my eyes and fell asleep laughing.

XX.

Hale Enbo

I woke to a drizzle of rain dripping through the root onto my face. It was almost day. A watery edge off to the east showed a faint light. With a sigh for the lost delights of the cavern of the Khi, I sat and tried to arrange the boughs above me so they would make a better shelter. Then I set to and finished what was left of the bread and water.

I could tell that heavier rain was on its way, for a distant rumble of thunder was walking out of the northwest toward the camp. With full daylight came a thunderstorm, accompanied by a downpour that could have drowned me if I hadn't kept my chin down. My roof of branches was swept down with the first gust of wind, leaving me to gasp in the streaming torrent.

The Ginli guards never varied in their rounds, though they ran with water from helmet to heels. When they and I were all but drowned, I heard the rasping tinkle as one of them consulted his timepiece. Eight death-rattles sounded from the thing, and as the last gasped to silence, Number Forty emerged from his hut.

He looked at the lowering sky. He set his booted foot into a stream of water that was carrying away the runoff from his roof. It came almost to his calf. He looked across the compound at me, and I knew that my bedraggled state was giving him as much pleasure as those people allow themselves to indulge in. He turned his back and reentered the hut, and two new guards relieved their wet companions.

I didn't worry. Wet never hurt me. I don't take colds, and I certainly don't melt. I knew the Ginli shuttle would land in the cleared spot to the east, exactly on schedule. Even if the landing must be made in two feet of water or a raging tornado. The "book" on timing is highly important to Ginli. Their greatest fixation is promptness.

The brush roof that had fallen on all sides of me had concealed the fact that I was now the only one shackled to the pole. I waited with damp anticipation for the first prisoner detail to make the morning check. About mid-morning, three guards came tramping over to the pole and flung the tangle of branches aside. When they understood that I was now alone they stood for a moment, shocked into immobility. One of them went along the line of empty shackles, examining each minutely for signs of tampering. When nothing of the sort was found, they stared at me.

The "corporal" lowered himself enough to address me. "Hale Enbo, where are our lawful captives? You must know. You were here all the time!"

"What a pity you didn't watch the others the way you watched me," I yawned. "They evidently aren't the animals you thought they were. Apparently they're smarter than I am. I slept most of the night, but not too deeply, and I didn't hear a thing. Didn't you?"

He glared at me and turned on his heel to report to Forty. From the explosion of Ginli that erupted from the hut, I knew that Forty had been touched on the raw. I knew a lot of Ginli. What I was hearing was not the high-class language that was supposed to be used by officers.

I stood in deep mud and watched as every Ginli in the camp was pressed into the search. Without heeding the rain they poked into every existent and nonexistent cranny inside the fence. They tested the field at the gate. They sorted through my scanty shelter, leaf by leaf. They even turned out their own living quarters.

Only the arrival of the shuttle diverted them from their search. It came down, as I had expected, exactly on time (I could tell that from the pleased expression on Forty's face). The duty-force snapped into formation and moved out to meet the incoming detachment.

Though I couldn't hear from my isolated position, Forty's

stance as he reported to his superior told me much. Unless I
was badly mistaken, he was describing superhuman (super-
Ginli?) efforts expended in finding and subduing me. If I
knew anything at all about Ginli, he wasn't mentioning that
he had ever had any other captives, either. His kind thinks
more about what his service record says than about what he'll
have for supper or whether his socks are dry.

They went through their long and tiresome ritual of report-
ing and relief of ground-detail. The rain had slowed to a mere
downpour, but it might have been completely clear and dry
for all the notice they took. Before the new group had been
aground for ten minutes they were as wet as their peers. They
stood in formation in the middle of the compound and read
off orders, went through the formal drill as Forty turned over
command to his superior. Then that officer released the old
detail from planet duty and turned me over to them.

They loosed me from the pole and we all marched off to the
shuttle. They could have done everything necessary in about
two minutes without getting more than damp. The manual
said otherwise. I'd have bet anything you could name that the
Khi didn't have any rules at all, at least of the kind the Ginli
recognize. And they could have twisted the Ginli into multi-
dimensional knots that would have had them peering into
their great-great-grandmothers' coal-scuttles.

The shuttle was commanded by a pilot-officer. Not a
Ginli. From old pryings I knew that even the Ginli hadn't
managed to alter the laws of physics to fit the hypotheses of
planet-bound bureaucrats. Their ship-handling manuals
stuck pretty close to the facts of the matter at hand, but
non-Ginli were required for handling the unexpected things
that always come up when planeting shuttles or navigating
ships.

We got off the ground with a minimum of fuss and were
soon docked against the hull of the lab-ship. Once we had
been cycled through the hatch I had to stand around while
they filled and filed and fussed over reams of paperwork.
That done, they hauled me off to De-Con, where I was
stripped, scrubbed, tested for everything from Osirian Rot to
Tick Fever, and reclad in a fresh Scout's uniform. After some

fast talking, I promoted a meal on the ground that whatever
they intended my fate to be, I'd never know about it if I were
dead of hunger. They deposited me in a small room between
the refectory and the kitchens. There the rotund Valu cooks
plied me with smuggled dainties, along with regulation fare.
It was amazing what those big, quiet creatures could hide
beneath their aprons. If the Ginli had suspected that this
"inferior species" could conjure up doughnuts from the
protein-carbohydrate powder they got to cook with, they'd
have foamed at the mouth. One of their most sacred tenets
was that eating was somehow degrading and flavor was next
door to blasphemy.

I trudged off to the next stop with a supply of contraband in
my least-noticeable pouch, blessing the page in the manual
that prescribed the stance, position, and gaze-level of those
standing guard over a prisoner. The manual assumed that the
prisoner would always be standing. Sitting, I could get away
with murder, and did.

As we neared the corridor that housed the quarters of
Number Six, the highest-ranking of his kind aboard the
236-J-16 (her name had been Night Song, before the Ginli
took her on a long lease), I forgot my stomach and looked
inside myself again. The ship was a fascinating webwork of
lines. Each kind of metal, every impulse of power made a
slightly different-colored marking on my interior chart.

The Ginli now showed as blobs of purple. I could see seven
stationed along the dimly lit corridor, two in the commander's private dissecting room, three in his access corridor, and
one, the Great Six himself, in his cabin. My own escort
numbering two, that made fifteen in this area.

We paused outside the sealed hatch. One of my escort
pressed a panel beside it. While we waited, two more Ginli
came up behind us, dragging a wretched Varlian that seemed
too drugged to stand. I caught his eye, however, and saw a
glint of speculation in his dark green eyes that hinted that he
might be less incapacitated than he seemed. Without seeming
to do anything more than stretch, I made a sketchy sign for
the Khi, then a quick folding motion with my fingers. His

fingers twitched in reply. Then the door opened, and we were hustled inside.

Six was a big one. Though the Ginli ran to tall rangy frames, his was hung with a bear's bulk. Mostly muscle, if I knew my Ginli. His long, doleful face was less blank than most, and his pale eyes were shrewd. Though I had seen him vaguely from a distance, close at hand I found him impressive.

When the Varlian and I had been properly announced and ranged before his console-desk, he ordered our guards out of the room into the access corridor. When they were gone he sealed the door and rose from the metal chair, pushing as he did so another button that slid it out of his way against the wall.

"You have broken contract, Hale Enbo. If we should bring this before the Council of your world, they would view it very seriously." he grunted.

"You've broken worse than that, Six," I replied. "If you let me live to inform the authorities about Ginli activities on this ship—and probably on others you lease—your kind will be banned. You'll be limited to life on Gin until investigators are convinced that you're civilized enough to allow at large again. You don't intend to let me survive to testify to what I know. So just stow the unnecessary feces and say what you have to say."

He didn't like it. I saw his pale eyes narrow. His hands slowly balled into fists, then unballed just as slowly. "The insolence of the lesser Primates is intolerable," he said. "It will be well when we prove beyond doubt that you, too, are simply beasts that have learned tricks. We will then eradicate you *all*, and the Cosmos will be cleansed of an offense."

"Oh, can it!" I interrupted. "Even the Varlian, whom you are beginning to fear as well as hate, can do things that you never dreamed were possible, using technologies borrowed from every kind of being in the galaxies that ever wielded so much as a screwdriver. You ask your commanders down on that planet. You'll find one who had a group of his men vanish from one spot and reappear in another. Just ask him how it was done. He won't be able to tell you, but I can. It was done by a couple of little green Varlian pretending to fold cloth. I'll bet this one right here can do it, too.''

Without waiting to see Six's reaction, I shot as fast a stream of Varlian as I could lay tongue to at my companion. He straightened up, lost his disoriented air, and began to fold his invisible cloth. Six winked from sight. I didn't know where the Ginli had been put, but I didn't really care. I patted the Varlian on the shoulder.

Using the sign language I'd learned from Lime, I asked him why he was here when he could have folded himself away home. For several exchanges he seemed unsure of what I was asking, so I spoke to him in Varlian while repeating the question with my hands. When he was sure that he understood, he began an intricate reply that required my entire attention to catch.

He was not alone, he began. His family had been surprised, asleep, away from their community and had been captured by something that stung them from a distance and put them to sleep. He could not leave his mate and their young, even if he could fold himself away. But he had never known that one could fold *himself* away. His kind only folded those who threatened them.

The Khi probably had good reason for withholding this vital information from a developing species. I felt, however, that the time had come, with Ginli all over Khi-Ash, to teach them a new trick. I sat down behind Six's desk-console, after retrieving the chair, and checked the button that sealed the door. Then I motioned for the Varlian to sit opposite me.

It wasn't easy. I didn't understand, in the here and now, exactly how folding was done any more than the Varlian did, though when I withdrew into that inner place it was clear to me. I did know very well that my first experience of folding myself was triggered by the desperation of personal danger. So I described the things that Ginli do to sentient beings. His big eyes grew bigger, a darker green, as I talked and gestured. He looked ill.

Then I described to him my predicament on the logs with the sharks all around me. I made it quite graphic, for he sat forward on his stiff chair and nodded with interest. When I described my blind attempt at folding myself ashore . . . and the result thereof . . . he stood and took a fast turn around the room. He was chattering and making sign language so fast that his hands were a green blur.

I didn't catch half of it, but I thought he was clarifying the idea to himself. When he came to a stop, he reached across the desk and patted me vigorously on the head. Then he stood in the center of the cramped room and folded with care and precision. When he had that done to his satisfaction, he closed his eyes and was gone.

I would have bet tomorrow's dinner (whatever and wherever that might be) that every Varlian on the ship was now back on Khi-Ash.

XXI.

Hale Enbo

After my small friend left I sat for a time in Six's hard and uncompromising chair, munching on a doughnut from my pocket. The console before me was not too unlike those the Scouts used in registering reports. I studied it for a time, getting its setup firmly in mind. I played with the different standard programs until I felt competent to deal with the computer to which it connected. Then I rummaged in a pile of printouts for Six's authorization code.

I found it at last, a long string of numbers that would have been terribly impressive to another Ginli. To me it seemed stupid to use fifteen numbers to retrieve information when a simple six-digit combination would have done just as well. Still, I punched it in, saw the "clear" light wink on, and asked for a listing of all animals captured from the world below. Arranged by species-analog and accompanied by a listing of testing done or to be done, together with the locations of the beasts on the ship.

The computer, of course, was not made by the Ginli. It was Fssa. The cat-people have been building thinking machines for longer than we Primates have been walking on the ground. It was a fine bit of equipment, and it always amused me that the Ginli had to use the product of a non-Primate culture in order to further their mad project. The Fssa probably got some quiet feline laughs out of that, too.

The printouts began to roll out (the Ginli eye found images on screens very difficult to decipher), and they were, of course, all in Ginli. That made me doubly glad that I had troubled myself to learn the language, in defiance of all the regs. As I had suspected, all the Scouts had been recalled from the planet and put into suspension. There were, therefore, only a few specimens aboard, instead of the hundreds that ordinarily would have been captured by now. Of those few, about fourteen had been Varlian. They were, I well knew, now gone, though the computer hadn't been informed of that fact, as yet.

I only had to worry about twenty-seven creatures of several kinds. None were Ssseelt. Several were the orange-furred spiders. Two were bearlike creatures. There were numbers of smaller beasts like the many-toothed black animal and the scarlet monkeys. I intended to leave none of them to the tender mercies of the Ginli.

Carefully, using the computer printouts as a guide, I located all my charges on my internal grid-chart. Then I folded them, one by one, to spots I remembered on Khi-Ash, as well suited to their needs as I could manage. When that was done to my satisfaction, and their life-patterns had moved to assure me that they were alive and mobile, I turned again to the computer.

Regretfully, I keyed in the central bank of working programs and instructed it to abort all existing data and instructions. The ship-working and navigational banks were totally separate, I knew from my engineer friends ("inferior" Primates like myself).

When I had done all the damage I could think of that wouldn't actually harm anyone, and the internal hum that was the Khi was purring with contentment, I thumbed the button that unsealed the door. Those doors were intended to seal out space itself, at need, and the efforts of the Ginli on the other side to force entry hadn't even been audible inside the cabin. That they had been busy was evidenced by scars, scorches, and various acid-marks on the outer face of the hatch.

The thing opened slowly. I waited. A Ginli head peered round into the cabin.

I grinned at it, and it ducked back into the corridor. A babble of Ginli was audible for a while. Then the door was pushed to its widest. Number Six strode in with a hero-about-to-die-for-his-country expression on his face. I motioned for him to sit, as two guards followed him in and leveled their shipside light flamers at me.

With a twitch of my fingers, I folded the weapons out of their hands and onto a long bench against the bulkhead behind me. Then I folded the guards back into the corridor and sealed the hatch behind them.

Six sat across his own desk from me, his skull showing plainly through the flesh of his face. He expected to die, I knew. That would have been the kindest of the punishments he would have inflicted on me, had our positions been reversed. Enjoying his discomfiture, I yawned, stretched, and stood.

"On the planet below us, which in your ignorance you probably don't know is called Khi-Ash by its dominant species, there are no less than six intelligent kinds of living beings. I have seen four of them. At the top of the heap are the Khi, who are not only not Primate, but are most likely not even detectable as life-forms in this dimension. They make you and me and the Varlian look like those little red monkeys, by comparison with them," I began.

Six stirred, opened his mouth, but I raised my hand. He closed it quickly, looking from me to the weapons on the bench behind me.

"Your people's theories about the occurrence of intelligence among species are totally ignorant and erroneous. Why any halfway bright beings would take up such a crackbrained project is beyond me . . . unless you're so unsure of yourselves that you need bolstering by looking down on others. Whatever the case may be, you have begun to be dangerous to other creatures. I'm about to begin educating you. Unless you absorb what you're about to learn, the days of the Ginli as a spacefaring race are over—and possibly your days as a living race as well."

His Adam's apple bobbed in his long neck, making a wobble beneath the turtleneck of his tunic. Before he could say anything there was a muffled "boom!" at the door. Six turned even paler than his usual hue and looked at the communicator in front of me.

"Be my guest," I invited, and he grabbed it and shouted, "Belay that! There will be no further efforts to open this hatch until I order it!" He looked at me again, and I nodded.

Then I picked up the com and said, "Forty, old sprat, your commander is going to need a Scout uniform and planet boots. Get somebody to get them to the hatchway. Then buzz the com when they're ready."

Six rose to his feet. "I will not go down! It is unfitting that a Less-Then-Ten should set foot on an uncivilized world. Kill me if you must, but do not dishonor me."

I looked him in the eye, my patience frazzling fast. "You are about to be honored far past your deserts," I snapped. "You are going to learn the truth about yourself . . . the first of your kind to do so in eons, if ever. And maybe . . . just maybe . . . you'll be allowed to meet the Khi. That's entirely up to you and to them."

He sat there after thumping back into his chair, rebellion in his eyes. To take his mind off that, I said. "By the way, while we wait, you might take the com and check on the specimens—all of them—that you had on the ship." I emphasized the word *had*.

When he learned that every last specimen had just vanished before the eyes of the techs he sat back, stunned and silent. At last he said, "Long ago, in the dark period of our people's history, there were those who claimed to have unnatural powers. Matters that came from trafficking with demons of darkness. I never believed, but now I begin to wonder . . ."

"Well don't!" I said. "There are many powers, both within and without this continuum. You haven't even scratched the surface of them because of this stupid fixation your people have. Just sit there and wait. You'll begin to learn something useful, for a change."

In a bit the buzzer sounded. I opened the door to admit a wary Forty, who carried a pile of clothing and supplies for his commander. He looked questioningly at Six, but that worthy stared at the wall and said nothing. When Forty was again sealed out, I instructed my prisoner to don the jumpsuit and boots, and he did it, if reluctantly.

I consulted the computer to find the point upon which the shuttle had landed last. Then I concentrated on the planet below, making certain that I could determine the exact spot upon which I wanted to land.

When I was sure, I folded us both away.

XXII.

Hale Enbo

Those damnably familiar bushes brushed my face as I found myself looking through them again at the white beach and the purple wavelets. I heard a muffled grunt at my side and turned to see a greenish Six, who was sitting on the ground after dropping the short distance from what had been a chair-seat one instant before. His eyes stared wildly, as he rose to his feet. I grinned at him and helped him regain his balance.

It was almost sundown, though the heavy clouds made it just about dark. The rain had stopped, but the air was moisture-laden, and the soil beneath our feet was spongy. In contrast to the heat of the past days, it was almost chilly, at least to me, though Six seemed to be sweating. I stood there for a time, considering. Then, my decision made, I turned my back on the beach and went toward that tree where I had met Lime.

"Come along, old chum," I said to Six. "We're going to have a refresher course in what it takes to be a real Primate."

He didn't like it. He stood there watching me walk away for a half-dozen heartbeats. Then he hurried after me, and I felt his grip on one of the back pockets of my uniform. When we reached the big tree in which I had spent my first night, he stood glaring up at me for a long time after I had leaped for a branch and swung myself up.

It got darker and darker. I drew together some leaf-thick branches to make a bit of comfort against the damp night. Then one of the red-brown beasts came grunting from its hole beneath the next tree but one. I found Six sitting beside me on

111

the broad limb before I'd realized that he had moved. He was only a dark shape, by now, but I could hear the rasp of his breath, and I could feel, through my elbow, the faint trembling that was shaking him.

I suppose there's nothing in the universe so pitiable as a once-all-powerful being who is forcibly removed from his own sphere and placed in a situation that he can neither recognize nor control. We lesser creatures are used to feeling helpless and endangered. *They* have no practice at it. It really gets to them. I fumbled in one of my lumpy pockets and pulled out a doughnut.

"Munch on that," I suggested. "Then we'd better get some sleep, because that creature that assisted your climb is only one of many in these woods. It's faster than anything you can think of, too. We'll be traveling above-ground in order to stay clear of his kind and several others just as unpleasant. It isn't easy for those with our kind of arms to do that, so you'll need all the rest you can get."

He didn't answer, but I heard chewing and swallowing in the darkness. When he finished I offered him another doughnut. It was accepted without thanks, but also without any snide comments about the fixations upon foodstuffs displayed by inferior intelligences. I chuckled silently and settled into a position in which I could sleep without falling out of the tree. I offered no suggestions to my companion. A large part of education is learning to use your own judgment.

The sun rose the next morning, clear and bright, and I was intensely grateful. It would be enough of a job to teach that stiff-necked Ginli to swing through the trees without having to do it in trees slick with wet. As it was, we were soon moving through a haze of steamy mist, as the hot sun turned water into vapor.

My pupil wasn't the most cooperative. He objected indignantly to sliding on his rear along dampish branches. He protested the impossibility of traversing the thick tangles by swinging from his arms. In a word, he bitched. I ignored him and hustled him through the trees as fast as possible. Finally he sat down and refused to budge.

Luck was with me. As I dropped to his branch and sat

facing him one of the pseudo-bears stalked into view below us and fell onto something that had denned at the roots of our tree. As the creature was dragged out, I could see that it was one of my toothy friends. Without saying a word I pointed downward.

Great as the size-differential was, the bear didn't have any free meal. Those wide jaws with their rows of teeth (I never did find out how many rows) clamped semicircular chunks from the hide of the bear, even while that creature was detaching the head from the body. Six's eyes followed the gory battle with fascinated disgust.

When the bear had ambled out of sight, leaving behind only a smeary patch on the forest floor, I rose and said, "Well, that's what's down there. I'm going to a village I know. There I can rest in safety, eat well, and communicate with interesting people. You do what you want." Then I climbed out along a limb, chinned myself to one on an adjoining tree, and moved away with the fanciest technique I could manage. As I had learned, by this time, to chart my path ahead, I didn't have to make any embarrassing back-tracks before I was out of sight. I wanted to rub it in that I could do well what he couldn't do at all. Once I was out of sight I waited for him.

It didn't take long. He made almost as much noise going through the treetops as his kind did moving along the ground. Once I heard him fall, the upswish of the branch coming a split instant before the thump of his landing. I hadn't realized how nearly expert I had become at this mode of travel until I had a chance to compare my present capacities with Six's. Though I was no Varlian, Six was a long way from being a Hale Enbo.

He scrambled noisily into another tree and continued his progress, while I waited at ease and listened to the hum in my head that was the Khi. It was leading me, as it had once before, in the direction in which I wanted to go. I was quite sure that I would find the Varlian village, dead center, by following the hum. Six had no such direction-finder, and he would have missed me entirely if I hadn't been keeping an ear trained in his direction.

I headed him off when he came near enough, and took up
the task that Lime and Owl had done for me. As he was now
trying his best, we made better time than we had been doing.

Lime and I had reached his village in a day. Of course we
had gone rather fast afoot for a while before taking to the
trees, but his expert guidance aloft had sent us along at good
speed. It took Six and me three days to do the same distance.
In that period he collected calluses on his hands and ate things
that he would have condemned any of his men to death for
consuming.

Well into the second day, after I had run entirely out of
doughnuts, he said, ''I feel the need for food. Such effort
depletes the body. I cannot go on without something to eat.''

I was hungry, myself, but I wasn't going to admit it before
he did. Now I said, ''There are many edibles in the forest.
Just rest. I'll go down and find enough to keep us going for a
while. Or, if you want water, you may come with me.''

He wasn't ready, as yet, to go down into those carnivore-
infested depths. Leaving the tree, I slid cautiously down and
went to find a bread-pod thicket. Luck was with me, for in a
small clearing I found bread-pods, my orange-colored ''lemons'', and even a small jelly-fruit bush. I returned with every
pocket stuffed full.

He seemed surprised to see me so soon. I think he'd
envisioned me staggering blindly through the wood, trying
and gagging upon all sorts of unpalatable things before I
could find anything edible. As it was, I was back long before
he was rested. When I spread out an array of the stuff on the
branch where he sat, he looked at it doubtfully.

''We have determined that it is physiologically sound to
limit food intake to artificially manufactured substances,'' he
said pedantically. ''This eliminates any unlooked-for side
effects, as well as subduing the animal impulse to notice
tastes and textures. We are strictly conditioned against eating
native fruits, nuts, or any other natural foodstuff.''

I waited, but he seemed to have run down. Then I picked
up a jelly-fruit, opened it at the top, stirred with a clean twig
until the jelly at its base was thoroughly mixed with the
creamy filling, and began to lick it from its leathery skin.

"You know," I said between mouthfuls, "if you don't eat the unorthodox fare, eventually you'll grow too weak to hang onto a tree. You'll fall out, and one of those creatures we've seen will eat *you*. But it's strictly up to you. I know what a religion you Ginli make of following rules, even if the man who wrote the rules doesn't have to starve alongside you."

I licked the fruit again, and its fruity-rich aroma settled around me like scent around a blossom. Finishing that one, I cracked open a bread-pod and dug into it. Six watched me, his eyes missing no motion of my tongue or jaws. His own salivary glands were working overtime, as I could see easily. He was, after all, a Less-Than-Ten, used to imposing rules upon others but not quite so intent upon living up to them himself. I could see his mind working.

As if deciding that it was the least sinfully delicious item there, he picked up a bread-pod and, watching me crack another, opened it. He bit into it with a martyred expression. Then he closed his eyes, as the subtle flavor got to him. I may not have given the bread-pod its due. It is nutty, slightly yeasty, the tiniest bit sweet. Aside from that, it was probably the first thing with any taste other than bland or nasty that he had ever put into his mouth.

As he finished that (very, very quickly), I opened and stirred a jelly-fruit beneath his very nose. He reached for it without pause for thought, and he ate it to the last sticky drop. By the time he reached for a "lemon" he was lost.

I resumed the journey, quietly contented. Alone and un-aided, I had corrupted the morals of a Ginli. A Less-Than-Ten! From now on, he would never face his daily ration without remembering the seductive flavors of the forbidden fruits I had given him. The difference that would make in his outlook on life held infinite possibilities.

I've never seen a study done on the effect food habits have on racial behavior. I feel certain that if such was done, it would be found that that effect is decisive. Never underestimate the power of a taste bud!

With the food to fuel us, we forged ahead. That night I was confident that we would reach Lime's village the next day. As we rested, I felt the internal hum gaining intensity.

Six was learning. Though he was less suited to the arboreal life even than I, he tried very hard. His greater bulk was a hindrance, and his lack of practice was a worse one, but he did have muscle. So we moved steadily, if not speedily, and in mid-afternoon I found that we had reached the clearing.

I dropped to the ground. Six, coming up behind, looked around for me, saw the clearing, and slipped down to stand beside me.

"You've done well . . . for a Ginli," I said. "We've arrived at our first goal. I didn't think you had it in you."

Six ground his teeth. He was so furious that his colorless face was splotched with angry pink. When he could speak at last, it was a splutter of extremely rude Ginli.

"If I were your superior, you would have demerits for un-officerlike language," I said mildly, when he ran down. "Now I expect you to be both civil and helpful to our hosts. They are, believe it or not, very intelligent and most efficient at the things they consider important. Besides that, they're kind and friendly."

"Those . . . are *errhampfet* BEASTS!" he gasped in a strangled voice.

"The one in your office was the one who folded you away into the corridor. Or have you forgotten?" I replied.

He had forgotten. Remembering, he quieted, watching the Varlian in the grove as they went about their evening tasks.

I wasn't waiting for him. I stepped out of the wood and raised my voice in as good an imitation of Lime's whoop as my vocal chords could achieve.

The scene dissolved in an explosion of green-furred shapes. A babble of chattering Varlian rose, and a familiar shape came hurtling down a tree, across the clearing, and into my arms. Lime hung about my neck, talking a mile a minute, patting my back with hard, quick little thumps. I was grinning like an idiot. I had wondered if Lime was working strictly on orders from the Khi in his treatment of me. Now I knew he hadn't been.

Disentangling him, I bent to shake hands with Owl. She took my hand in a swift, warm grasp, then she gestured for us to go to the grove. I turned to the Ginli. He was speechless

with a mixture of shock and outrage. Nevertheless, he be-
haved himself, which I attributed to my reminder about his
folding-away.

The vine ladders came down. I looked up and saw Lime's
young ones descending at breakneck speed. As I disappeared
beneath a flying wedge of young Varlian, I saw Six's face. It
was a study in frustration.

XXIII.

Number Six, Lab-Ship Commander

It is with deep shame that I find myself in this predicament. No Less-Than-Ten in the history of Gin has been so beset with inexplicable happenings and problems that should not exist at all.

First, of course, there was the prying of Hale Enbo, Scout First Class, into our top-secret procedures. Who might have predicted that an inferior Primate of dark skin could be either so fast or so inventive in escaping? Yet that circumstance, in itself, should not have been any major disaster. We have located escaped Scouts before this and eliminated them without any suspicion falling upon us. It is out of the question that one of that sort should be allowed to inform the authorities of our activities. This is simply a matter of our being right and the laws governing exploration and examination of remote worlds being wrong.

Who could have thought that a Primate intelligence could be hidden among those of the animals that inhabit the planet? Always, the lower sorts have exhibited drastically differing impulses on the scanners. Yet when we scanned this world, no less than a half-dozen major patterns emerged, none of them differing dramatically from those of our kind. This is a matter to be erased from the computers and from the log-books, of course, but it made a terrible dilemma for us.

I will admit to this journal only that we only found Hale Enbo by sheerest chance. Forty maintains that he was caught in one of the spring-traps our techs have brilliantly devised for catching specimens. Yet even at that I wonder . . . he

118

removed us both from the ship to the planet, without the use of any discernible device. This gives me the insidious thought that he could have removed himself from the trap . . . and did not. For what purpose? My capture? And if so, why should he desire that?

I can see no pattern to his behavior. His arrogance, always an issue, has become intolerable. His abilities disturb me profoundly, smacking as they do of prohibited practices.

Now we are in what he calls a "village," surrounded by small green vermin who live in woven nests instead of steel and concrete apartments as intelligent beings must. These creatures greeted him ecstatically, swarming over him as if he were one of their own. This gives me to wonder if we have assessed Primates of his color accurately. It well may be that they are so inferior as to be unworthy tools for my kind. Certainly, he shows no resentment at the familiarities imposed upon him, even by the young of this filth.

He has done all that he could to convince me that these are rational beings. They may, indeed, have one inexplicable (except in the most dire terms) trick, but that must surely be parroted from some other, greater race than theirs. Their ways are without the iron discipline required for a true culture, and their individuals go their own ways without recourse to authority.

Gherzhum! He proposes to leave me among these things, going his own way. He pretends that they will bring me to join him, but even a child could tell that I am to be sacrificed for some bizarre cause. May I die like a citizen of Gin!

XXIV.

Hale Enbo

Though Lime's youngsters kept me busy all evening, I stole a moment, now and then, to watch the Ginli. He tried his best to pretend that he was dealing with trained animals, but the exquisite courtesy and warm hospitality of the Varlian made that difficult. When Lime and his family insisted upon knitting still another room onto their house, exclusively for his use, he seemed bewildered.

"They put one on the other side just for me," I told him, sitting beside him on a branch that had been trained to a comfortable curve and upholstered with velvety brown moss. "After supper, we'll have a visit from the Elders. They are the nearest thing the Varlian have to authorities. Even they, however, can't—or don't—compel anyone to do anything he doesn't want to do. Yet those five could probably fold your lab-ship to the other side of the galaxy—and possibly Gin right along with it. Don't forget that."

"Many animals have well-organized troops or tribes . . ." he began.

I raised my hand. "I know better," I snapped. "If you must keep trying to con yourself, do it silently; the spiel makes me want to toss you out of the tree. It's a long way down, and if you broke anything I'd have to haul you all the way to the Khi. That would be a terrible job, as much as you weigh."

Before he could answer, Mrs. Lime and her family came from the house with bowls for our evening meal. We all sat, with much polite conversation that Six couldn't understand at all and that I caught a lot more of than I had before. Encouraged by my increased ability, I asked about the folding-away that had happened just as Lime, Owl and I were about to go into the valley of the Khi.

Mrs. Lime bent double, hiding her face in her lap as she laughed the chittering Varlian laugh. Even the children broke up, while Lime nearly fell backward out of the tree.

When he had composed himself, he lifted his youngest (the name was k'k'k't't, as best I could catch it) to her feet and instructed her to tell us the tale. "It is, after all, the children's story," he told us.

Without shyness, the tiny creature said in very slow Varlian, for my benefit, "The Elders were teaching us to fold things away. They had finished with the older ones and were showing us, the smallest, how to fold pebbles from one spot to another and how to put them accurately on the very place they picked for us. We had done this many times. We were tired of such simple things. T'a'k't had just asked if we might not practice at folding one another away when there was a noise, far away in the forest.

"The Elders called us high into a tree, and then we waited. After a time many tall, pale things came to the edge of the trees and looked out through the bushes. The Elders pretended not to see them, so we pretended, too. While we were pretending, the Elders told us that we could practice on those creatures. We should all work together to fold them away to the rocky beach beside the river.

"Those things like him" (she pointed to Six) "began to make fire come toward the grove. The Elders said, 'Now!', and we folded them to the river, just as we were told to do." She sat down again, and I reached over to tickle her chin-fur.

Then I turned to Six, though I was shaking with laughter, and said, "Would you like to hear what actually happened to a group of your people who wound up on a riverbank, instead of being allowed to burn out this village?"

"No such thing could happen to Ginli!" he protested.

"It happened, all right, though I pity the poor officer who had to report it to you. This child here and her companions

were having a lesson in elementary folding. The Elders
allowed them to practice on Ginli!''

He sat, stiff and silent. I let it drop, knowing that the
knowledge was eating its way into his obdurate brain like
acid into metal. One more lesson he must learn was being
digested. I didn't disturb the process.

Now came our jolly food-server, with his bread-pods and
broth. When the bowls had been filled and emptied, the
children sent to the sand-pit to clean the dishes, we sat
quietly, waiting for the Elders. Midsummer had evidently
passed, for full dark had come before they arrived.

They must have been communing with the Khi. Or they
had highly developed intuition. They arrived, not by climbing quietly through the trees, as before, but by folding themselves onto the branch where we waited.

I wondered, even as they appeared, one by one, why they
knew how to fold themselves and that other Varlian had not.
Of course, it could be that they, being Elders, kept a thing or
two to themselves, to be used only in an emergency. Then my
mind slid into gear and I saw the problem. Varlian, like most
living creatures, tend to take the easiest way. With the ability
to move about their world without effort, they'd lose their
physical abilities in short order. This way they had to stay
sharp. That settled to my satisfaction, I turned my attention to
the Elders.

It was too dark to distinguish features, but their shapes
were as I remembered them. One was short and square, one
tiny and frail, one tall and thin, one medium-sized, and one
tall and stocky, with one shoulder higher than the other from
some old injury.

I leaned to take their hands, one at a time. "When I came
among you first," I said in careful Varlian, "you met me
with help and kindness. Now the Khi have given me a task to
do. It brings me here again. This Ginli who sits among us is
the leader of those who have disturbed this world. We are
trying to teach him the meaning of intelligence and of good
will among thinking beings.

"We have brought him, unarmed and helpless, to learn

what you alone on this world can teach him. The Khi have told me that I must come to them now, folding myself away. But he must come to them as I first came, with the help of the Varlian. Are you willing to take upon your people that task?''

There was a rapid-fire discussion, too quick for me to follow. Then the voice of Lime said, very slowly, ''We will do this. We can see the need. Go you to the Khi, Hale Enbo. Tell them what they already know. We will bring the creature to them.''

I touched all the hands again. Then I rose and embraced Lime and Mrs. Lime and all their children. ''I am going now, Six,'' I said to the Ginli. ''You will come with one or more of the Varlian, as fast as it can be done. Forget your prejudices and your rules of behavior. Learn their sign language—it's easy and comprehensive—and pay heed to what they tell you. You're in good hands.''

He came to his feet and caught me around the shoulders. ''You cannot leave me here in the wilderness among these alien creatures!'' he cried. I was encouraged to note that he didn't call them beasts. ''You brought me from my own place, where I was in command. It is the work of a monster to leave me so, after tearing me away by force!''

''Well, Ginli, the shoe is on the other foot, isn't it?'' I laughed. ''Little did you or your men or your superiors back on Gin care whether they forced alien species off their own worlds, where they, too, were in command of their lives. Did you ever wonder how your victims felt, dying beneath the scalpels of your henchmen? What of the blind terror and despair of those beings, intelligent as you in their own ways, that you have kidnapped and vivisected? In defiance of the laws governing spacefaring kinds? This small inconvenience is nothing!

''If our Councils operated by strict justice, you would have much to fear. If the Khi held you liable, sin for sin, for all the things you've ordered you might well tremble. But both have leavened their justice with mercy. You are to be taught, not tortured. You won't believe that, most likely, until the end of this road is reached, but it's true. Goodbye.''

I folded myself from him and the Varlian about us. The black tunnel spun about me, and I felt a vertigo worse than any I had felt before. When I came to myself again . . . it was not to my*self* at all.

XXV.

Hale Enbo

"Forgive us for diverting your folding," said a familiar voice within my mind. "We have reason for this action . . . those who are beyond the diamond wall wish to examine you again. When you faced them before you were untaught, unaware that many of the matters they can teach you existed at all. Your perceptions had not been sharpened to a point at which they could grasp the Hril. Now the Hril desire to compare your present capacities to those you possessed before. The work they have in store for you is demanding, and you must be in all ways prepared."

I tried to settle my consciousness into being a puddle instead of a vortex. "Where am I?" I asked. Something like laughter vibrated about me.

"You are here with us, in the dimension adjacent to that one in which the Hril approach us most nearly. Your body is safely within the room where you slept. We have only borrowed your real self for a short while." As Khi-Sang spoke, my vision cleared. I could see darts and flashes of light that had to be the Khi.

She answered my surmise. "Yes, you are now as we are. The self that exists here is more a troubling of the light than a visible, tangible thing. Come, now, to see the Hril."

The "come" was rhetorical, for the space (or whatever) that surrounded us seemed to stretch itself, becoming a clear transparency that seemed deep, without being distant. Within this I could sense motion. The sensation reminded me of long-ago physics lessons that taught of subatomic particles so swift that only the disturbance of their passage revealed that

they had been there at all. The Hril must be something like
that, I decided.

There was tumult in my—not *head* for that wasn't with
me—thinking processes. I surmised that this must be the
result of the probings of the Hril. It wasn't frightening,
though it gave me a weird "multiple" sort of feeling. There
were no voices in my mind, but I sensed dartings and rip-
plings in the field that was my thought. I didn't doubt that the
Hril were drawing from me exactly what they wanted to
know.

Then I began to see things. Not with eyes, for they too
were not there. These were like hallucinations, but somehow
I knew that the things I was seeing actually did exist somewhere, in some form. I was aware that my mind was forming
comprehensible analogs for the ungraspable in many cases,
but there was an underlying reality.

I saw a path of glittering substance that wound in precise
curves between shining domes. Plantings that seemed random grew along the way. When I looked closely, however, I
realized that the positions, the heights and textures, the colors
of the growing things were entirely too logically satisfying
for them to have been natural. The overall effect was that a
mathematical genius had been moved to calculate a perfect
city, and his designs had been followed to the letter.

Shapes moved along the paths, in and out of the domes and
among the flowers. They were very real-seeming, though
upon occasion they passed through walls and plants. I felt my
mind translating those shapes into a form that I could grasp,
so as they examined me, I examined them.

They were faceted. The light did fandangos off their surfaces, which seemed to be of the same diamondine stuff as
the wall in the Khi's cavern. They shone with such brightness
that the shapes were not clearly defined. The flashes they
emitted or refracted or reflected lit the shining domes and the
path to a glitter. Even the plants sparkled.

As I watched, the probings into my mind intensified. A
figure turned toward me and approached, growing larger and
more terrifyingly lovely at each step. Step? Perhaps *glide*. As
it came near I could see that its top—head?—was a peaked

and angled cone, in which a well of darkness seemed to be an eye. That eye came near. The shining scene evaporated at the edges of its blackness. The probings into my inner self stilled.

The eye became all of existence, deep and velvety and without end or beginning. I couldn't move. It seemed that I leaned into the eye, and it swallowed me. For a time not to be measured I *was*. The Hril *were*. We interacted. Information, instruction, understanding moved effortlessly between us. I knew the Cosmos from beginning to end. I understood matters that had puzzled my kind for all its history. But as well there were acceptance, trust, and the beginnings of affection. I was Hril. The Hril were Hale Enbo.

Then I was again whirling down the tunnel from which the Khi had removed me. I woke lying on the couch in the cavern. The three Khi stood above me. I looked at their softly glowing faces and forms, and tears poured down my cheeks.

"I was . . . I was . . . I can't *remember* what I was. I knew things, could see how everything fits together, how the universe is made. I can't *remember!*"

"I know," said Khi-Sang. "It has been the same for us. We were as you are, in the beginning. Rooted upon our world, relying upon technologies to implement our dreams. Then the Hril educated us, as they have begun to educate you, and we were no longer prisoned in flesh, subject to limitations of time or space. We grew wider, deeper, even though we could never hope to cling to the terrible truths our teachers had shown to us. We went out into the worlds, explored and marveled . . . and meddled. We found the dimensions between, where our spirits could grow, unshackled by physical things.

"There we flourished for aeons, dabbling in the affairs of races whose business was none of our concern. Until the Hril interfered, which is a thing they seldom do. Though we were their children and their pupils, they punished us and bound us to the vow that we must not break.

"Yet we long, even now, to reenter the web of their living creation, which encompasses all that we know. We cannot remember, either, the truths that we learned then, but they are within us. Though we cannot deliberately recall, those truths will emerge when they are needed. For you as well as for us. And the fact that we have had that knowledge has shaped us into what we now are. We meddle no more, believe me, except indirectly and in time of direst need.''

I lay thinking, tears still wet on my cheeks. At last I sat and looked closely at Khi-Sang. ''The Ginli are *their* creation,'' I said. ''They have spoiled themselves and their world. They're trying to spoil the rest of creation. Were they a *mistake?* Can the Hril err?''

The gentle voice replied inside me, ''By our standards, we would think the Ginli an error. But the Hril did not intend perfection. If we understand what they have taught us, they intend that every species undertake its own journey toward its best destiny. When a species, or even just one member of it, reaches a point at which it stands mute and worshipful before the loveliness of that which is, this wonder reaches the Hril as joy.

''The Ginli have moved in another direction. Their depredations reach the Hril as pain. The pain has reached such an intensity, evidently, that the Hril have decided to alter the course of the Ginli. Their reasoning is beyond our comprehension, but we have not the information or the wisdom to question it. They would not allow us to break the old pact. Instead they chose you as their instrument.''

It took a bit for the full implications to reach me. I recalled the intricate web of circumstance that had brought me here. Chance, foolhardiness, and stubbornness had all played a part. Those things were not mine alone—they held true of most Enbos, as far back as records of the family went, even to Old Earth. Had I been bred, through all those generations, just for this?

Khi-Sang pulsed with laughter. ''No! No!'' she said, taking the thought from my mind. ''For many things. More important things. This is merely your first major task, your training ground, as it were. You and we and each one of every sort of being in all the Cosmos has its own purposes. Never doubt that!''

Khi-Rehm touched me on the shoulder, her glowing hand intangible but giving off some kind of tingle. "Hale Enbo, you must eat. Your body has drained itself, in sustaining your other self. It needs fuel and rest."

I looked at her, astonished. Nobody had ever had to remind me to eat. I felt inside myself. My stomach replied with a growl. My salivary glands responded. But my entire attention didn't focus, as it always had, upon the coming meal. I sighed. My father told me, with I was eighteen or younger, that food wouldn't always be the major motivating factor in my life. I hadn't believed him, but perhaps he was right after all.

The table appeared, laden with all my favorite foods. Somehow the single-minded concentration that lent eating so much pleasure was no longer there. I had outgrown my physical appetites by a small but decisive margin.

Khi-Sang managed what might have been a sigh. "You are growing wider already, Hale Enbo. Much more quickly than we did. It is well for your task, but we took joy in your untrammeled youth and gusto. It is no unalloyed gift that the Hril bestow."

"I'm finding that out," I murmured. Before I could continue, there was an interruption. A feeling something like that in a forest just after lightning has struck nearby tingled through me. Leaving the food unfinished, I folded myself to the surface, beside the stone doorway.

XXVI.

The Hril Who Watches

We have chosen a worthy instrument. He has absorbed the teachings of the Khi and the lesser beings with the acceptance of the very young. He has melded with us in full accord. We find no cruelty within him.

Best of all, he now contains the Great Powers, yet he will not, we feel, be corrupted by them. He identifies with all living things, and that will be his protection. The longing for power that is the curse of incarnate beings is not a matter that will concern him.

We are almost sure of that.

XXVII.

Hale Enbo

It was midday. I had no particular idea of which day, for there was no frame of reference for the passage of time in the dimensions of the Hril. The golden-orange tweed of the grasses glowed like flame in the sunlight. The creamy foliage of the trees floated above in almost disembodied serenity.

Once again I watched the approach of a Ginli. He was, as I had been, led by two Varlian. I found to my joy, as they neared, they were Owl and Lime. They held Six firmly by the elbows, as if they expected him to run amok and begin tearing up the countryside with his bare hands. He looked, I thought, as if rearranging scenery might be the last thing on his mind.

He looked up from his feet and saw us waiting beside the stones. His shoulders went back. A bit of the old Ginli stiffness came into his carriage. He marched up with bravado, but it melted away as he absorbed the reality that was my companions. As he gaped, I looked beyond him.

A small blue butterfly was wavering on the breeze. It was followed by dozens more. I glanced at Khi-Sang. We said nothing, but we were both smiling as we opened the doorway and led the speechless Six into the tunnel. As the door reformed behind us Six clung to my arm, but the glow of light reassured him. He loosed his grip and straightened again.

We went to the topaz room, where the table waited with replenished supply for the newcomers. Lime and Owl cleaned their hands and sat at once, but Six surveyed the scene with deep distrust on his rigid features.

"I just finished eating those very same things, right here at

this table," I told him. "I'm hale and whole" (he didn't get
the pun, which was a shame) "and the food is very good and
extremely nutritious. Sit down and stop acting like an infant."

He didn't argue, for once. With considerable gusto, he dug
into the foodstuffs. He was growing fonder of good food,
which seemed to me a hopeful sign.

Lime and Owl finished quickly. The three of us then sat on
the couch and exchanged news. While my sign-assisted tale
went far over their heads, theirs afforded me with much
amusement. Lime's account of their handling of Six when
they were approached by a contingent of Ginli was graphic.

Here came the Ginli, marching through the wood. Here
were Lime and Owl in a tree, trying to sit on their oversized
captive and keep him quiet, simultaneously. Here was Six,
wriggling furiously, biting any hand he could get his teeth
into. Suddenly Owl reached above her head and pulled a
half-grown nut off a twig. She popped it into Six's mouth, as
he opened wide to bellow. With a thump she rammed it down
until his eyes watered and strange gurglings came from him
(Lime did the honors inimitably).

There went the troop marching away, slashing right and
left with their flameblades. Here were Lime and Owl now
desperately concerned with saving their Ginli from choking.
Back-thumping, prying down throat, nothing seemed to
help. Then Owl, with her usual aplomb, kicked him out of the
tree. He landed on his back with a resounding thump, the nut
flew from his mouth with the deadly accuracy of a projectile
and hit Lime on the shin, just as he reached the ground to
check on Six's condition. Owl dissolved into laughter, Six
rose and began running, and it took the two of them to head
him off and get him settled again.

I laughed myself into tears.

By the time we'd finished catching up, Six had completed
his meal. We had been quiet, and he had been faced the other
way, so he didn't know I'd been told about his misadventure.
It was almost impossible to look into that stiff, humorless
face without cracking up again. Even the Khi, who had been

much amused by the Varlians' tale still glimmered fitfully.

Nevertheless we straightened our faces and settled the guests for the night. I found that I could now conjure up couches as well as Khi-Sang herself. I made several extras, just to see them pop into view. When all were settled for the night, I went out of the room with the Khi.

We didn't exactly fold. It was more as if we were gaseous clouds that drifted through walls that were no more tangible than we. The room in which we found ourselves was a dream of darkest blue. It was like being in the center of a gem the color of the eastern sky just before sunset. I almost gasped for breath, for I felt as if I were under water. Then I realized that my lungs were no longer working . . . or necessary.

It took a bit to get used to this state of being. The Khi looked almost the same, yet I could see that they, too, had moved somewhat out of phase with the physical world. When I looked down at myself, my solid, muscular body was shimmering with light that shone entirely through it. The light was the darkest possible golden color, in contrast with the sun-gold of the Khi. Behind it, where opaque flesh should have been, was a vibrant something shaped as I had been but totally different.

"You are *becoming*," said Khi-Sang. "It required many ages for us to reach the point at which you stand. But the Hril had not a special, driving need to develop us quickly. And we were not as apt as you. You hold no anger in you, Hale Enbo, though you have had much reason to be angry. The only thing we can detect is a clean fury at the cruelties of the Ginli. No one with deep personal hatreds could be trusted with the powers that are being placed in your hands. You have the open, honest heart of a child, and that is a thing we envy you. The Hril, always wise, have chosen someone new and clean, without prejudgments or too much experience of the horrors that living beings are capable of."

"But will I be the self I have always known?" I asked her.

Khi-Sang turned from the blue wall and said, "You, even as we, will be able to exist on more than one level of being, taking with you your physical self, at need. That self will be

altered, to some degree. It will look as it did. Yet it will be
able to travel between dimensions. You will be able to go, as
we do, where need calls you, by ways that those still rooted in
three dimensional bodies can neither understand nor emu-
late."

"But you will be able, if you wish, to enjoy the body, even
in its altered state," added Khi-Lohm. "It will not *need*, as it
once did but it will still be able to take delight in food and
beauty and love and the variety of existence."

I didn't answer . . . something inside was a bit dubious
about the entire arrangement. Life had been hairy at times,
that was true. I'd been hungry and cold and tired and afraid.
Everything had not been pure fun, but the thought of being
without any physical need at all left me feeling orphaned and
lonesome. By the gods, I *liked* Hale Enbo, with all his faults.

As if she knew what I might be feeling, Khi-Sang drew
near and touched my shoulder. Before, I hadn't been able to
feel the touch of the Khi. Now the golden glow of her
not-quite-flesh was warm . . . a comforting tingle that crept
through me. She caught my hand, hers pulsating and vibrat-
ing within mine.

She turned me toward the wall. "You need practice at
using your selfhood. Come into the blue jewel wall with
me. We will take delight, work wonders, exercise your new
powers . . . and perhaps even more than that. When we
emerge you will be capable of turning the Ginli from their
journey toward darkness."

We drifted toward the many-faceted wall . . . through it.
Veils of sapphire mist touched us as cool wisps as we went
deeply into the blue dimension.

"This is a world to which we come when weary," said
Khi-Sang. "Here we find rest and happiness and exercise for
our most potent capacities."

We moved out of the mists. There before us was a world of
joyous blues in every shade and tint and tone. A forest of
splintered sapphires rose on either hand. A road of velvety
blue dust eased our not-quite-touching feet along its way. At
the curve in this road an azure dell was centered with a

lacework pavilion of the tender blue that is almost white.
Tables and benches sat beneath its roof, and we went in to
admire the dappling of sun through the fretted patterns of that
roof onto the blues of the mosaic floor.

After a time, Khi-Sang brought into being a pitcher of
greeny-blue liquid that smelled of fruit and wine. With it
were goblets like halved spheres of midnight-blue glass. We
drank, and her tingling touch trembled through me.

As we sat, a cloud of blue butterflies drifted along the way.
I turned to Khi-Sang.

She smiled her tremulous glow. "True. It was from this
place we stole the treasure that now flits in our valley. To
replace it was a thing most difficult, for none of the things in
our world are blue. We owe this world a debt.

"But now I have brought you here, and you have wondered at its beauty and smiled at its butterflies and taken joy in
it. So the balance is restored . . . the weight of your pleasure
has restored the equilibrium. Now we owe the debt to you,
Hale Enbo."

The tingle of the wine and her touch had run through my
spirit, making it feel light and young. "Let's run!" I cried to
her. "With the wind making tangles of our—my—hair.
Kicking up great clouds of powdered sky!"

She glimmered assent, and we sped down the gentle curve
of the road, effortlessly as in a dream. A great trail of blue
marked our passage, though our feet didn't seem to touch the
dust at all. Because I wished it, I drew up panting and
laughing, though I wasn't truly breathless.

Khi-Sang matched my mood, and I turned to her and laid
my hand along the curve of her shoulder. She did the same,
and we stood there in total stillness, as our selves moved
away from their insubstantial containers and drifted together
as if they were clouds of mist. Every atom (if of such we were
composed) entwined: Knew-thought-felt-understood among
them all that could be known of Khi-Sang and Hale Enbo.
Then we drew again into ourselves, and the glow of our joy lit
that corner of the blue world to gold.

Something clinked at my feet. I stooped to pick it up, and it

was a stone, rounded on one end, curved inward at the other.
It was marbled with blue and gold and emitted a faint, infant
shimmer that charmed me. I handed it to Khi-Sang.

"What is it?"

"That is the child of our love," she answered gently.

I took it into my hands again, rubbing my thumb along the
curve. "This is a stone," I said. "No living thing . . ."

"Hale Enbo!" she chided, "use your gifts. Feel what that
is for yourself. It is, as I said, the child of our love. We are
neither of us corporeal beings, with their complex and painful ways of birth. We shall take this small life and set it in its
place. Though it will never have a body it is a creature of
mind and soul, nevertheless."

I looked inside myself to find the gridwork pattern. It was
clear, now, certain as my own existence. On that weft of
perception glowed a strong impulse, radiating from that
small thing in my hand. I laughed. "We have a loud little
thing, whatever it may be," I said. "But how will we know
its place?"

"Everything in this dimension has one true place. No other
can fit into it. Come with me slowly, now, and it will become
apparent to us."

We drifted along peacefully. The glow above that I had
taken to be the sun never changed its position. The dreamy
stillness was unbroken by anything sharper than the rustle-
clink of leaves touching or the fizz-plop of insects (all shades
of blue) taking off and landing. When we found our child's
place I knew it at once.

Beside the road at a bending rose a careless-artful mound
of stones. The lowest layer was ilex green-blue, the next
bottom-of-ocean blue, and they paled as they rose higher. In
the side of one curve was a smooth chink that cried aloud for
something to fill it. The stone-child fitted perfectly. The
pattern of gold-marbled blue completed the sculpture in both
form and color. We stepped back to admire the effect.

Khi-Sang glimmered her smile. "We have done many
things. Now it is time for work. Here you must gain control of
your powers, for this is a place where you can do damage to
none."

I sighed, for I knew that was true. Playtime was over. We moved into the forest. There I worked harder than ever before in my life, driven by Khi-Sang, who was a taskmistress with much patience and more perseverance. When I had exhausted even the insubstantial self that had come into this dimension, I was master of the things that the Hril had set into me, for their own inscrutable purposes.

XXVIII.

Hale Enbo

When Khi-Sang drew me again through the blue gem wall, I was all but another being from the one who had left the chamber with her. I understood what I could do and what I *must not* do, which was more important. I greeted the other Khi with new recognition, for I now could see the realities of their beings.

They gave me no time for reflection. "The Ginli grows restive," said Khi-Lohm. "He expects terrible things, here in the caverns. You are the only one here whom he will try to understand . . . he finds the Varlian intolerable, and they have been returned to their home.

"He refuses to think about us. We are not, of course, firmly rooted in flesh, and he will not admit, even to himself, that such as we can exist. His mind is a turmoil of trying to find ways to *coerce* such as we. He will not listen to our voices within himself, though we learned his language from you. We suffer for him—he is in such distress."

"The time has come," I agreed, "when he and I must begin our journey. That will distress him more than anything, yet it must be done. You have done your parts well, but now the task has passed to me. The Hril are hard taskmasters. I don't relish the job, but if it is not done the Ginli are lost. The Hril will erase them, if nothing can turn them from their course."

The Khi's glimmers paled at the thought. They hustled me back through the corridor to the topaz room, where Six sat glumly on a cushioned chair. He looked up as we entered, then stood abruptly.

"You have left me among hallucinations, surrounded by unholy magics!" he shouted. "Whatever your mad purpose may be, it cannot justify that."

"Oh, can it," I said, disgusted. "The only thing unholy that I see is you. The Khi are here just as much as I am" (which was literally true, but not quite candid), "and they've looked after you well. Your worst trouble is selective blindness—and deafness. Refusing to know the truth is worse than being unable to know it.

"Still, I don't have time to bother with you. We're going to Gin, after one short delay."

He looked at me, his eyes filled with hope, fear, and doubt. "You have been proven untrustworthy . . ." he began. I grabbed his arm and hustled him down the corridor to the diamond room.

The Khi remained behind, and I was glad. This was my own work, that the Hril had laid in my hands.

I held Six in front of the diamond wall into which I had first looked. "Listen," I said. "You won't believe what I'm about to tell you, but without that as a cushion for your mind you might go mad—or madder. You are about to see—almost—the creators of the universe we know. They can see you. They will winnow your mind to the last whisper of an idea. You are their creation, as am I and the Khi and every other kind we know. Hold onto this thought: They want you to exist. They have gone to a *hell* of a lot of trouble to see that your kind is saved from its own stupidity. You can love them or hate them or resent them, but you cannot doubt them. Now brace up!"

I can't tell you what he saw. It wasn't what I had seen. The deepening glints in the wall held the motes and gleams that I had seen, though now I could perceive something of their meaning.

Six gave a terrible cry as the wall began to shimmer in its depths. I had to hold him still, for his entire body convulsed, his muscles reacting with random impulses to the disruption of all his most cherished notions. He struggled in my grip, but though he was bigger and heavier than I it was no effort to hold him. I suspected my new self had capacities that it would take a lifetime to learn.

Whatever he saw in the diamond wall, it was a vastly different Six whom I turned away from it. His eyes were fixed, as though he looked closely at something an arm's length from the end of this nose. His face had relaxed into an almost infantile placidity, though his frame still shook occasionally.

I sent him into sleep. Popping a couch into being, I laid him on it and then lay beside him and closed my eyes. I willed myself to sleep also, though I no longer needed that sort of rest. Morning would bring the great task itself, and I was anxious to have it behind me. So we slept, the Ginli and I, while Khi-Ash turned on its axis, and the distant blazes that were the stars wheeled across the sky above the valley of the Khi.

I roused myself when he stirred. Once he had awakened thoroughly, I took him to the washing-room and left him to his own devices while I enjoyed a hot bath, which I may or may not have needed in my present state. It did my morale a world of good, anyway.

After breaking our fasts, I took my charge out into the sunlight of the valley. I had lost track of the weather while dallying in other dimensions, and I found that a delicate mist softened the forest, blotted out the mountains, and made dim shapes of the foothills. The valley was filled with fog, and only the grasses at our feet were visible. I breathed in the gray dampness and stepped close to Six.

"We are going to Gin. You'll be dizzy and disoriented, but don't let that worry you. You'll feel better when we get there."

I folded us to a spot that the Hril had pinpointed in my mind. The dark tunnel sucked us away from Khi-Ash, and we whirled madly. I was now able to keep a semblance of balance, as well as a consciousness of the nearness and well-being of Number Six.

We opened our eyes to find ourselves standing in a circular chamber whose walls were adrip with conduits and staring with viewscreens and lighted telltales. In the center of the room was a chair that swiveled inside the low circle of a control console. In the chair sat a Ginli whose pale eyes were wide with shock.

The sensors went crazy. There was such a humming of mechanisms, shrieking of alarm systems, clicking of emergency relays that I felt out along my perceptions and shut off the main source of energy for the entire complex.

Then I turned to Six. "Tell this man to call his superiors. We must arrange a meeting of the full ruling council of Gin, and it must begin as soon as possible. While he's getting his own people here, you will give me the whereabouts of the headquarters of the rest of the Less-Than-Twenties on Gin."

Six stared at me. He was shattered and naked in a world so cold and unfamiliar that he was like an infant left parentless. I was the only thing left from his past. He nodded.

I turned to the officer on duty. "Call your superiors, in order of rank. Tell them that Number Six of lab-ship 236-J-16, assigned to sector four thousand eighty-seven, has arrived by way of a revolutionary new technique. There must be an immediate meeting of the Council. Use Code Number 000111000."

The Ginli began tapping out his orders on the dead console. When he gave up in despair, I caught his attention. "I will give you the power . . . now!" I said airily.

I waved my hand (purest theatrics) and at the same time converted the material in the nearby waste-bin to energy and introduced it into the console's system, neatly phased to work flawlessly. I felt a moment of sheer pride in my own artistry . . . then I thought wryly that this business would turn me into either a show-off or a power-mad monster. I hoped the Hril had foreseen and forestalled both possibilities.

I had intended to monitor the assembling of Gin's rulers, but that code number that Six had provided kept sticking in my craw. Even while I assimilated the coordinates of the locations of all the headquarters complexes and plotted them on my internal "map," I kept a weather eye on the ramp leading into the chamber.

Just as well, though even when being stealthy the Gin cannot keep quiet. I shook my head sadly at Six when the stamping and clanking became audible.

"You know better than that!" I said. My tone reminded me of the voices of parents and teachers, long ago on Big Sandy.

Six hung his head. His colorless face flushed faintly. "It was my *duty*," he muttered.

"You're engaged in saving your people from destruction," I said. "*That* is your duty. They are a threat to their own existences. *Remember* that!"

I waited until the troop reached the head of the ramp. The first line started down, weapons at the ready, and I folded them back into the hallway from which they had come. A mistake . . . I had seen a portion of the hall when we arrived, and I'd calculated it to be large enough to accommodate everybody. It must have had some offset that narrowed it, for when the leaders piled back among their peers I could hear crunching groans, clatters and bangs and pops. We could see legs waving wildly, flamers sliding across the floor, followed by a tumble of off-balance bodies.

Abashed, I did no more folding but wove a field across the wide doorway to keep out both men and energy-bolts. As an afterthought I made it impervious to projectiles.

Relieved of that problem, I completed the needed data and began folding Ginli bigwigs into the chamber where we waited, beginning with those most distant and working inward. As two-thirds of Gin is ocean, there wasn't a terrible distance to cover. It wasn't long before the room was crowded with bewildered officials. Before the locals arrived (it was the middle of the night where we were) all the rest were assembled.

I had been keeping a bit of my attention on the corridor. When I felt the locals coming, I let down the barrier for them. A few overeager guards got tumbled back into the hall when they tried following, but I did it more gently this time. The newcomers arrived in some disorder, which became worse when they found their control center filled with milling compeers from all parts of Gin.

I folded Six and me neatly across the expanse of confused Ginli and into the circle of the console. It was a bit crowded, so I ejected the duty officer.

That bit of business nailed down the attention of everyone in the room.

XXIX.

Hale Enbo

I had learned from the Hril an important thing about changing the thinking of intelligent beings. Words are useless. Oh, in one case out of millions talk might do the job, given an open-minded subject. But those are rare indeed.

Now I was faced with a roomful of restive Ginli, some of them in dishabille that bordered on the risqué. One big fellow had arrived in full uniform, medals and all, except for his trousers. Below the waist he wore nothing but socks. I conjured him up a pair of pants, partly from sympathy, partly as a practical matter. A pantsless male has no attention left for anything else.

That, too, created a stir. But I nudged Six, and he stamped his heels and achieved some quiet. Then he spoke. "Fellow Less-Than-Tens! Less-Than-Twenties! We are in terrible and unsuspected danger, all of us. I have been seized by beings whose existence we never knew. My mind has been turned inside-out by them. They have shown me truths that our race has forgotten. Listen to me!"

They didn't, of course. They thought he was crazy. While their attention was focused upon him, I summoned the full power that had been put into me by the Hril. I opened all their minds. They were like glowing nodules, differing in intensity, some giving off very strange hues.

Pulsing energies surrounded me, feeding my own. I knew that the Khi were lending me their strength. Confidently I reached into Six's memory and brought forth the skein of impulses that had recorded his confrontation with the Hril.

I spun that skein out over all their minds, exposed and bare as they were. Six continued shouting, his audience listening or ignoring him, but all were now caught up in the teaching of the Hril. As each of those minds absorbed the truth, the colors of those nodules steadied, losing their flickering and their muddy hues.

When I had finished, Six was speaking quietly and reasonably. Those who stood in the room were nodding agreement. Six was outlining the changes to be implemented among all the Ginli complexes, all the educational facilities.

As he went into the specifics, I felt myself fading out. It was a peculiar sensation . . . I was drawn out through dimensions until I found myself again in the diamond room in the caverns of the Khi.

Khi-Sang was waiting. "It is done," she said, her interior voice a bit sad. "Now you may choose your own path, Hale Enbo. Do you want to go forward with us, trans-dimensionally, working the will of the Hril? Or do you want to go back to being what you were, at least in seeming? Anything you choose will be done, for the Hril can warp individual time-lines back upon themselves."

I gazed at her glowing shape, rounded and dear and familiar. I thought of an eternity spent with the Khi, doing great things in the worlds of the many dimensions. I remembered my pleasure at finding new things on new worlds.

I turned to Khi-Sang. "The time will come when I'll want to walk the strange ways with you. Now I'm still young and ignorant . . . yes, ignorant, though the Hril have taught me things I never thought I'd know.

"I'd like for those new things to recede from my memory, keyed to some symbol that will release them at need. I'd like to go back as nearly as possible to the self that I was . . . learning, feeling the worlds with my old senses. I shall want to return, but now I would go back."

The room shimmered away. The receding roar that was the shuttle that had set me here to explore this new world for the altered Ginli receded over the horizon. I turned and looked about.

The bushes were thick and springy, covered with leaves that blazed with fantastic color. Peering cautiously through that autumnal foliage, I could see the beach plainly . . . a strand of white sand that curved gently inward and was lapped by gentle purplish waves.

I smiled and moved forward . . .

XXX.

The Hril Who Watches

The first task is completed. Well completed. Our choice was good, strange though it might have seemed to those who cannot see into the hearts of living beings. Only one with the strength and determination of a man and the straight vision and loving heart of a child might have done this thing for us without damage to himself or to others.

Even the Khi . . .

Most interestingly, he has chosen to return to his former state, being wise enough to understand that he had not matured in his former condition. For one to turn his back, voluntarily, upon such powers as we had to teach him is astonishing. Even to us, whose thought he is.

Now he works amid the teeming worlds, learning from the creatures there, interacting with the sapient beings, interlacing his instinct and his thought even with the trees and the growing things and the stones. We did not have to hint to him that this was best . . . he knew it instinctively.

Many times we have turned our thankful thought toward those whose creations we are, ourselves. Only by infrequent fitful glimmers of perception do we know them to be there, yet they, too, must be involved in the forthcoming confrontation. They caused us to be wise enough to choose Hale Enbo to face the terrible thing that is to come.

XXXI.

Hale Enbo

It was a blue voice. It went echoing away down the maw of this alien place, setting up reverberations among the fangs of ice that studded all the labyrinth that I could see. Its words were even more alien than the caverns in which I found myself . . . but the voice matched the light, for that, too, was blue.

I rolled onto my belly and pushed myself up. I felt about a thousand years old, and possibly that long dead. My bones grated together every time I moved, and my muscles seemed made of rusty wire. Whatever the situation might be (and for the moment I couldn't remember a thing), I knew that I was *not* a doddering septuagenarian. Nor yet a physical wreck. The one thing that stood firm and unwavering in my limited universe was the fact that I was Hale Enbo, and I was twenty-eight years old.

As for the rest—such as where I was and why I was there—the hell with it for now. Two things demanded top priority, and they were going to get it if it was possible. I was freezing to death, and I was starving.

Deciding that the voice had had the stage to itself long enough, I took a breath and shouted, "Heyyy!"

A shattering deluge of echoes battered me to my knees, hands over my ears. The vibrations threatened to set up a gonging inside my skull. It was as if thousands of voices shouted back at me, with the blue devil of a *vox daemoniam* rising triumphantly above them all.

So much for shouting. I got entirely too much answer for

comfort. Next I'd better see if I could make my unsteady legs
walk. Even though every direction looked the same, I knew
that this spot held nothing that I needed. Elsewhere couldn't
possibly be worse.

Standing, I lost the little warmth I had managed to conjure
up by huddling into a ball. It was so cold it reminded me of
that classical Hell that I had read about back in school on Big
Sandy. I could now sympathize with those long-dead heretics
who found themselves frozen for eternity in the bottommost
circle.

I lifted a foot and slid it forward. So far so good. The other
managed the same feat (a pity there wasn't anyone to share
the pun), and I found myself walking painfully slowly along
the right-hand tunnel wall. As I moved it became easier
to negotiate my stiffened body. My blood began to flow
faster, generating a faint warmth.

The voice was still going, shivering the icicles that hung
from the arching roof. When I began to move it receded into
the back of my consciousness. The language was so alien that
I had no idea what it might be . . . it rang no faintest bell of
familiarity.

As I moved along the passage I found that the voice went
through all the tunnels. I couldn't leave it behind, which
suggested a speaker system distributed throughout the entire
system of caverns. That, in turn, suggested some sort of
living beings who existed here. Living beings eat. *Ergo,* if I
could find them, I might find food along with them. That
sped me along considerably.

The tunnel narrowed to a funnel-like neck, bent at right
angles. Then it widened out into a large chamber. There the
blue light was brighter than I had yet seen. In the center of the
cave lay a mirror-smooth pool of black water that reflected
the other end of the room so faithfully that I almost walked
into it. Stalactites of blue-lit ice reached down from the arching groin above. Stalagmites of blue ice rose to meet them,
surrounding the pool with surrealist columns.

It was very beautiful—and unbearably cold. I began to
wonder if any being capable of existing here for long periods

could possibly be kin enough to my kind to share anything useful with me. Food, principally. At the thought, my stomach gave a doleful growl.

There was a path around the pool. I found it simply because my feet recognized it and began following it, while my eyes were still searching for a way. The trail wove in and out among the pillars of ice, ducking once beneath an archway frozen into sapphire stasis above.

It was, without doubt, a path worn by feet. Or hooves. Or pseudopods. Here and there a fragment of ice was crushed into glittering powder. Once or twice I saw a stump where a minor icicle had been snapped from its base. Once, in the middle of a patch of rime, a print was set. Leaf-shaped and very small, it was a frost-etched proof of the passage of some living thing.

Though I was only mildly claustrophobic, as a usual thing, the meandering about pillars of ice was beginning to tell on my nerves when I came out of the maze into a small circular "room." The light was stronger, bluer, and the voice was so loud that it made the icicles ring with faint, shrill notes. But I wasn't listening. I was examining the room closely.

I would have bet my next meal, whatever and whenever it might be, that this was an office of some kind. The table in its center was far too low for a desk to fit my kind, and there was no chair of any sort. The equipment that squatted around the edges of the "desk" was totally unfamiliar. But a filing cabinet is a filing cabinet is a filing cabinet, wherever you find it. When Hale Enbo bets a meal, it's on a sure thing.

On the other side of the desk was a sort of glimmer. I could make out shape, now and then, as it moved and the light slid up and down thin limbs, but its continual motion blurred its unfamiliar contours. Once I had seen, in a museum on Argo, a set of incredibly delicate animals from old Earth. They'd been shaped in some fashion from glass, and they were true to the finest detail. And only the size of my thumbnail. This creature reminded me of those.

I cleared my throat. It jumped, exactly as anyone else would have if interrupted when he thought he was alone. The motion stopped, and I could distinguish its true form. It was four-legged. I felt certain that at the ends of those frail legs were set tiny leaf-shaped hooves. Its trunk was svelte, moving upward from the front legs to a long narrow head with neat round ears. They were set above a short neck that sported two slender arms that ended in delicate hands.

It looked at me for a moment. I could see, now that I knew how to look at it, that its pale grayish brain was pulsing inside its skull. Its inner workings, in fact, were quite visible, though they, too, were so nearly colorless that it took a bit of effort to make them out. It was impossible to see any expression on the glassy face, though. That was a shame, for my chocolate-brown skin and dense texture must have had considerable impact upon such a transparent creature.

Feeling apologetic, I cleared my throat again and said, ''I hope you know Terranglo, my friend. If you don't, we're in trouble.''

The creature jumped again, cocked its head onto one side, and darted a hand toward one of the mechanisms. It flicked something, and at once the blue voice snicked off. A round disc lit up at the side of the mechanism.

A brisk voice said, ''Give me your papers. In triplicate, mind you. I haven't all *ehrm* to waste on you.''

''Now wait a minute,'' I answered, ''I haven't any papers. Not that I know of. I just waked up, back down the tunnel, and I don't remember anything about where I am or why I'm here. I know that I'm Hale Enbo. I'm twenty-eight years old. I was born and reared on Big Sandy, and I've spent the last few years scouting for the Ginli. That's as far as I go. If you want papers, you'll have to look somewhere else.''

''Oh, *gresh!*'' said the voice, with that complaining tone that must be standard issue with every bureaucrat in the universe, ''I get all the unorthodox ones. Amnesiac? Hmmm . . . now who . . .'' He touched something else, which lit another dial. He spoke in that incomprehensible language of his.

I had the uncomfortable impression that I was a buck that was in the process of being passed. A few minutes later, I was sure of it. Two blown-glass shapes appeared in the arch beyond the desk. They carried a pouch that my companion pounced upon and disemboweled with relish. It contained filmy wisps of something, and I would have bet my second-best boots that they were the "papers" that authorized my transfer from the bailiwick of Number One to that of some so-far-invisible Number Two.

The wisps were stacked neatly and slotted into one of the machines. It spat out a yard or so of the stuff. My transparent friend snipped it into lengths, marked it with the equivalent of a rubber stamp, and put it into the pouch. This he returned to the bearers. They took the pouch with something like res-ignation and Number One said, "That's that. You will go with Shhhp and Slnnn, here, and they will show you where you belong."

He returned to his mysterious activity, dissolving into a glimmer again. I walked around his desk toward my escort. As I passed, I reached down and pushed every button I could see. Bureaucrats do something weird to me . . . and I like to reciprocate in full.

The blue light began to pulse frantically. The voice rose in an ascending volume to an intolerable wail. Dials flashed, irate voices boomed and muttered and mewed from ten direc-tions. Number One backed away from his suddenly de-mented desk with a doleful squawk, and disappeared among the ice-pillars. My escort, tearing their dark blots of eyes from the spectacle, grabbed me by the hands and dashed down the path by which they had come.

Behind us the noise rose to greater volume. Then there was a crashing and crushing and smashing . . . as if ice were falling onto rock. With a twinge of conscience, I realized that that was just what was happening. The vibrations from all the cacophony must have loosed every icicle within range.

I didn't have time to worry about it. Shhhp and Slnnn were scurrying down the slippery path so fast that I could hardly keep up. Off to right and left, as we flew by, I could see shiny pipes of reflections that told me others of their kind were also moving through the caves. I must have passed them on my way without knowing it.

We sailed around a sharp bend. My feet went ahead of me. I slid into the new "office" on the seat of my pants.

XXXII.

Hale Enbo

My slide ended painfully as the icy pathway turned into a graveled surface. Shhhp and Slnnn stopped exactly at the end of the ice and handed me the pouch of "papers."

"Give this to that one in there," said a tinny voice that had to be a canned instruction issued to the messengers for use with speakers of Terranglo.

I rose to my feet, slapped the grit off my rear, and stepped forward rather gingerly to see what sort of official might be here. The place was warm—warmer, anyway, than any I'd yet found. It was lit with good yellow light, not the frigid blue of the other caverns. A curtain of blown air walled it off from the icy breath of the tunnel, and my escorts stayed well away from the warmer area, strengthening my suspicion that they just might melt at higher temperatures.

As I looked about, noting the presence of a large, comfortable chair behind the equipment-ringed desk, a fruity voice said, "Come in, young Primate. Warm yourself. Those *pfersneeft* caves are cold enough to freeze the fur off a Varlian."

I walked toward the desk. A low chair was tucked into a space between it and the far wall, and I sat down. But the owner of the voice wasn't immediately visible. Something about my present location seemed to favor disembodied voices.

I pulled the chair about, testing its strength. It held me securely and rose beneath my weight enough to let me stretch out my fairly long legs. I leaned back and looked up. In the arched curve of the cave roof above me there was a large shadow that seemed to be moving across the groin and down the wall.

"Forgive me," said the voice. "I was having my after-snack nap. I do try to save the feelings of non-Epfelen visitors—walking on the ceiling seems to make them giddy—but we hadn't a thing on the docket for today. You must have given the Sdnnn fits. They do hate anything out of the ordinary, unscheduled and undocumented."

The shadow reached the lighted area and became a flat furry creature that looked something like a bearskin rug. It floomped across the graveled floor and draped itself onto the chair. Thereupon it shook itself, assumed a rotund shape, and extended a furry paw to take my pouch from the desk-top.

"Ahhh . . ." it grunted. "Aha! No warning, no memory. You just appeared in the Records Office as if Transferred direct. Hmmm. No idea why?"

"Not one," I replied. "But I'm hungry as a bear . . ." he looked at me quizzically, and I raised an apologetic hand . . . "as can be, and I was about to freeze to death until I came in here. I don't suppose you have anything suitable for a Primate?"

"I hardly think imported swamp-fern with fungus would suit," the Epfelen answered. "But I can remedy the situation in a moment. Rest and get warm . . . I'll be back immediately." He rose and trundled out, a substantial figure, now, having lost all trace of the flatness of his on-the-ceiling shape.

I leaned back in the chair again. This let my eyes wander idly over the arching stone above. There were more shadows there, from middle-sized to very small. I surmised that my host preferred taking his nap surrounded by his entire family. As I watched, a smallish area began inching along the rock toward the wall.

Down it came, just as its father had done. When it reached the floor it stood erect and fluffed itself out into a podgy shape of dark fur. Shaking each of its limbs in turn, it worked until its hirsute covering stood out with electrical vigor. Last of all it bottle-brushed its short tail. I lost control and laughed aloud.

It turned and looked at me with eyes as large and black as its parent's. Though I was sure it wouldn't speak Terranglo, I said, "I'm sorry, little friend, but yours is a kind of being I've never met before. And you look much like a toy I had when I was a youngling."

The small Epfelen gave a baritone giggle and moved quickly to the desk, where it pressed a button. Then it said, and the mechanism translated, "Now you can talk to me, Hairless One. Why did you laugh? *You* are the one who has had *errsu* and lost all your fur."

I explained that I wasn't one of its kind, and while we were getting things sorted out the adult returned with a creature I'd heard about but had never seen. In all the worlds governed by the Council, robots are outlawed. There are too many beings who need a reason for being for any work to be allotted to machines of that kind. Yet this was indubitably a real working robot. It looked like a low, wheeled cart, with its sensory organs contained in a round knob in the middle of its table-like top.

It had a voice. It said, "Food suitable for Primate, *Homo Sapiens*. Warm on left, cold on right. For liquids, turn knob."

Taking a bowl, I held it beneath a wide orifice on the warm side. Thick stew oozed into the container. I made short work of that, then held another bowl under the cold side. And there came lime sherbet . . . my favorite food of all. Back on Big Sandy it had appeared only at Festival time.

The small Epfelen moved up beside me and peered into the bowl. "I like?" it asked.

"I don't know . . . or even if it might make you sick," I answered, turning to the father. But he nodded his furry head, so I held another bowl for the young one. He sat down and devoured it with single-minded energy that reminded me of myself at that age. By the time we'd finished, we were boon companions and fellow lime sherbet addicts.

After the robot trundled itself back into the tunnel, I sat back in the chair and asked him, "Do you have any notion what I'm doing here? I was going about my business on a little old ball of rock inhabited by a race that looked more like

scorpions than is entirely comfortable, when suddenly I
skipped a beat and woke up here. The Ginli don't treat their
Scouts that way, so who sent me here and why . . . and even
how?'' But somehow I had an uneasy feeling in my interior
that I knew the answers, if only I could remember them.

The Epfelen chuckled a rich bass gurgle. ''Inquiries are
being made. But you are in the Ice Caves of Sennlik, which is
the home world of the Sdnnn. We are, in fact, a bureaucracy
created for handling interracial and interspecies transactions
of all kinds. These caverns are deep below the surface of
Sennlik, cut into rock, which allows the creation of almost
any kind of habitat.

''The Sdnnn are born paper-shufflers and nitpickers,
which is another reason why Sennlik was selected for the
central routing and holding offices. We other kinds are here
to deal with the more relaxed sorts who are sent here. Many
of the warm-bloods have problems in dealing with the Sdnnn.
The Epfelen, the Fsssa, most Primates, and almost all ursinoids have a terrible time holding their tempers with our
transparent brothers.'' He chuckled again, and the young one
joined in.

''But that means that I'm involved in some sort of transac-
tion . . . between species?'' I was thinking furiously.
''Surely I'd have been told.''

He leaned back in his chair. ''Oh, you should have been.
You should indeed. Someone has slipped badly.'' He looked
uncomfortable and twiddled with the translator, though he
spoke perfect Terranglo. ''I think—this is only my own idea,
understand—that you have been offered as hostage in some
Exchange or other. That would explain why no purpose of
your own brought you here. But you should have been
consulted . . . you truly, truly should.''

Hostage? All my Enbo don't-try-to-push-me-around blood
rose to my head. It must have turned my brown cheeks
purplish, for the Epfelen watched me nervously. Still, I managed to swallow my anger and to cool down a bit (a feat
impossible in my younger days).

''What did that first Sdnnn put in those papers he sent
you?'' I asked.

''That was only a detailed physical description, right down to fingerprints, retinal patterns, and the exact chemical composition of your exhalations. All that junk on his desk measures and detects things like that from a distance. A lot of nonsense, really. I could *see* what you looked like. But poor old Slrrr couldn't bear to send you out paperless. It's like asking a Fssa to make love to a serpent . . . a racial impossibility.''

He tucked his offspring into a corner of his lap and said, ''By the way, I am Heff. This is Grynn. If you'll look upward, you may see my mate Renn (she's the biggest shadow—there at the rear of the arch), and our other young ones. Living in such close quarters with the Sdnnn has somewhat eroded my manners. They are content to refer to themselves by their office title, and to others by number or title . . . don't find it a bit ridiculous. We Epfelen are much less starchy.''

I found myself liking the big Epfelen. I had encountered many kinds of intelligent beings in my years of working for the Ginli. Every time I had a new one I measured it on my internal scale of one to ten. Heff was easily an eight-and-a-half. Maybe nine. Only once had I met a ten, and that memory refused to come clear.

He brought my musing up short with his next remark. ''You know, hostages have very . . . variegated . . . careers. My jurisdiction lasts only until you are properly classified and your destination is determined. I seldom have opportunity to come into contact with those in your position, but when I do I always offer them a bit of advice . . . totally unofficial, mind you, and if you say I said it I'll be horrified and indignant. Seize any opportunity you may find to get away from the Sdnnn. They won't mistreat you. Heavens, no. But they'll bore you to the verge of catatonia.

''When they remove you from my office you will find that there are many smooth-bore tunnels leading upward from the principal passageways. They lead to the surface of Sennlik. The Sdnnn don't guard or obstruct them, for they consider the surface to be a totally hostile and deadly environment. For them it is. But it's only very hot and desertlike. With pretty

frequently occurring natural water. Not a bad place at all
. . . we take holidays there occasionally, though we don't
admit that to the Sdnnn.''

He winked solemnly. I winked back. Then he said, ''Nobody has ever taken my advice. Some of them have been
sitting in holding apartments for years. Wishing, I don't
doubt, that they'd escaped when they could. The Sdnnn
provide entertainment materials with all the interest of the
Ratio of Sand-Gravel to Fuel-Stone Trade Among the Orin-
dan Systems. Together with educational holograph shows.
Mostly about amoebae, I hear. Think about it, Hale Enbo.''

I sat there thinking about it until two Sdnnn came to the end
of the ice outside. Heff sighed and nodded toward the air-
curtain, and I rose to go.

As I stood, I said, ''My thanks, Heff. I'm impressed by the
amiability and . . . wisdom . . . of your species.'' I winked
again.

His dark eyes brightened. He raised one fluffy paw in
farewell. ''Perhaps we shall see you again,'' he said. But his
voice held no conviction.

XXXIII.

Hale Enbo

The ice-studded tunnels were even colder, now that I'd had a taste of the warmth of the Epfelens' quarters. My tough coverall was designed to give maximum protection from any sort of weather, adapting itself to climates ranging from frigid to searing, but the insidious bone-creeping chill of these caves seemed to go right through to my marrow. The freezing touch of a Sdnnn hand on my arm didn't help any either.

Shhhp and Slnnn must have been on other errands, for my new guides were considerably different. Translating the ribbons of light that defined (somewhat) their transparent shapes, I thought that these two were more like attenuated miniature elephants than like deer. We passed, as we went, members of that species who had giraffe-like necks, no necks at all, fourteen matched pairs of arms, six irregularly-placed legs, and others too involved to sort out at a glance.

We also passed a number of the ventilation tunnels. They angled upward from my shoulder-height above the floor of the passageways. Blasts of cold air whistled down them . . . they certainly gave no indication that they opened onto a broiling desert. As we drew near each one I tried to examine it without being obvious about it, but my escorts were extremely attentive. I was driven, at last, to pretend to have a gravel in my boot that required immediate attention.

I stopped almost opposite one of the vents and knelt to undo the straps of my right boot. We now were in a tunnel that came to a dead end a short way further on, and my

companions seemed to be in a real snit. They babbled away in
their incomprehensible slippery tongue and made urgent gestures with their hands. There seemed to be no canned speech
suitable for making a prisoner stop taking a stone out of his
boot, so I pretended ignorance and removed my boot with
agonizing slowness.

The blue light didn't penetrate far into the vent, I found
from my low angle. Still, I thought that there was a curvature
just beyond sight in the smooth opening. Behind my position
was an angle in the tunnel that would block the sight of that
vent from anyone in the outer tunnel. This dead end, though I
suspected that it must have offices up ahead, would be a good
place to make a break.

As do many best-laid plans, this one went rapidly aglim-
mering. A voice like a nail scratching glass came hooting up
the tunnel toward us, just as I got my boot strapped on. My
two blown-glass elephants grabbed me by the elbows and
literally shot me down the slick tunnel, into an arched opening framing another pool-centered office, complete with ice
pillars and filing cabinet.

The voice was raising so much Cain that the waters of the
pool quivered nervously from the vibration. Stalactites of ice
were chiming faintly in a key just audible above the voice.
My companions were trembling so that I feared for their
stability, but I was annoyed at having my plan stifled before
its birth.

This office was bustling with Sdnnn, some hurrying about
gathering "papers" from various machines, some sitting (or
standing) before desks tapping out unintelligible matters on
anonymous equipment. I thought immediately of Ginli sec-
retaries in offices in the old days, terrified of not seeming
busy enough to justify themselves to the reigning bureaucrat.

The reigning bureaucrat in this office squatted in the midst
of its kingdom on eight spidery legs amid an obstacle-course
of ice-chunks. Its voice never stopped. I stalked up to it,
ignoring the fragile assistants scurrying out of my way, and
said, "Pipe down. You're making too much noise."

The result was interesting. A blob of scarlet appeared in
the middle of its body. From that central redness a flush

spread out along the centers of every limb. The effect was rather beautiful—a scarlet spider encased in ice might look just so. I suspected that I was seeing a classic example of what happened when a Sdnnn got angry, which was quite all right with me.

A deluge of slurred and slithery Sdnnn-ese broke about my head, accompanied by emphatic gestures that made blue light wriggle along the creature's contours in dizzy patterns.

I grinned at it, took from my pocket a crisp fruit from the robot-cart, and crunched into it. The Sdnnn became totally scarlet, the color so dense that I could no longer admire the workings of its innards.

It seemed, suddenly, to remember itself. It jerked to a stop and waved at a "secretary", who hurried to activate a translator. Then I was treated to a masterpiece of dressing-down, and mine has been a life rich in such matters. Then I recalled the chaos I'd created for poor old Slrrr. I was reminded of that several times. It must have been infuriating to the official that I began to laugh uncontrollably halfway through his tirade. I do love discomfiting stuffed shirts.

When the VIP ran down he scrunched himself down on one of the ice-chunks. I winced, expected to see him shatter into transparent shards, but his fragility must have been only apparent. He crouched there, the red receding from his limbs, and glared at me, getting back his breath. Then he waved an arm, and a secretary put a pouch into the flexible hand that tipped it. Once more the translator came into play.

"You have been named hostage. Your employers, the Ginli, are engaged in making an agreement with the Oti of the newly discovered Otirian system. An exchange of information is in progress. We are Custodian of Record for both you and your Oti counterpart. Neither, be it known, could exist on the world of the other. The Oti are energy-gas intelligences.

"The negotiation in question is none of your concern, nor is the substance of the information to be exchanged. Your function, as of now, is to sit quietly and wait for the span of time required to put into operation a smoothly functioning system of information-exchange."

"How long might that be?" I asked.

If the thing had been human, it would have grinned with fiendish glee. There were traces of that, even in the canned voice of the translator, as it answered, "If it runs true to form, they'll forget about you entirely . . . you'll be with us for years."

"And where in this frozen maze do you keep an energy-gas intelligence?" I inquired.

"We have accommodations for any life-form known," he said. "We have put you and your opposite number into adjoining apartments . . . that is one of the advantages of living sensibly underground, with every wall impermeable rock."

"Do my immediate employers know my present location and duties?" I asked. "I was assigned as Scout to the J-105-W, under the command of Number Eighteen, at this time."

"They were informed at the time of your removal from the moonlet that you were examining," he answered. "The decision to use you was made at the highest Ginli level. I cannot imagine why."

That sounded like an insult, and I felt sure that it was meant as one. But I let it pass . . . I was determined to escape from the Sdnnn as soon as possible. While I mulled that, a vision of a softly glowing golden shape moved briefly through my memory. But it was a fleeting thing, gone before I could grasp it.

I was brought to attention by the reappearance of my guards. Old Spiderlegs was almost completely transparent again, and his gestures were a web of flashes and glints. My guards took me firmly by the arms and led me from the office, making a wide detour around every piece of equipment.

The tunnel through which I had intended to escape stared at me reproachfully as we passed. In order to loose myself I would have had to shatter both my companions. It seemed a bit extreme to demolish intelligent beings just to escape being bored. I sighed and went with them through the complexes of chambers and ice passages and ice-studded grottoes.

It was almost worth it just to see that fantastic place. No two spots were alike, or even similar. Like snowflakes, each had its own unique pattern of growth and development, and I grew dizzy with admiring each as it came. Whether through artistic sensitivity or practical unwillingness to trouble themselves, they had mostly left their underworld alone. The tunnels wandered around pools and pillars. Offices were put where there was space for them without disarranging the natural arrangements. It seemed a pity that such loveliness was seen only by scurrying bureaucrats and bemused hostages.

Where they had needed large spaces or enclosed chambers they had tunneled into the rock and carved out just what was needed. I remembered Old Spiderlegs's office and wondered if such were reserved for the VIPs or for the extremely paranoid.

We passed many vent tunnels, and I looked at them wistfully, moving gently against the glassy hands about my arms. But they were firmly clamped onto me, and I shrugged in defeat.

Once we reached our destination I wished that I had taken my chances on demolishing the guards. We stopped before a smooth panel that closed an arched opening in a sheer wall. I never saw a more solid piece of work in my life. The door was swung from a pair of steel rods, one of them fixed into the stone of the wall, one into the door itself. A series of wide steel collars joined them, allowing the door to move smoothly. It opened to a long oration in the Sdnnn tongue, and I gave up any idea I might have had about picking the lock. It hadn't any recognizable one. Three oblong bars were sunk into the edge, and three corresponding openings in the facing stone showed that they must slide into them, barring the opening effectively. What made the thing move was invisible.

The tunnel behind was very dull, after the splendor of the ice caves. It was lit with blue light, but there was no ice to reflect nor pool to mirror it. Dark stone, hewn smooth and lit with streaks of gray, met my eyes. The doors sunk into those walls were as featureless as the stone, being of brown metallic stuff. There were no gratings or windows through which the tenants might see or be seen.

I thought of Heff's words . . . "They will simply bore you to death." I was beginning to believe him.

We moved down to the third door, all doors being on our right, and it, too, opened to a Sdnnn soliloquy. With stiff courtesy, the guards led me in and gestured toward the two-room complex within.

The canned voice said, "These will be your quarters for the time of your stay. You will be provided with equipment for exercising, with literature of an improving nature" (I groaned internally) "and with other interesting and educational materials. Any request you make, so long as it is for materials that will enhance your character and education, will be honored."

I nodded, thought for a moment, and said, "Might I have a book—*The Carthagoan Mythos*, in Ginli? And would it be possible for me to undertake the study of your own most interesting language?"

There was a long pause, and I felt sure that my request had been relayed by means of the communications equipment on the collars about the wide necks of the blown-glass elephants. In a short while the tiny voice replied, "Your request has been evaluated and granted, though the *Mythos* is on the borderline between acceptable anthropology and obscure folklore. Your request for instruction in Sdnnn is most unusual, but it is one that we respect. No other hostage in our experience has had the intelligence and taste to recognize its value and beauty."

I chuckled, deep inside, as the two about-faced and left my apartments. Even as I chuckled, I was committing to memory every syllable of the unlocking-code, which they used to reopen the door.

XXXIV.

Hale Enbo

The Sdnnn had a fair notion of acceptable accommodations, to be sure. My rooms were large, high-ceilinged, and finished in a matte-textured covering in shades of cream and beige. On the long stretch of wall that faced my float (which doubled as couch and sleeping accommodation) was a handsome mural of a lake backed by mountains, with misty haze rising from the water and first sunlight just touching the forests and peaks behind it. The more you looked into the picture, the more there was to see. Animals and birds and even insects were there for the seeking eye. It took me a week just to find all the deer.

At the end of three weeks I could pinpoint everything hidden among the foliage or in the ripples. Every otter or beaver or bird. Every wood-mite. I could see the damned thing with my eyes closed. In my sleep. In my nightmares, which began to be frequent.

The *Mythos* was some comfort. I'd been itching to read it since learning that the Ginli kept it in the Less-Than-Tens-Only file. It was a fascinating account of a culture that developed rapidly and grew to be an efficient and overbearing technocracy. It had been overthrown by a cult that had sprung like fungus from the ranks of the regimented. The "people" (actually a kind of rodent) grew mortally weary of total control of their lives being in the hands of a few. Before their reformation, the Ginli had been on a terribly similar path. It could have been overthrown by anyone desperate enough to imitate the Carthagoan Quadrate, which had brought that other culture down . . . and down . . . and down.

Perhaps those little beings were happier, now, but theirs could no longer be called a culture. Internecine maneuvering for power, I decided by reading between the lines, had blown the revolutionaries higher than the revolutionaries had blown their established government. A sad case of the cure being worse than the ill.

Between the *Mythos* and studying that damned mural I killed off two months. Then I tackled the Sdnnn language, and that was a real battle. The approximations that could be achieved by Terranglo speakers were distant, at best; it had no alphabetical equivalents. The Sdnnn, when speaking their own language, went off both ends of the scale, creating new sounds all the way. The grammar was involuted, convoluted, irregular, and hellish. But the real problem was the fact that the concepts behind the language were alien to any warm-blooded being.

It's amazing how much of the basis of any language is rooted in the physical needs of its users. Entire methods of thought, however coldly rational they may be, are still outgrowths of a folk who need food and shelter, warmth and love and sex, stimulation and achievement.

A Sdnnn wades into one of those black pools once a week (their actual time-measurement would bore you to tears) and absorbs the liquid and its rich mineral content. Once every three years it deposits a spoonful of cells in a steel tray held by a collection-robot, for the purpose of propagation of the race. Shelter was not a factor for them, happy in their underground world. An entire spectrum of needs that shape the thinking of my kind is totally invisible to the Sdnnn. They probably have some spectrum of their own, but it seems to be equally invisible to me.

Therefore learning the language was a very tough go. I persisted, for I come from a people who need challenge as they need air. I was forced to ask for sound-tapes at last, for the allegedly phonetic renderings of the word-sounds were too confusing for use.

I was able, after a time, to find attendants who would remain for a short time to make conversation with me. It was funny—the elephant-shaped ones were strictly business. The deerlike ones were shy but a bit more friendly. They'd sometimes stay for a few words. The best of all were the giraffe-necked ones.

Two of those visited me often, bringing books and filmstrips and taped lessons, not to mention repairing the various mechanisms that dispensed food, water, clothing, and such for my use. These things broke down more frequently than I'd have thought a bunch of nit-pickers like the Sdnnn would put up with. I always rejoiced when Lrrr and Lthhh appeared at my door.

Those two were curious about everything. Sometimes we'd spend their entire time (while they worked, of course) talking about places I'd explored for the Ginli. It gave me good practice at their language, but it was fun, as well. They were the only Sdnnn I ever met who were curious about the upper world of Sennlik. They'd even, in their wild youth, gone up one of the vent tunnels, past the layers of ice that chilled the incoming air, to the height at which the heat became dangerous to their bodies.

I learned a lot from them about the Sdnnn and the ways they lived. They told me also about my fellow hostages. There was a Hleror on one side of me, securely situated in his liquid mercury, entertained by telepathic contact with his home world. I envied him, though I had a niggling feeling in the back of my mind that I could do the same, if I could only remember how.

On my other side was the Oti. He had to have semi-vacuum with no humidity at all. That hadn't been difficult to achieve, but my informants hinted that getting him to his quarters unharmed had been a real problem. They had, I gathered, made a one man (pardon, Oti) force field. When I asked how he passed the time, they could only say that he enjoyed a random jolt of electricity, at intervals.

We three were, at the moment, the only inhabitants of the hostage quarters. Most hostages could be quartered on the worlds involved in their transactions. Though I had to approach the question from oblique angles, I learned that it had never occurred to either Sdnnn or hostages (so far) that escape might be possible. If Heff had indeed suggested trying the vent tunnels to others, they hadn't taken him seriously.

It took four months to learn Sdnnn well enough to suit my purposes. In normal circumstances I doubt that I could have learned it at all, it was so difficult. But here I had unlimited time, no distractions, and driving need. They had started providing me with the amoeba films.

I have nothing against amoebae. Some of my ancestors were indubitably amoebae. But the Sdnnn found them fascinating in the most exotic sense of the word. So different were their lifestyle and their biological processes from those of the Sdnnn that they held an almost morbid interest for the blown-glass people. From what I could gather from my studies and my guards, the Sdnnn were formed of a crystalline material which reproduced by a simple method of depositing a few "cells" in a solution that caused the crystals to multiply rapidly. Added minerals at intervals assured a fully formed, completely adult Sdnnn.

The activities of noncrystalline life-forms interested them mildly. For some reason the mindless divisions of amoebae held them spellbound.

I couldn't say the same.

Before the sixth month was over I was ready to risk life and limb to recover my liberty. They had provided a wide variety of study materials, when I asked. My custodians were completely devoted to my welfare. Yet I found that Heff had been right when he warned that they would bore me to catatonia.

Yet escape was a real problem. I had no equipment suitable for tackling an unfamiliar desert (or even a familiar one). I had no idea what might be above ground that might be edible for my kind. Though I knew that Heff and his family had found water up there, I didn't know if their idea of water was the same as mine.

So I didn't rush it. I gave myself plenty of time to consider every apect. As part of this, I decided to try my best to make contact with my fellow prisoners.

It's useless to knock on a stone wall that's yards thick. Only a blast of thermite would have made a sound that could penetrate. But I knew that Hleror was a telepath, and I decided that that was the only feasible way in which to reach out for him.

Though the memory was terribly dim and blurred, I thought that on an assignment several years before I had had some sort of mental contact with at least some of the inhabitants of the world I was exploring. The inability to recall clearly infuriated me. I could usually rely on my memory. Still, I seemed to remember that I had shown some aptitude for telepathic contact, and I was determined to try reaching out by that method.

A day came when I said goodbye to my guards after their daily visit, knowing that it would be at least twelve hours before they returned. I felt that I could safely count on a good long time in which to make my first attempt. If the chambers were bugged with cameras it wouldn't cause a problem, either . . . a relaxed and receptive state is indistinguishable from sleep.

I stretched out and closed my eyes. I must have drifted off for a while, but I woke to a sort of tickle inside my head. If you've ever, when very young, gone back to archetypal radio equipment and built one of the basic kinds that picks up atmospherics as static, you can imagine the sort of sensation that was jiggling around inside my skull. Eerie . . . but somehow familiar.

There were no pictures within that sensation, no words. Not even a regular pulsation that might be a code. Yet it was definitely something that originated outside myself. I let myself ride with it, using deep meditation techniques to allow it to sink into me.

There was a pause. A question inhabited the nothingness. Something was waiting for an answer.

I sighed. If my thought processes were as foreign to it as its were to me, it was going to be a long night. I concentrated on a picture of myself (as nearly as I could manage) and did my best to transmit it. When I thought there had been enough time for that to soak in, I kept the framework steady and peeled off the skin to show the musculature and nervous system. Then I did my best to trace out the circulatory system (my perusals of several good Ginli libraries helped there) and at last I stripped myself down to the skeleton. Then I let us both rest.

There was a long pause. I was beginning to think that I had lost contact when there was a burst of energy that washed through my mind as a chaos of color and movement. I sank into sleep and dreamed of a golden shape, rounded and glowing. It said to me, ''Do you want to wake, now, Hale Enbo, from your forgetfulness?''

But something inside me said no. The refusal left me still sad when I woke to the rising of the lights in my room that signalled the beginning of a new day.

XXXV.

Thheeer, the Oti

I drift between rough textures, lost from my own and unable to orient myself with any other mind that is akin to mine. The gases that wisp thinly through my semi-vacuum are not those of Otir, though they serve well enough at keeping life focused within me. The energy with which my hosts seek to titillate me at intervals is a dull, mechanical sort, not the fountainhead of lightnings that plays across my world, engaged in creating and stimulating my kind.

Time, a thing that my people have always regarded as an arbitrary standard imposed upon That-Which-Is by those imprisoned in flesh, has begun to be real. It drags at my consciousness. I never dreamed, back on Otir, how much of myself was made up of interactions with the physical and mental existences of my fellows. Now I am learning that a single Oti is a maimed creature, its delight in the processes of thought and learning blunted for lack of a sharing relationship. I, Thheeer the Thinker, am bored!

And this exchange was, in large part, my own idea. Naturally, when a hostage was required I volunteered. I wonder now why it seemed so vital to understand the rationale behind the reformation of a disruptive species. I have regretted my curiosity many times over.

Thought itself is less comfort than I conceived possible. But by using the limited information we possessed about the Sdnnn, in addition to observation and close attention to the sound-codes they use for communication, I have arrived at some understanding of them. They, too, are dull, even though I have proven the usefulness of my Rational-Intuitive Technique in studying them. How useless that feels—the total wattage of creative output in the Caves of Sennlik would not tickle a newly formed mind-bud.

The other hostage, Hleror, has touched its mind to mine. A well-honed ability, true, but a mind so enmeshed with its relations with its home world, as well as so closely linked, chemically, with its liquid mercury environment, that there is nothing of common interest.

I know that my counterpart will arrive on Sennlik soon. It will be interesting, I hope, to study a Primate. Our worlds being mutually inimical as well as distant from one another, I find the opportunity intriguing. The notion that intelligent life could possibly develop within the soupy atmospheres of the overgrown worlds is still strange to my kind. How could the initial stimulus set their processes in motion, there amid heavy elements and thick gases?

Ah well, I shall learn before long. Until then I shall send myself into semi-stasis. That will, at least, obviate my boredom.

I woke in mid-span, my energies tingling with excitement. Something has changed in my immediate vicinity. I suspect that my fellow hostage has arrived. The presence I feel is nearby. Unique. The Sdnnn are not so energy-emitting nor is their wavelength the same. In addition, their life-sparks move about. This one remains fixed in one location.

The shape of his energy-field is fascinating, alien to any I have encountered. He transmits strongly . . . impulses that seethe with power and a youthful sort of vigor. I cannot as yet translate those emanations into anything understandable. This is not going to be either swift or easy.

I have, however, learned one thing about him already. That is a being of logical and methodical habits. When first the Sdnnn left him in his quarters, he stood for a time in the center of the room as if he were sensing his surroundings. I believe that he felt my probe to some extent, but he evidently discounted it as something natural to this new place. After orienting himself, he went around the walls of every chamber, examining each from top to bottom with his upper limbs.

It was not the reaction of a trapped animal. This was the act of an imprisoned creature that wants to ascertain the exact nature of its prison. Who intends to escape! So . . . there is more similarity here than one would suppose. Though the atmosphere of Sennlik would be instantly fatal to my spark, though the difficulties will be great and the dangers all but insurmountable, I intend to go out with my fellow hostage . . . if I can make contact with him.

He busies himself from sleep to sleep. His consciousness is either aswarm with impulses or deeply sunk in that strange other-function that physical beings require. He is learning . . . and I can perceive that he believes that the things he studies may implement his escape. All I can do is to keep a part of my thought attuned to him and to be ready to respond if he ever reaches out with his mind. I seem to be able, now, to attune with his deeper self . . . strange that one who has never been troubled by a body should connect with the emotional plane of a Primate's selfhood.

There is something surprising about my subject. Deep inside himself, he is divided. Not solely into the much-discussed conscious and unconscious levels, but into a great self that sleeps beneath an imposed compulsion and the self that he knows at this time. About that great self I can sense intense powers . . . more wide-ranging powers even than my kind has encountered in all our investigations. Is this Primate normal for his kind? Or is he one with unusual aspects? Fascinating!

I find that I am learning the language of the Sdnnn along with my subject. I seem to be absorbing it directly from some part of his mind. Being without means of making sound other than a gentle hissing, laced with poppings, I will never be able to speak that strange tongue, but the ability to understand it may be useful. And I find it amusing to learn through another's efforts.

Before we took up the study of Sdnnn we were involved in

a complex matter concerning some sort of being that was subjected to compulsion. The concept being totally unfamiliar, I was not quite certain what it was that we were learning. The exercise left me unsettled.

It had not occurred to me that the mere fact of being trapped in flesh would make it possible for a rational being to become entrapped in other ways, as well. Once I had entertained the notion, I found it logically sound. One who cannot osmose through material things must remain within the bounds about its body. If those are not of his own making, and if those who impose upon him will it so, he, so to speak, is a spirit trapped in a body trapped in a chamber. Shackles, I understand now, were devised thus, binding that carnate trap still further.

The habits of thought compelled by that fleshly bondage could lead to more esoteric bondages still. The scope of possibilities was appalling, and I spent several spans in fascinated pursuit of all the permutations of possibility that I could conceive. Truly, it was a frightening idea, that of being encased in so vulnerable a body. It gave me even more respect for the sturdy courage of my fellow hostage. Though it was likely that he had never actually examined the full terror of his situation, still he was sufficiently intelligent and inward-looking to grasp most of the grimmer potentialities of his state.

Armed with new understanding, I set myself to learn more about my neighbor. I looked out through his emotional reactions when he sat studying the mural on the wall. It was some time before I was able to grasp the fact that inhabitants of the green-grown planets are linked, perhaps through actual evolutionary linkages, with their worlds. They love them, if they resemble him, with an almost physical yearning. Yet they also love them as an idea of perfection.

But, as do I, he grows weary of seeing the same thing, span after span. He has grown to hate the scene on the wall as much as he loves it. I can feel his yearning to find just one of the depicted beasts moved from its proper location, or to see a new ripple on the surface of the water. His desperation has gone deep into him. It is disturbing me, in my close-knit relationship with his inner feelings. Soon, now, he will reach the limit of his endurance. Then . . . we will, in some way, find a method of escape that will neither kill me nor impede him unduly.

Meanwhile I wait and watch. I wonder at the almost infinite resource of this Primate. If all of his kind are as determined and disciplined as he . . . but no, I forget. The Ginli are not—or were not until their inexplicable about-face. Though he is not Ginli, he has been long associated with them. No, he may be unique.

Patience, Thheeer! T'Thhisss, in our last synthesis before we parted, warned me that the outer ways of the universe were not subject to the conditions and the habits that govern our lives on our rocky worlds that spin near our superactive sun. He indicated that he wished-feared that my lifelong habit of patient and unruffled calm might not survive contact with the outworlds.

If I could but fuse my thought with his, I could assure him that he foresaw accurately. It hasn't.

XXXVI.

Hale Enbo

The day dragged as if it wouldn't end at all. Even a long session with Lrrr and Lthh failed to hold my full attention, though I had wanted to sound them out concerning the guard that might or might not be set in the corridor of the area where I was. This question was a sticky one to maneuver. Even the Sdnnn might have suspected something if I had asked, "Are there guards outside?"

I calmed myself and managed to wangle the conversation around to the vital importance of the work done by the Sdnnn of all kinds. After being told in detail the particulars of forty kinds of paper-shuffling and message-carrying, I sighed guiltily.

"What a pity it is that the valuable time of your kind must be wasted in standing guard over hostages!" I said. "It makes me feel as if I must be a burden on your system!"

I think they would have looked shocked, but transparent features are the very devil to read, even if they used the same expressions that my kind does.

After a confused babble of Sdnnn, Lrrr said slowly, for my benefit, "Hale Enbo, we are not wasters of time. No hostage has ever troubled our world for an instant. We would be less than wise to burden any of our own with such a senseless task. Think no more of this, we beg you. For you to feel guilt over something that does not exist is folly, indeed."

I brightened, though I didn't have any idea whether they could read me any more than I could them. Pretending much relief, I turned our attention to a really difficult phase of Sdnnn grammar. They tried so hard to help that I began

176

feeling *really* guilty at leading them up the garden path so shamelessly. Of all the Sdnnn I encountered, then or later, those two were the only ones with whom a being of my kind could attain any fellow feeling.

I saw them off with relief and drew my second "meal" of the day from the slot in the wall. Though I usually ate rather greedily, I had made it a practice to consume only two meals a day. Those were very modest, for I wanted to shrink my capacity, which might be of real value if I managed to escape. But I had programmed the food-dispenser to issue four light meals a day, two of them austere ones of dried fruits and hard biscuits.

Those extras I stashed beneath my float, that being the only concealed spot in the rooms. Try as I might, I couldn't figure out a way to carry water with me, however. There was simply nothing in the chambers that would serve as a carrier. And I could hardly ask for a waterbag. The thing worried me considerably.

I just decided to play it by ear as I went along, and I shelved the problem. On this particular evening I gave it a fleeting thought, but I was too anxious for the dimming of the lights to let it worry me. I wanted to stretch out on my float and wait for developments as I reached for any mind nearby.

The last hour was torment. I didn't know if my quarters might be bugged . . . it was likely. I had to seem normal in all ways. It was time at last, and the lights dimmed to pitch blackness, as I had requested. That eliminated distractions and let me empty my mind of anything except receptiveness.

I felt the mind waiting for me, impatiently and hungrily, as if it, too, had suffered through long hours of waiting. With a tingle like a mild electrical shock, I felt a connection form. I opened my mind wide.

I saw . . . something. For a time I couldn't make out a comprehensible pattern. Then, quite suddenly, something clicked into place, and a shape was there. The key was the memory of my lab training, early in my apprenticeship as a Scout. The experiments with electrical charges . . .

The shape that I saw was a continuing electrical display

taking place in a clearly defined area shaped something like a
melon, though considerably larger. Once I had grasped that, I
could see that tiny "lightnings" were continually playing
through the entire area that formed the being's body. That
eliminated Hleror, for I knew the shape of his kind, and this
wasn't it.

So . . . I must be in contact with my Oti counterpart. He
must be, I felt, as desperate as I for a change . . . for escape?
Perhaps. I had sent him a portrait of myself. He had recipro-
cated. Now we must work out a mutually comprehensible
code. He obviously had no organs for speech.

Languages are, principally, codes devised for communication within a single species. Languages have always been my
passion, and I have learned at least the rudiments of almost
every one I've ever encountered. Thheeer (the Oti had indicated that the best he could do in the way of sound was a sort
of hiss and pop) was totally logical. His memory was an
integral part of what he was, if I understood correctly, in
something like the way the blood circulating through human
bodies is for us.

Therefore, the invention of a code wasn't terribly hard. As
I was its principal inventor, I had no difficulty in remembering it, and Thheeer was incapable of forgetting it. From now
on I shall convey our conversations as if they were spoken
aloud in plain Terranglo, instead of pictured symbols, emotional responses, snappings, and hissings. It will save a deal
of trouble.

The first truly clear message we shared was that of our
mutual need to escape. Thheeer had a better notion of the
surface conditions of Sennlik than I did, for he had studied
the planet before volunteering as a hostage. His first concern,
now, was humidity, for even more than semi-vacuum he
needed dry conditions. The desert satisfied that need, within
reasonable tolerances. Otherwise, he told me, he would short
out and dissipate into nothingness.

The semi-vacuum could, he thought, be maintained if I
could find where the Sdnnn kept the "bubble" in which he
had been conveyed from the Transfer to his cell. As he had no

weight, and as the bubble weighed only a few ounces, I felt
that I could take him along without any trouble at all. We
were, so to speak, in this pickle together. Besides, the more I
talked with him, the more I liked him. I liked all sorts of
people . . . and things. Once I had a spirited argument with a
rock . . . but that's another story.

As for my needs, I figured on making do with what I
found. It hadn't occurred to Thheeer to investigate the needs
of a Primate with regard to the surface of Sennlik . . . in fact
he had no idea at all what those needs might be. But he
assured me that real water existed in small quantities above
ground. That, with Heff's assurances as to the livability of the
surface, assured me that I could probably make out well
enough. I'd done well on less, in my time with the Ginli.

Within a few weeks we had established our code so firmly
in our minds that communication was almost as easy as
normal conversation. We had ironed out every difficulty we
could think of before the fact, and we had worried ourselves
and each other into snits over those we had no way of
foreseeing. When it became obvious that we had done all that
we could and were retrogressing by waiting, we decided that
the time had come.

It wasn't easy to jam the food dispenser deliberately,
though the thing had no trouble at all conjuring up its own
foibles. I did manage to foul it up in a manner that didn't
suggest sabotage; then I waited. I hoped that my two friends
would form the repair party. And they did.

I had never asked questions about my fellow hostage, after
the first few days, so I felt it safe to do a bit of probing, now. I
hoped to get a hint of the location of his bubble. I felt that Lrrr
and Lthhh would know something about that, for they did
much of the work in this hostage section.

I led the conversation, very carefully, around to the nature
of the Oti, about which I pretended utter ignorance. My
repair Sdnnn were never so happy as when they were dispens-
ing information, so I got a detailed run-down on the elec-
tromagnetic composition of the Oti, the suitability of the
planets of Otir, huddled as they were about their superhot and

madly active sun to the formation of that odd form of life.

I marveled. Then I said, "You said once that it was difficult to transfer the Oti to his chamber. It seems to be that it would have been almost impossible. You can't get an energy field into a spacesuit, and surely the damp of the caves would have been fatal to such a being. How did you manage it?"

Lrrr managed the equivalent of a deprecatory shrug. "We often have need to safeguard exotic life-forms, Hale Enbo. We have created a device for protecting such as the Oti. When in use, it is a bubble of force. When it is stored it is a tiny packet that would fit into your pouch or pocket. We keep it always nearby in the storage cabinet, lest some catastrophe disrupt his air-tight seal."

I marveled some more, leading them gently into other subjects. I thought that they'd have little memory of being asked about the bubble. When they finished their work I felt real sadness to see them go. I seem to be able to make friends with any sort of being at all. I felt that here were two I might never see again.

Yet when the light dimmed for sleep I was wide awake and tense. Thheeer was also emitting veritable frenzies of energy that soon had every hair on my head prickling. We waited until we felt that all had settled for the sleep period. Then I silently drew on my Scout's jumpsuit and the boots that I'd been wearing when they Transferred me. I stashed my food supply in a tunic that I had sewn across the bottom to make a bag. I tied the sleeves about one of my shoulders and stuffed into the pack one of the light, compressible blankets from my float. I thought wistfully of the constant supply of water, but I dismissed the thought immediately. Win or lose, it was time to go.

I crept to the door and began speaking to it the words I had gleaned from listening to my guards. If anyone were listening in on my chamber, I hoped they'd think I was practicing Sdnnn in my sleep.

It wasn't easy to pitch my voice to the glassy thinness that the Sdnnn produced, but I gave it my all. And the door moved

. . . it swished softly as it slid back. Thheeer felt my surge of excitement, for I felt his thought racing with me into the corridor.

There was dim light . . . I had no trouble finding the "cabinet" that had neither lock nor catch. It was set into the wall beside Thheeer's door, and the packet that held the bubble was on the bottom shelf, together with directions for its use (in Sdnnn). I couldn't read them in the dim light, but Thheeer had put the thing on before. I took it to his door, slid it into the airlock, and touched the switch that evacuated its air into the hall. Then I waited again.

XXXVII.

Hale Enbo

I was getting a bit antsy before the waiting was done. I could envision a troop of angry Sdnnn descending upon us and locking me in so tightly that we'd never be able to get out again. But nothing happened. Until, that is, Thheeer's door slid back quietly (must have had other than a sonic lock on that one) to disclose a bag of sparkling mist bobbing about in the airlock.

Once when I was a child on Big Sandy my father had taken the family to Zimbwe, the largest (and only) city on our dirt-scrabble planet, to an historical exposition. It was an affair that the Earth Origins Society had assembled and arranged to show on every world whose inhabitants' forebears came from Earth. It reproduced the ways of things back on Old Terra. There my father bought me a balloon—the first I or any of the family had ever seen. I held onto the string for two days, until the thing shriveled and became a limp, rubbery corpse.

Thheeer was a super-balloon. I tied a ravel of the yarn from my blanket onto the tip at the bottom of his bubble. He bobbed along above my right shoulder, sparkling excitedly and thinking volumes at me. My spirits popped up as far as possible. We were going to make it!

At the second door, leading into the Ice Caves, I tried the words that had opened my own door. They weren't the right ones, and I had suspected that, all the time. But I had spent months rehearsing in my mind the set of then-meaningless syllables I had heard my guards use when they brought me into the hostage section.

They worked. I was a bit proud of myself, for those memorized sounds with their alien intonations rolled off my tongue slickly. The door swung back on its silent steel rods, letting a gush of icy air into the corridor. The light beyond was even bluer than I remembered, glancing coldly from the stalactites hanging from the groins of the roof. Thheeer went off like a dozen small electrical storms, his thoughts flashing madly about his being until the charge made my hair rise on my head. But he was too excited to encode his ideas, so I might share them. I tugged him along on his string, making for the vent that was a short way along the main stem of the tunnel. I thanked my stars that the Sdnnn weren't telepaths, for the psychic racket my companion was making was deafening.

There were no Sdnnn in sight. They observed resting spans matched to those in the hostage sections and left only key personnel on duty. I wondered what Lthhh and Lrrr would feel when it was discovered that we were gone. The thought made me a bit dismal . . . I liked those two. I thought it unfair that they were condemned to the life of Sdnnn, when their inclinations were so different from those of their fellows. But there was no way I could help them. Taking them from a life of dullness only to melt on the surface wasn't a really good choice.

The blue voice was still maundering. Now I could understand the message. It consisted of constantly updated reprises of all accounts being handled, all paperwork due and soon to be due from every department, duty schedules for every Sdnnn in this segment of the Ice Caverns. It was, if possible, even duller than the amoeba films.

As we crept (and bobbed) along, taking care not to disturb so much as an icicle, I heard steps approaching from the direction in which we were going. Moving cautiously into a maze of ice stalagmites, I hid behind one with a conveniently placed opening. This window was fretted with a web of ice formations, which effectively concealed me while allowing me to look out. I tugged Thheeer down to my level so that he, too, could perceive (he didn't actually see) what went on.

A creature exactly like the blown-glass-spider VIP went many-legging it down the way, accompanied by some dozen of the elephant-types. They marched up to the door we'd closed behind us and began their spiel.

We didn't wait. I maneuvered my way out of the maze and made for the vent with all speed that three generations of chasing things the Big Sandy winds blew away had bred into my family. I made some noise, but the crew at the door made so much more, aided by the blue voice, that it did no harm.

By the time they were moving into the hostage section, I was scrambling up into the vent. I dug my elbows and heels into the smooth sides to keep from slipping right out again. Thheeer was something of a problem. I needed my hands; if I held the string in my teeth he bobbed around so I couldn't see where I was going. So I finally tied him to one of the straps on the back of my scout jumpsuit, which I had resumed for our escape. More than once the many pockets, strings, straps, and other oddments of that versatile garb had stood me in good stead. It did now.

Hands free, I made better progress, moving far enough up the sharp slope so that nobody looking up from below could see us, though light from the caves reflected much farther up the shaft than I'd have predicted. When darkness closed about us at last I was more relieved than dismayed. It told me that we were well into the vent, past the point to which any normal Sdnnn would think to probe in search of us. Lrrr and Lthhh had still shuddered at the horror with which the darkness had filled their young spirits on their youthful adventure.

One of the handy adjuncts of my jumpsuit was a squeeze-generated flash, designed around a concept so old that it had only just been rediscovered. Though I wanted light, I left it in its zipped pouch. I had no wish to have its glint catch the eye of any searching Sdnnn who might look up the vent. The stone was shiny-smooth. So we proceeded in darkness—or semidarkness, as the Oti's little lightnings played constantly, making a firefly glimmer.

Before we'd gone much higher I could hear the slurring tones of Sdnnn echoing up the shaft. I couldn't know if those below were searching for us or not, but the chances, at this hour, were that that must be their mission. I braced my back and knees against the slippery walls and was very still for a long time. I could hear strange scrapings and irritable Sdnnn-ese at the mouth of the vent.

To take my mind off my discomfort, I envisioned some fragile and ungainly Sdnnn attempting to climb into my hiding place. Difficult as it had been for me, it must be awkward in the extreme for one of them. From the sounds I heard, which resembled glass scraping against glass, it was all but impossible.

They were persistent, however. With, I judged, much boosting from below, the scraping moved along the tube. I could imagine the desperate anxiety of the unfortunate who was making the inspection.

"Relax," I said to Thheeer. "No Sdnnn can come this far, I think. Not without suction gear like that Lthhh and Lrrr used in their escapade. We'll just wait until he gives up and move on past the ice layer. Then they *can't* follow."

Code poured into my skull. When I'd sorted it out, Thheeer had said, "This Sdnnn comes in fear of worse things below than could be above. I cannot read his thought, as I can now read yours, for there is no mutual code, but I can feel what he feels. His fear is behind, not before, him. Can you move up silently?"

Jarred from my complacency, I scrooched around into climbing position and carefully hunkered my way upward. I had to make some noise, I saw at once. I stopped, moved back into a holding position, and said, "Can't be done, friend. He'll hear me, and then he'll surely come on up. Maybe if there's no sign of anything unusual he'll give up and go back."

There was no answer to my silent comment, and I knew that Thheeer was feeling his way along the tunnel with our pursuer. Tense now, also, I listened to the ominous noises moving up the vent toward us. Before long a glint of light glimmered through the darkness, reflected upward by the polished stone of the wall.

I watched the light crawl up, and I set myself grimly to rush downward in a controlled slide and shatter the unfortunate

one who was coming. Killing was never my way, but another
session with the amoebae would leave my mind in tatters.
Perhaps, too, I might push the pursuer down hard enough to
send him scooting out into the caverns, unhurt. Or at least
alive.

The glass-on-glass sounds drew near. Only one more
curve now barred us from the full glare of the light. I set my
elbows and knees against opposite sides of the vent, laying
forearms and legs against the walls so as to give as much
friction as possible. A glassy hand came around the curve,
followed by an equally glassy head.

I braked myself abruptly.

"Lrrr?" I asked aloud.

A flurry of rapid Sdnnn answered me, though he slowed
quickly to a comprehensible speed. "Hale Enbo, I am sent to
pursue you, even to the surface. They encased me in a
force-suit much like that bubble in which the Oti rides. It will
allow me to enter the warm places unmelted. They threaten,
if I return without you, to . . . to . . . melt my hands!"

Guilt flooded through me. I should have known that that
unmentionable VIP would send my friends after me. He was
that sort of being; I'd known that from the start. There was no
way that I was going to injure Lrrr, any more than I was going
back with him.

"Lrrr," I said, looking into his reflection-rippled face,
"how would you like to come with us?"

In that peculiar light, alive with reflections of reflections,
there was no way to read his features, even if I'd known how.
There was really no need, though, for he said, "It has been
my dream, to see the surface. Lthhh, too . . . but if I must go
without him, then I will. I have not been one with my people
since I reached the time of thought. I will go. Perhaps Lthhh,
too, will find a way."

He clung there, holding his light, his giraffe-like neck
curving around the bend behind which his body was hidden.
At last I found an expression on that shimmery face. It was
one of pure happiness.

I cleared my throat. "You don't suppose they'll do anything to Lthhh, do you?"

''My people don't think in that way. They will punish one who fails or disobeys, but it wouldn't occur to them to injure one innocent of error, simply to unsettle his friends,'' Lrrr said. He began to wriggle upward. His neck was fully in view, and the rest of his svelte body appeared in the vent.

''Then we'd better move,'' I said. ''We can be up and out before it will occur to them that you aren't coming back . . . I hope.''

Thheeer was crackling with lightnings, and my head was full of his conjectures and comments as we began to climb again. He bobbed along over my head, twinkling madly, and it occurred to me that there was no reason why I should keep him tethered when he could float up the shaft as easily as a bubble rising through water. He was aware of the thought at once. Wedging myself, I freed one hand and untied the string.

I watched the Oti waft upward with a feeling of abandonment. Though the air streamed down the shaft toward the caverns, the energies and odd properties that Thheeer possessed bore him away as easily as those long-ago balloons at the fair had risen into the heavens of Big Sandy. I felt a similar loss, but I began climbing again. I could hear Lrrr coming along behind.

We'd moved a fair distance when I saw a twinkling light on the shaft-wall. In a moment Thheeer was bobbing at my side.

''We are almost to the level of ice. Another short span of time should bring you into it. There the way is nearly level for a distance; then it begins climbing again. I went far enough to see that then I returned. I feel . . . lonely without a mind with which to interact.'' If a mix of crackles, pictures, codes, and moods can sound wistful, Thheeer managed it.

The small levelling-out of the tunnel had helped the Sdnnn in his own efforts. He seemed to be getting the hang of moving up the slippery vent, too. How he managed, I couldn't say—if my own legs (four of them) had been set to extend only straight down, and if my arms (two) had been set at the base of my l-o-o-o-ng neck and were too short to reach from side to side of the opening, I'd have had more problems that I already had. Never think the Sdnnn aren't both nervy and smart. Some way or another, that one figured out a way and traveled almost as fast along the tunnels as I did.

There was no rest for us; keeping still was just as much work as moving. Or more. We were in no position to eat (at least I wasn't, and the other two *didn't*). There was no reason to stop until we reached the ice. It was touch and go, I'll admit. I felt as though my stomach was glued to my backbone before the chill and the leveling off allowed me to know we were truly at the end of this first stage.

XXXVIII.

Hale Enbo

I dropped onto the first flat spot I found and began digging into my pack. Thheeer bobbed back down the tunnel to the side of Lrrr, and they came slowly up it together. Even the positively outré picture they made in combination didn't distract me. My parents, had they been able to see into the future, would have named me Hungry Enbo.

I could feel Thheeer's exasperation at the waste of time. Lrrr, however, was as glad of the rest as I. I had a hunch he wouldn't have refused a nice wade into one of the black pools, either, but he said nothing.

By the light I carried, I had my first good look at the "suit" they'd put on him. Its glisteny look was similar to that of the Oti's bubble, but its shape was really strange. Of course, Lrrr's shape was odd in the extreme, too, yet the suit managed at once to follow his general outlines, maintain a cooled gap between itself and his outer integument, and add a subtle lumpiness all its own to his figure. A Sdnnn *au naturel* is strange enough. One in a force suit is something else again.

Explaining to Thheeer the phenomenon of weariness wasn't easy. But at last he accepted the strange fact that creatures encased in flesh of any kind must have periodic rest. He had thought that we slept at night solely because it was too dark to do anything else. Once we reached a stage in our evolution at which we could make artificial light, he assumed, we had been so much in the habit that we hadn't thought to stop.

He probably never did arrive at any real understanding of what a tired body feels like, but he did accept the reality of it,

in time. I didn't worry about that but fell asleep before
our discussion was more than begun.

Before all my weariness was dissipated, I was awakened
by the discomfort in my bones. Lrrr, too, seemed a bit stiff
and sore, though I felt certain that his discomfort stemmed
from his climb rather than his standing sleep amid the ice. To
his delight, we found one of the black pools partway down
the tunnel and he was able to nourish himself before ventur-
ing out into the dangers of the desert. I helped him out of the
suit, then chewed on dried fruit and a biscuit while he stood in
meditative silence, awash to his shoulders.

Then we all made for the foot of the climb that would lean
into warmer and drier areas. I felt concern for the Sdnnn, but
his suit must have been highly efficient. He clambered after
us at a good rate, even after the temperature had risen well
above melting-point.

It was a long way up. We slept three times before Thheeer,
scouting ahead, returned to say that we were almost to the
light. That spurred us to greater efforts. Soon we could see a
tawny glimmer against the shiny walls. Lrrr extinguished his
light.

It grew steadily brighter. The light was dusty yellow,
much like that on Big Sandy. A sudden homesickness for
desert country went sliding through me. Lrrr, just behind me,
began to mutter in his slippery tongue so fast that I couldn't
catch what he was saying. Still, his excitement came through
strongly, and I smiled to think that he was having his great
adventure at last.

Thheeer, though he was bursting with curiosity, had
waited for us at the mouth of the tunnel. Even in the strong
light, I could see his lightnings playing inside the bubble, as
he drifted beside the opening. His flood of coded thought
came to meet me.

"This is a world not unlike my own, Hale Enbo. The clean
surface is similar, though it is still far too humid. The sun is
much weaker, and the radiations from it must be infinitely
less than those which power our beings' beginnings. Still, it
makes me think of times I have known and minds with which

I wish that I could mesh. This is the first time that I have ever seen the surface of a world other than my own!''

"Funny, Thheeer, it's a world much like my own home world. The desert out there calls to me. Let's go out, all together!'' I motioned to Lrrr, and we all moved forward, the Sdnnn and I side by side, the Oti bobbing between us, into the warm, bright air of Sennlik.

At first I thought it might be unbroken desert. When my eyes adapted to the hard light, I could detect, at the edge of vision, a dim line of something darker than the sands, off to our right. My Big Sandy instincts rose within me.

"There's water over there!'' I said.

We stood in the lee of a low dune that looked just like all the others undulating away to the skyline in three directions. The tunnel from which we had come curved sharply, just inside, so that the outward opening looked to be only a wind-eddied hollow in loose sand. But that particular dune was stable as any stone, though indistinguishable from any of its fellows to sight or to touch.

Beyond, the desert swept outward like some weird ocean, devoid of plant or beast. Except for that dim line, I might have thought this a segment of one of the totally dead worlds I had visited.

Still, I had faith in my own water-sensing, not to mention the word of the Epfelen. Followed by my Sdnnn friend, led by the Oti, I started slogging through the weary reach of sand that lay before us.

It was hot. The sun stood five degrees from zenith (it would be a bit before I could know if it was rising or setting), and its blazing yellow seemed to be redoubled by the palls of blown dust that swept over us at times. The Sdnnn began to lag, and I went back, fearing that its cooling system might be inadequate for such work.

Lrrr sank half his leg deep at every step, struggling along with desperate effort. I realized that he'd never make it, unassisted. His slender legs and tiny hooves were sinking into the loose sand, and it was wearing him down. It was hard going even for a being with wide feet and heavy-muscled legs. I explained the problem to Thheeer, who was so intrigued by the entire concept of weight, gravity, and sinking into sand, that I thought he was going to be of no help at all.

Then, with the unexpectedness that was the one thing I could expect from him, he said, "In this atmosphere, I can exert a bit of lift. I never thought of myself in that context before, but if you caught up one side of the Sdnnn and tied me onto the other, we might give him enough . . . 'upwardness?' to help him along."

By golly, it worked. We didn't lift him entirely clear of the sand—even in the lighter gravity of Sennlik, his weight, added to my own plodding progress, would have burdened me. But with my boost on the right and Thheeer's on the left, Lrrr rose to the surface and tipped along it, providing his own forward momentum. Even so, it grew dark, for the sun had been moving down, before we were halfway to the line of greenery that marked the course of a stream.

Tired as I was, I almost lost the night of sleep because of the stars. Sennlik, as was logical, was near the hub of a galaxy. Its night sky was awash with suns and planets and comets and meteors enough to make any watcher dizzy. As a bonus, the dust-laden atmosphere, while it obscured much that we might have seen, lent color and movement to those bodies brilliant enough to be seen through the thick envelope. Lrrr, child of the deep dark places, was struck dumb with wonder. I think he lay all night, eyes wide, looking up into that wondrous display. (Lying down, itself, must have been torture for him, but the heavy sand gave him no choice.) Thheeer, having no vision as we knew it, was enthralled by our reactions. It was at that time that he began his real progress in communicating with Lrrr. His delight in those dancing suns cried out to be shared, and Thheeer was there, ready to share. Their understanding came about quickly for much of the coding had been done when Thheeer learned to "talk" to me. And we found that the Sdnnn did, indeed, have latent telepathic powers enough for such communication.

I slept at last, dreaming brilliant dreams. First light roused us, eager to move before the sun rose. In the night the dust had settled somewhat, so that we could now see the line of trees more clearly. It was a relief to my scoured throat, too, for there would be no water until we reached our goal.

As we marched over the sand, my feet flumping heavily, Lrrr's going "flip-flip-flip" as he was half-carried, Thheeer, whose perceptions were so utterly different from mine that I will never grasp them, said, "There is one ahead of us!"

I raised my eyes. Plodding along, I had kept my gaze downward to avoid the glare as well as to spot sinkholes. There in the distance, wavering across the morning-lit desert, was a shape.

I thought at first that it was a dust-devil. Still, the morning wasn't warm enough to have created such a strong updraft. Then I realized that the shape was wrong . . . pale yellow sand-color, it tapered from high to low, true, but two-thirds of the way up a pair of winglike protrusions spread on the light breeze. They whirled rapidly, like rotors of a craft designed for atmospheric flight. The shape below them danced lightly across the surface of the desert. It moved toward us, though the wind was at our backs. The feeling of intelligent purpose was unmistakable, even without Thheeer's designation of it as "one."

As it drew nearer, I could see a veritable tornado of sand kicked up at its base. I tugged Thheeer down and crammed him into my tunic, though it stretched the tough fabric almost to bursting.

To his queries, I replied, "That one could blow you so far and so high and so fast that we'd never find you again!"

I set Lrrr on his feet and pushed downward, planting his sharp little hooves deeply into the sand. Then I laid my arm over his back and braced myself as well as I could. If there had been a ditch, I'd have dived into it. Strong winds are one of the diversions we have on Big Sandy.

It was awe-inspiring. The kind of awe that brings out goose pimples. That tremendous shape skipped to within thirty yards of us. As though judging to a nicety the amount of buffeting we could stand without being blown away, it stopped and spun lazily, regarding us with something—it had no eyes, that was certain.

Aside from a really vicious backwash of wind-driven sand,

we were secure from being sucked into the vortex. I relaxed a bit, eased my grip on the Sdnnn, and looked at it as well as my dust-tortured eyes could manage. Inside that envelope of debris was something . . . something I could almost discern amid all the tumult. A slender, chilly something, almost like a very long tapered metal rod. But the moment I decided I had really seen something it would disappear and I would doubt my eyes.

I became aware . . . I can't tell how . . . that some sort of communication was taking place between Thheeer and the thing. It was an exchange of energies, actually, but I knew enough about the Oti, now, to realize that communication could be accomplished in many more ways than those recognized by my kind. The sand-creature was twitching with excitement. Thheeer was bouncing inside my tunic, fit to split the seams.

I fired a burst of our code at him. "You sure you know what you're doing?"

"YES!" he shouted, if an overwhelming burst of code can be qualified as a shout. So I loosed him and watched him bobble out to meet that elemental creature. I felt more dismay than I liked to admit, too, seeing him go.

A wing swept by and enveloped him. I could see glimpses, now and again, as he sparkled in the midst of the whirlwind. As there seemed to be nothing to do but wait, I sank to the sand beside Lrrr. We leaned against one another and suffered the abrasion of the sand in silence.

I wish I had a picture of that. Not a holograph, but an old-fashioned two-dimensional photograph. It must have been one strange sight, a Primate and a Sdnnn snuggled together for comfort in the presence of an intelligent tornado in the middle of a desert.

It took a while. At last the thing slowed to a lazy twirl, then the sand sank almost entirely and Thheeer was drifting out of the column of dust. When he was clear, and I held the string firmly, the creature bent in the middle as if bowing; then it whirled away at an angle to our line of march.

I could feel Thheeer, even down the length of the string, pulsing with a new kind of energy. His lightnings were sparking madly. His thought swarmed all over mine so rapidly that I couldn't make heads or tails for quite a while.

At last he calmed down enough to encode. As we moved toward the now badly-needed-by-me water, he told me of his encounter with the Sheeash.

XXXIX.

Thheeer

Not in all the span of my thinking life have I intuited a fraction of the wonders and delights that are to be found in interacting with incarnate beings. None among my own kind has ever seen fit to pursue such an exotic pastime, which leaves a terrible chasm in the firm base of information that we transmit from mind to mind among ourselves. The store of learned facts that we assume to be sufficient knowledge concerning such beings is a paltry thing. It lacks any real understanding of these matters, as I am learning more fully at every moment.

From the instant when I came forth from my place, encased in the bubble of force, and Hale Enbo tied me to a bit of string raveled from his blanket, I have been borne along upon a tide of sheer excitement. The escape up the vent, though not terribly eventful, was filled with discovery. My companion's calm in dealing with anything that might befall—even when that held the possibility of being rendered suddenly discarnate—struck me as admirable. His care for the Sdnnn who came after us fulfills every requirement of the Oti philosophy of interspecies concern.

The Sdnnn itself is far more than I had intuited its kind to be. Curiosity is a necessary concomitant of intelligence, and this specimen of its kind is, by that criterion, highly intelligent, not to mention courageous. Its chances of being suddenly bereft of its tangible envelope are even greater than those of my Primate companion. Any failure of its layer of force could leave it to melt instantly in the heat of this sun. Still it goes forward with both determination and interest, grasping every new phenomenon with much eagerness and delight, almost intoxicating me as I fuse with its emotions.

As for myself, I find that existence is far more than I had thought it to be. I have meshed with two divergent kinds of physical life. I have felt their fears and their joys, and I have entered and melded with the Sheeash. That in itself is an experience that makes my long span of thinking life fruitful. No other Oti has experienced such things. When I return and flood this new knowing into the pool of knowledge, my people will be enriched beyond imagining.

My first sensing of the thing—the being—I cannot quite define it—came while we moved over the desert, tugging the Sdnnn between us. Though I could tell by looking out through his eyes (I have learned to do that now) that Hale Enbo was seeing a towering column of sand topped by whirling wings of dust, my own sensing was of another kind. I felt a questing mind, cold, terribly powerful, smooth and chill, with the feel of *metal* to it. I saw a flame in the midst of the chill, but it was a cold flame. Its fuel was no element that I had ever known. Almost . . . it seemed that a tiny opening had been made into a universe where warm and cold were reversed, light and darkness interchanged. But all of that sensation did not come from the Sheeash.

My companions, limited to physical means of sensing, were stunned by its size and power, but excitement filled me, forcing me from the shelter of Hale Enbo's garment into the full fury of the thing we faced. I knew that I would not be swept away, though I felt it possible that I might be swallowed up into that vortex of energy, to become one with it. That thought brought no terror, only exhilaration.

It was a being unlike any I had imagined. Though partially carnate, it was also pure energy. Gifted with the ability to move material things, it also was able to manipulate the most delicate particles with the unaided power of its thought.

It was neither cruel nor kind by any standard arrived at among the Oti—or, I would guess, Primates. I found it, while enmeshed with it, to be insatiably curious, inflexibly intelligent, totally unmoved by its own or any other sort of life. No sense of feeling had ever impinged upon it; it had neither a concept for love nor one for hatred, even such tiny amounts as I was beginning to realize were the lot of the Oti. It objected neither to suffering nor to pleasure among others, and it was incapable of either.

Borne up into that towering form, I was almost bursting with energies generated by its physical nearness. No code of symbolism ever devised can express the things that moved between us as I went toward its core. My thought processes moved more swiftly than ever before, and I absorbed instantly a store of data that will require a long time to assimilate. In one surge I was set into contact with every other of its kind on the desert of Sennlik, taking into my swelling awareness an entire system of being.

There were not many Sheeash roving the surface of the planet. I could see, from some interior place, the entire world, bright desert where we stood, shading to gray and black as it curved away toward the night side. The small, mineral-thick seas were there, and the streams that ran infrequently through the lands, fed by snows on distant peaks. All were marked out in my inner seeing.

As I took, so I gave. Everything I knew, which was most of the carefully garnered and shared knowledge of thousands of aeons of Oti, was sucked greedily from my mind into its unlimited memory. Thousands of races were introduced into its knowledge, tens of thousands of disciplines, great and small. Worlds that I had never seen but had learned of from the minds of others poured into the creature. Even the underground world of the Sdnnn went with the rest, and when that was passed I felt a change.

The exchange halted for a moment, as the Sheeash mused upon the Ice-Caverns below it, so near in space yet so inaccessible. The Sheeash knew the Sdnnn more intimately than the Sdnnn knew themselves. Their probing minds moved down through the layers of rock and ice and locked into those of the crystalline people without shock or Sdnnn awareness. The Sheeash were, in their strange and aloof way, amused by the Sdnnn. They looked upon them as some species look upon pets or livestock. They had known, in their timeless and deathless state, when the first crystal formed in the first pool, growing, atom by atom, into the first tiny and limited ancestor of the Sdnnn. But the Sheeash had never seen the caves, as I had seen them through the eyes of Hale Enbo.

Of their beginnings I can understand only a little until I have the time to exist in quiet and sort through the information now tumbled into my memory. The history of Sennlik is a different matter, for it is one of endless sun and wind, night and wind, sun and wind, broken only a few times in all the ages of its existence by the intrusions of others.

Among these there were, incredible as it seems, a few Sdnnn, through the ages. They arrived on the surface, one at a time, over very long spans of time. All were melting at the time they arrived, and all simply stood and looked over the desert as their bodies faded away beneath them. Once a ship came down near a sea. It bore many-jointed creatures that took samples of everything in sight before leaving.

Two minor species had evolved on the surface of the world in relatively kindly geologic ages, but returns to harsher conditions had erased them. Only a few crawlers and peepers now lived among the sands or along the courses of the miserly rivers. The Sheeash had no companions in their lone tenancy of the surface.

Over the tremendous spans of time that their memories contained only six races had stopped here to break their journeying among the teeming planets of this galactic hub. Four of them were beings that must have been extinct for aeons, for in none of the records of the Oti knowledge-pool is their like to be found.

The fifth were Ginli. They seem to have gone everywhere.

The sixth . . . the sixth were Khi. I had never encountered Khi. Few have, even those who exist, as we do, on the borderland between those who live in flesh and those who exist only as minds. Yet they are known to us, for we have felt the touch of their spirits as they move through adjacent dimensions, going about their mysterious work. Those who have made a study of them insist that they can exist in any form, on any world. They also believe that there are those

beyond the Khi who are accessible only through the golden
people.

The Sheeash had been awed by them. Great though they
are, powerful enough to tear Sennlik into shreds and shards,
they had gathered about the small golden forms as they
appeared silently upon the desert. They had had no hint of the
purposes of the Khi, though they had followed at a respectful
distance as the glowing folk moved to the line of greenery
bordering a nearby river and busied themselves there for a
time.

I saw it all, though the strange sense of the Sheeash. I, too,
was puzzled. It had been long ago. Not ages, as those earlier
visitors had been, but still long ago. For what—or for
whom—they had set glowing patterns among the stunted
trees of the river course no one could say. Those patterns
were now invisible, for I had seen with the Sheeash as they
faded from sight after their formation.

After the Khi dissolved into sun-shimmer, there were only
sun and wind, night and wind, sun and wind again until I saw,
through the senses of my host, our strange party of three
emerge from the dune and make their way toward the river. I
felt sadness well through me, and I wondered if it came from
the Sheeash, learning, at long last, the feel of loneliness. I felt
its spinning slow, the tensions of the vortex ease. I knew that
it was time to return to Hale Enbo and to take up the adventure
again.

My friend met me with a surge of warm feeling. It was a
grateful thing, after the chill embrace of the Sheeash. Even
the Sdnnn seemed happy at my return, rising upon its pointed
feet and lifting its long neck to place its face near my bubble.
We watched together as the great being bent to look at us
once, then moved away in a cloud of spun sand.

After their long rest my companions were ready to move
with good speed, though I could feel the thirst that tormented
the Primate. He had had no water since we reached the ice
layer, having no way to carry with him the ice as it melted.
Lrrr, after his soaking in the pool, was fit for many days or
weeks before he would suffer from want of nutrient. For Hale
Enbo's sake we must soon reach the river.

I conveyed to Hale Enbo that the stream did, indeed, contain the fluid necessary for his kind. That knowledge gave him renewed strength. We made our way rapidly, and the line of trees came clear. To me they were vertical lines of energy drawn through a maze of roots below the soil, through slender trunks, then radiated outward and upward in a shaped field that discharged both moisture and an electrical aura into the air. Even the small growths below contained their own charged entities. I felt for the first time a vivid sense of the springing life that is in plants.

Hale Enbo felt my thought and said to me, "You are picking a bit of that out of me, Thheeer. I love and value growing things, for my kind evolved among them and with their aid. Even on the dusty world where I was born we nurture bits of forest, though it takes water and energy and work to maintain them. It is worth all that, for it brings us such joy."

I knew it to be true, but I was still touched with wonder. On my world there are no growing things. Only swirling winds and charged particles that ride them, waiting for the spark that will join them into brief union, the fruit of which is another mind for the Oti.

As we came into the shadow beneath those trees I could sense humidity. Strange that an element that meant life to my friend would mean death for me. We were most ill-assorted beings, we three. The comfortable habitat of any one of us would mean discomfort, if not death, to each of the others.

I watched as Enbo knelt beside the moving water and cupped a handful to his mouth. Meshed into his entity, I felt the relief of it wash the grit from his throat, cool the burning in his body. When he had drunk and washed the sand from himself, he and the Sdnnn felt need for a short term of unconsciousness. I took the opportunity of their resting to begin assimilating the mass of information that I had acquired from the Sheeash.

I look forward to the bringing back of such a treasure of knowledge with me to Otir. I had gained understanding of a kind of being that nobody dreamed existed, together with its unique vision of the nature of reality, for the Sheeash almost

bridged the gap between Primate and Oti. It thought in terms
that I could absorb without the clumsy coding that Enbo and I
had to use: and it gave me, for the first time, an understanding
of the necessity for sleep. It seems that the body is a constant
distraction to the thought processes. At regular intervals all
bodily concerns must be set aside to allow the mind to move
in its own untrammelled directions. I found to my astonishment that most of the creativity and insight shown by carnate
beings have roots in that dark obscurity they call sleep.

That is, of course, only one echo of the flash of understanding that shot through me, but it gives an idea of the
comprehensions that were boiling about inside me.

There was no understanding of the reason for the presence
of the Khi on Sennlik. Or for those shining webs they wove
among the river trees. I found myself wondering with half my
attention what we might discover when we moved along the
river. Woven into my wondering was a strange conviction
that Hale Enbo, of the three of us, would understand most
readily the cryptic actions of the golden people.

XL.

Hale Enbo

I woke wonderingly to a mesh of green boughs overhead, the sound of running water, the joy of free space about me. As I lay on my back, absorbing the feel of this new planet through my flesh and bones, I could see Thheeer bobbing quietly just above the river. Without turning my head I could see a glassy haunch, as Lrrr stood sleeping beside me.

As soon as Thheeer realized that I was awake, he bobbled over to me and urged me to get a move on. This was so unlike his usual habit that I sat and gaped at him. The notion of time had seemed to be something he hardly grasped.

Something had lit a fire under him, anyway, so I set myself to winnow out the torrent of coding that he sent flooding into me. Ordinarily he was cool and precise—a sort of disembodied computer with personality. I soon realized that never before since I had known him had he been *really* excited. He was now.

Mingled with the information he gave me came a name. A picture in my mind. Khi. Suddenly I was as excited as he. I knew that name, those round golden shapes. Hidden in my memory as something I couldn't jog loose, but it filled me with a sense of power and gladness.

Thheeer was still conveying information, however, and I focused on that. The Khi . . . on Sennlik! In this exact area.

I saw through his mind, at second-hand from the Sheeash, the Khi moving among these very trees. They were doing something to the boughs, using their minds as instruments. Shining patterns glowed for a while, and then dimmed to invisibility. A half-memory niggled at me . . . the Khi did nothing without a purpose. I could almost sense the meaning of their activity beside the river, the significance of the patterns among the trees. It seemed personal, as if the entire exercise might be aimed, somehow, at me.

I was now ready to move, but the Oti was still pouring information into me. I sighed and settled to wait him out . . . then something caught my attention.

"Whoa! Back up, Thheeer!" He did so, and I concentrated on getting every last nuance of the item he had skimmed over the first time. Somewhere on Sennlik, according to the Sheeash, there was a power or a source of power that was troubling all its kind. All the Sheeash tingled with a sense of danger, though they could not pinpoint the origin. Something about that single item in the flood the Oti had relayed set up my own alarm systems. As if something long dormant had been triggered, I felt compelled to follow up this tenuous lead, wherever it might go. But first I must find those webs among the trees.

My reaction stopped Thheeer short. The frantic sparkle that was his thought concentrated into a tiny area of near-incandescence. The lightnings played furiously; then he turned his thought to me again.

"You saw this and recognize it as important without hesitation. I did not differentiate it from the mass of material the Sheeash gave me. How is this?"

"Well, you're temporarily overloaded with data," I soothed him. "The creature caught up in a whirlwind doesn't notice individual dust-motes, I'm certain. And you must realize that I have a sort of instinct for danger. No rational explanation for it, it's just there. That bit you picked up from our tall friend set off all sorts of alarm bells. All of it was interesting, but that one *threatened*—threatens more than just the Sheeash."

"You are doubtless correct," he agreed, bobbling near enough for me to reach his string. "I sense that you are now as eager as I to find those webs the Khi strung in the trees. Let us go find them. I feel certain that I will sense them as soon as we are near."

I had a notion that I would sense them long before he did,
but since I couldn't explain it I kept that thought away from
him. I climbed to my feet, shook out my tunic a bit, adjusted
my pack onto my shoulders. Patting Lrrr on his rump, I led
the way downstream. Our encounter with the Sheeash had
taken a good while, and my nap at the river had taken more
time. The sun was now down, but the nights on Sennlik were
so starlit that it was never very dark. We kept the murmur of
the scanty river beside us, and moved carefully. My feet,
used to finding paths on alien worlds, felt out the ground
automatically. I gave no thought to what we were walking on
until Lrrr gave one of his slurred exclamations.

"Hale Enbo, there is a path!"

Now I had gleaned, from among all that ruckus Thheeer
had flung at me, that there was no life on Sennlik capable of
making a path. The Sheeash would have torn a highway
through the sparse trees; they could never have made a *path*.
This one was nicely foot-fitting, powdered with quiet dust
like many a cow-path I'd walked along on Big Sandy, bringing Ma-Moo home for the evening milking.

The Khi must have left it as a guide. They could, I knew
without knowing how I knew, gesture a path into being with
one thought and hold it there despite the passage of time and
wind. I felt my heart begin to step up its pace.

"Something is ahead of us," I said to Thheeer. I felt his
agreement.

I've often wondered how the webs would have showed
themselves by day. However it might have been, it couldn't
have been so wondrous as the spectacle we found by the
million-starred night.

I felt something . . . something physical, nearly like a
mesh of spiderweb across my face and the exposed part of my
forearms and hands. I felt something inside myself that
seemed like a small light popping into being.

Thheeer felt something, too. His tiny lightnings sparked
and flashed until he almost distracted my eyes from the stars
that flicked between the overhead branches. Lrrr, quietly
following, moved up beside me. The combination of starlight

and Oti-flash reflected from his force-suited and blown-glass form would have made the fortune of anyone in the business of inventing new arts.

The dry, dusty smell of the desert, the water-plantish smell of the river were lost, suddenly, in another scent. Ozone? Something like that. I felt my body-hair tingle upright, my skin crawl. We were approaching power.

The trees were dark, straggly shapes against the stars. The path, now that I knew to look at it, gleamed innocently dust and shadow-colored as it went between them. I walked on, caught in a compulsion that was irresisitible. As we reached the outthrust edges of a branching tree a gleam began to wax among the interlaced limbs. I moved forward still.

Lrrr, at my elbow, gave something like a bleat. Thheeer was storming with electricity. I kept on, and the web began to take shape, golden against the dark branches, triumphantly golden even against the spangled sky.

I reached the first filament. It drooped as if to caress my face. The instant it touched me, the entire webbing of the wood lit. The beauty of it took my breath, and I sank to sit on the ground and stare up into the supernal glow.

The grove was linked into the pattern by the festooned webbing. Geometric as the work of spiders, the patterns were not those familiar concentric lattices. They formed shapes that explored, exhausted, and redefined the geometries I knew. Thin lines of light, they were spangled at intervals that seemed random, but were not, with globules of pulsing energy. Some webs were colored, pale shades of rose and green and azure. Some were golden as the Khi themselves; some were silver, with a sheen to hurt the eyes. Part by part, they enchanted the mind. All together, they opened it into a flowering of understanding that was both wordless and completely satisfying.

And now I remembered the Khi. I remembered myself. I recalled those weeks on Khi-Ash, and I relived, within one flash of time, the painful and grueling training that I had been forced through by the three Khi. I knew the powers that I had earned through necessity and stress and direst need. I remembered that I had asked that they return my knowing self, as nearly as they could, to a normal condition for my kind, at the completion of the first task.

Now I sat beneath trees that waved their flame-tangled branches in the breeze of Sennlik. I knew that need had arisen—perhaps that greatest of needs that had caused the Hril to choose me as their instrument. The Khi, being independent of time, had set this trap for me in order to wake me to myself again.

Thheeer brought me alert again. The pressure of his thought broke through my abstraction, and I found him flashing about my face.

As soon as he realized that I was again "with him," he said, "Hale Enbo! There was an anomaly about you—I noted it early in my exploration of your inner self. A greater being was hidden inside you that never made itself known to your conscious self. That was my very thought . . . and so there was!

"I moved in your memory with you. You—only you!— were the cause of the Ginli reformation that has puzzled the populations of the nearer worlds for many cycles. With potencies such as you possess, you could have mastered any world, any system. That being the thing that most carnate kinds desire most, why did you not choose to do it?"

I shrugged. "Thheeer, I need no powers. I am a happy man, given a new world to explore, new beings to learn about. The ability to transform matter is nothing, unless you have a driving need for it. The capability to say to my own kind, 'Go there!' or 'Come here!' and have them obey holds no charm for me. I am free. My only desire is that everyone else may be free, also. Even the ability to fold yourself instantly across time or space or both is only a convenience.

"I am young, still. I want to live the life of a physical being, with all its limitations. To learn through physical needs and compulsions, for how could I understand, otherwise, the needs of my own kind?"

"I never thought to find," said Thheeer, "a physical being who was so near to the thought of the Oti. We had assumed that the fact of imprisonment in flesh would necessarily warp the tenant mind to suit the exigencies of the bodily home. How is it that you are unwarped?''

I thought for a long moment. About the peoples I had met in my explorations, the dark-skinned folk of my own Big Sandy, my family.

Then I said, ''I know a few who are like me. Strangely enough, they are mostly from harsh and difficult planets that require them to be very strong and tough in order to survive. My own family formed me in their mold. We are not afraid. We suffer; we die; but we don't fear. That one thing is true of all the others I have known who are of my sort. They are unafraid. It is fear, I would guess, that makes men long for power.''

I felt his comprehension leap about, saw the lightning flickers that told me the Oti was carrying the idea through to its logical conclusions. When he was satisfied, he slowed enough for me to follow his rationalization.

Then I laughed. ''True! Fear equals need for power, equals slavery, equals revenge, equals bilateral fear. A nice neat self-perpetuating cycle of misery and two-way enslavement. When you remove the fear, you eliminate both the need for power and the syndrome that allows a being to be enslaved. You're right. Both are hinged irrevocably to bodies and their needs and weaknesses and gratifications. I'd never before realized how lucky I am, friend Oti, to have come from the place and from the people who brought me into being.''

He hung before me, winking faintly. I had not followed him far enough, evidently. Then I saw. ''Aha! You're telling me that unless I also take into account the fears of physical beings, all my other efforts will not give me an understanding of them. I must not actually become fearful, myself, but I must know the reality of *their* fears.''

He twinkled with agreement. I lay back on the dusty grass and looked up into the shining weft in the grove. Beside me, Lrrr stood, his long neck raised and his dark eyes fixed on the patterns. Their light ran along his surfaces as he moved, making him seem a part of the design.

Thheeer, too, almost merged into the thing. Only I, dark

and solid, was untouched by the light. But the pattern was shining inside me, lighting up crannies of my consciousness that I had not looked into for far too long.

Smiling up at the web and my companions and the stars, I closed my eyes. Sleep engulfed me in a dark tide.

XLI.

Hale Enbo (Ex Corpore)

I didn't dream. Though my body was left to rest itself in the grove, the other self moved outward. Not physically but dimensionally. Now that I was waked, once more, to the self that the combined efforts of Khi and Hril had made, I sought out my friends. And there was the glimmer that was Khi-Sang. We remained quiet for a time, warm with memories. Then we turned to the problem at hand.

"This danger on Sennlik," I said, though not with speech. "Is this the task for which the Hril chose me?"

"Yes. And it is gravest danger . . . for Sennlik, for you, for all our worlds, given time. We, in our present state of being, cannot approach it. You are the only being who might possibly cope with it. For that reason you were chosen as hostage and brought here."

I reached out my thought into the shimmering gases or mists or whatever it was that existed between dimensions. There was no feel of the other Khi there, only of Khi-Sang. "What is this danger—do you know?"

"The Hril have said that it is a part of outer blackness. It is not matter or mind or anything that we can comprehend. It is not of their creation but of another place, outside this entirely. It does not abide by the rules they set for their universe. It seems to be . . . hungry. It can, being immune to our physical and mental laws, absorb into itself all the things that the Hril have brought into being."

I had a feeling of illimitable darkness that reached out and drew into itself all that held light. A tingle of dread moved between Khi-Sang and me. The Hril had pictured for her a cosmos blotted out in an inky cloud that reeked of fear.

She went on, "The Hril, being who and what they are, cannot move to destroy this thing. Not only because destruction is not in their nature, but also because they are purest energy, and this thing devours energy. You are the only being in the physical worlds who has the abilities needed to remove this threat, linked to a physical body that it will not recognize as a menace. And . . . it may not be destroyable. It may take you, my love."

I would have sighed, but my lungs were back on Sennlik with my body. The Enbos are compulsive achievers, it's true, but taking upon myself the responsibility for rescuing the universe from outer darkness seemed a bit . . . presumptuous? My principal reason for returning to being the old Hale Enbo is that power sits uncomfortably upon my shoulders. Only direst need spurs me to exercise it. This seemed, no doubt of it, to be direst need, all right.

"Well, I'd better be at it. Can you aim me in the right direction?"

She'd followed my musings easily, and her glimmer was quivering with the Khi equivalent of laughter. "The Hril have set a compulsion in your physical body that will guide it without fail toward the source of the troubling," she said. The shimmer of light that was her voice seemed wistful. "We will be nearby, though we cannot aid you. Feel us near, Hale Enbo!"

Then she was gone, and so was I.

I hung high in the night sky of Sennlik and looked over the desert that gleamed in the swarming starlight as if powdered with silverdust. The darker streaks that marked streams meandered below me, and I could see disturbances blurring the pristine dunes that were Sheeash going about their incomprehensible business.

I felt a strange reluctance to return to my body. I needed to do something . . . I badly needed to. Remembering old techniques, I relaxed totally, letting my thoughts thin out until they weren't there at all. Then I knew.

Lthhh, Lrrr's boon companion, was still imprisoned in the
Ice Caverns. Now he had neither another malcontent to talk
with nor any alien hostage to feed him tales of the worlds. He
was alone, one island of curiosity and creativeness in a frozen
waste of bureaucracy. I had to find and rescue him. He had
some part to play in this game.

I folded myself away, down into the Caverns. The senses
that attended my expanded state pinpointed every spark of
life of any sort in any given area. I could see lives moving all
about me as I found myself beside the door that led into the
hostage section. Most Sdnnn were variations on a round blue
dot (nine million shades of blue!); the Epfelen were nice
spiky shafts of oranges and yellows. A swirl that resembled a
hole in space must be Hleror. Lthhh stood out as a steady
triangle of shocking pink.

I folded to his side. He stood before . . . shades of all
demons! . . . the desk of Slrrr, the buck-passer who welcomed me to Sennlik. Though the desk had been replaced and
its equipment was all shiny-new, there was no mistaking the
irritable precision of the blown-glass bureaucrat's manner.

He was accusing Lthhh, I realized very soon, of conspiring
with Lrrr and me in our escape. I let out a whoosh of wrath
and invisibly pushed all the buttons on all that equipment
once more. If a Sdnnn could turn pale, Slrrr would have done
so in the instant before his hasty retreat.

As I folded Lthhh away with me, I heard the unmistakable
sound of an office gone mad, complete to the tinkle of falling
icicles. Even while folding, I formed about Lthhh's frail form
a force-suit like that Lrrr had been put into. And then we
found ourselves standing in the grove with our two companions.

Poor Lthhh had no idea what was happening. I wasn't
visible in my *ex corpore* condition, but I slipped back into my
physical self and stood up, just as the Sdnnn seemed about to
sink beneath the shock of his sudden translation.

Lrrr stood mute. Then a stream of Sdnnn sped toward his
friend so fast that I could catch only an occasional word.
Lthhh didn't know the answers to any of the questions,
however, so I stepped between them and said, ''Wait a bit.

I'll explain everything in a while. Right now let's check out this suit to make sure that it functions as well as Lrrr's. Otherwise I'll have to take Lthhh back home.''

This brought them to attention, and Thheeer volunteered to run a check on its frequencies. Among us we managed to determine that I'd done a creditable job of it, and my Sdnnn friend stood in no danger of melting.

Then I arranged them about me and explained to them, as well as I could, my relationship with the Khi, my present abilities, and my trip below to rescue Lthhh from the tender mercies of Slrrr.

It took a while. When my Sdnnn grasped the fact that their world stood in real and immediate danger, their first impulse was to rush back into the Caverns and dump the problem into the laps of the VIPs. It took some doing to make them understand that interoffice memos would not do the job. That was up to me.

XLII.

Hale Enbo

There was strangeness all around me, as I stood in my flesh again. I could feel a tension as tight as a wire, drawing me toward the point at which night was now rolling away over the edge of Sennlik. Yet when I slid momentarily from my body and sought with nonphysical senses there was no token to guide me. That told me much. I knew that I must go about tracking down the enemy in the dogged ways my ancestors had used. There would be no easy shortcuts.

I tried folding myself and my strange crew toward my compulsion. I arrived nowhere. When we looked about the trackless sands I could feel my destination pulling at me from right or left or behind. It would have been so easy to save ourselves the labor of moving across the sand . . . too bad.

We started out again, this time more easily. Not for nothing had I spent my life making do on alien worlds. I made for the two Sdnnn a sort of snowshoe, using limber branches the trees and more yarn from my sadly depleted blanket. At least the odd contrivances allowed the creatures to shuffle across the desert without sinking to their hocks.

It was rough going, even so. With my newly-recalled abilities I had formed myself a water-carrier, which I could refill at need by using components of the air to zap up water. My food was holding out well, and I had no desire to extend it by artificial means. I had a gut feeling that the Hril intended me to tackle that strange entity as nearly *au naturel* as possible. I had an inkling of their reasoning, but it wouldn't come clear in my physical state.

We struggled onward, though I was the only one feeling

the terrible heat of the desert sun, the grit of sand in my teeth. Thheeer, floating serenely, had no body with which to feel such things. The two Sdnnn, in their force-suits, were insulated from their environment. Any chauvinism I might have held secretly on account of being a Primate would have been dried out of me, if I had ever considered that a matter of importance. I'd rather have liked to adopt Thheeer's mode of being . . . but it would have endangered our mission.

It took a long time. Once we dropped over the horizon and lost the line of trees there was no way to gauge the distance we covered. Only by days and nights could we estimate progress. But my inner guide held steady. We followed its lead. Night followed day relentlessly, and we—at least I— stumbled and sweated and cursed and groaned across that interminable desert. It helped not at all to try sleeping by day—with nothing to give a shadow (the dunes being too low), I merely lay in the sun and cooked. Sleep was impossible, even buried in sand to conserve internal moisture. There was only the difference between baking and pressure-cooking.

Ten days passed. I was wrung out to leather and bone. My skin, always a rich chocolate, was darkened to near-blackness. My hair was seared so that its ebony color was streaked with tan. I was a mess, and nothing less likely to strike terror into an unguessable menace could be imagined.

My companions, strange as they were, weren't frightening, either. We were, it seemed to me, engaged in a suicide mission that was bound to fail. Still I could feel, from time to time, a quiver of being nearby that told me the Khi were there. Though of what help that might be I didn't know.

Flesh is a curious thing. Having lived both with and without body, I can say with some conviction that it seems to create its own limitations. The doubts implanted in the mind by the fluctuations and minor malfunctions of the body can shape the individual's actions and reactions. Your own alarm systems often misread circumstances and give a push in the wrong direction. Just the fact of being tired and burned and thirsty and weary had sent me into a state of self-doubt that would never have occurred to me in the out-of-the-body existence.

At last we saw on the horizon a knobby irregularity. I was in no fit state to wrestle a rabbit, by then . . . and that was the reason, as I learned, for Khi-Sang's shadowing our steps. As we stood gazing at the ominous lump of almost-weathered-to-nothing that had been masonry, she came into my mind. I listened . . .

"There lies the enemy," she said. "It is great and dark and arrogant past understanding. For physical beings it has no regard at all, considering them all to be vermin for the scattering. No great nonphysical being has it met, as yet, the Hril tell me. There are no others in its own milieu—only it. Therefore it has no facts at its command concerning such beings . . . and we must not give it any.

"For that reason I can go no nearer to it than this. It would feel me as an enemy. You and the Sdnnn it may not even discern unless you bring yourselves to its attention. Thheeer is like no other life-form, and so he may pass as a natural phenomenon of this place, as do the Sheeash.

"Now you must bring all your powers under control, while remaining inside your flesh. Forget the complaints of your body, the baseless fears of your brain. Remember who you truly are. Remember that the Hril stand behind you, though you cannot detect them. Remember that in all but experience you are the equal of the Khi."

She glimmered once, inside my heart. Then she was gone.

I looked up at Thheeer. "Well, old friend," I said, "it looks as if we have found something at last. Should we go now or wait until night?"

"It is a thing of darkness," said the Oti. "Light, it seems to me, should confuse its perceptions, flooding its sensors with energies with which it is unfamiliar. I say we should go now."

The Sdnnn nodded their small heads, light running crazily up and down their long necks. "We are ready, Hale Enbo. Within our suits we are safe. You, however, are vulnerable, and that concerns us. You may be destroyed," said Lrrr.

"That may be," I agreed. "If that is the price for ridding

our worlds of this thing, then it is a small one. As you know, I do not require flesh now. Still, I will miss many things in the worlds that swing around the suns of the cosmos.''

Without further talk, we resumed our march, plodding through blown dust and blinding sunlight. It was just after noon, and the light set our shadows at our feet, glinting harshly off the Sdnnn. Even Thheeer's bubble rippled with yellow streaks, dimming his internal lightnings.

As we approached the ruin, I thought back over the information from the Sheeash. It held no hint that I could recall of any being that could have built such a city. I turned my thought to the Oti and asked if he would search his memory for some hint the Sheeash might have given as to the origin of the place.

''Those constructs were here when the Sheeash first looked about with knowing eyes,'' answered Thheeer. ''Those folk have little understanding of things material, no real interest in lifeless things. Yet even they have wondered, seeing the wearing away of the stone into sand, the formation of sand again into stone, the wanderings of the seas and the lands of Sennlik during the aeons of their watching, what sort of stuff the city was made of, that it might endure for so long without being reduced to nothingness.''

I looked toward the mounded but still sturdy structures before us. It was obvious that sand had covered and uncovered them countless times. Sand was banked in smooth curves against the windward walls, making, in part, the humpy impression. The shapes of the structures themselves were vaguely mushroomish also. We were now near enough to make out details. I saw to my astonishment that there was no break in any wall, though they were curved to make them seem ruinous at a distance.

A geometry not wedded to straight lines and right angles had conceived those buildings. No culture remaining among the worlds I knew or had studied had so divorced itself from the local versions of Euclid. I wondered (and still do) what long-perished forebear of one of our species might have stopped on this desolate planet for long enough to shape that weird city . . . and what its purpose might have been.

"There is no other city on all the surface of Sennlik," said Thheeer, his thought parallelling mine. "From this one, Hale Enbo, I discern an emanation of energy that is alien to all I know. This is indeed our goal. But what means, I wonder, did our visitor from otherwhere know that it might find safety and shelter from the light in this one spot on Sennlik?"

I had no answer.

By the time we reached the shadow of the outermost rank of walls, the sun was halfway down the sky. Our shadows paced us, stretching long as we neared the rounded elongation that had been an outer wall. Though no entryway was apparent, we had no trouble in simply walking up its slope and over, for the sand had all but covered it. When we stood on the top I could see that the city was at least half covered by sand. There was no way to know how high the wall, how tall the buildings might be if all the encroaching desert were removed.

Inside the wall some of the lower structures were almost totally buried. Other, taller buildings rose well clear of the sand-level, their rounded roofs well above my head. There were no windows. I assumed that any doors were buried near ground level. Only round holes gave any openings into the buildings. Most were no larger than Thheeer's bubble. Only a few were large enough for me to wriggle through, if I were forced to that.

We stood on the wall and looked. And inside that tumble something was, at last, looking back at us.

XLIII.

Thheeer

It is highly unusual for an Oti to be surprised. Still I must admit that Hale Enbo has continually astonished me, used as I have been to discounting the abilities of incarnate beings. His courage and determination were a revelation to me, from the beginning. The odd layering of his deeper self was intriguing from the first.

However, my discovery of his longstanding relationship with the Khi staggered me. It has only been in recent times that my own especially gifted folk have detected their existence and surmised their purposes as they moved quietly between dimensions.

The fact that Enbo, a simple Primate, had been chosen by them to become an initiate and an associate was enough to set my sparks into exaggerated motion. I followed his other self on its journey into elsewhere, when his body was resting by the river. I could tell that he was engaged in intimate exchange with the Khi whom he met in the not-world.

Though I was incapable of understanding the flow between them, I was still closely knit into his emotions. I caught a reflection of his feeling for the golden being. There was equality! There was an emotion that I could only interpret as love. Real love, as those of us unencumbered with demanding bodies and inadequate personae know it . . . that fusing into total understanding for the enrichment of both.

Only after he returned to his flesh and gathered us round to explain the matter did I grasp the most amazing fact of all—this Primate, subject to all the vulnerabilities of his kind, had chosen freely to return to his natural state, though he had the option of remaining as one with the Khi. Such restraint,

such maturity of choice would have been difficult even for an
Oti.

At that point I began to understand the intricately inter-
locked forces that had brought the four of us to this particular
time and place. I examined this closely. Not only Enbo, I was
certain, was specifically called there by the Hril, through the
Khi. Once I understood the relationships that linked the
worlds I knew to those of the Khi and the Hril, I was certain
past any doubt. We were all necessary for the success of the
enterprise.

I was attuned as finely as an Oti can be to the surrounding
desert, as we made our way toward that enemy that meant
death for us all if we should fail. I felt the bombardment of
solar particles against the sand and my fellows and my own
bubble of force. I felt the terrible magnetic pressure of the
gravity field that was held from my vulnerable self by that
atom-thick film. I felt the distant disturbances that were the
Sheeash.

I also felt, ahead of us, an energy so alien, so powerful, so
dark and forbidding that even I felt something that must have
been fear.

In the face of that force I was less than one sunbeam. It
could have swept aside every Oti ever coalesced without
noticing it. It was a drinker of energies. Its capacities were
fed, I thought, by the resistances that might have overcome
other kinds of danger. If it contained selfhood, I could not
find it. Only a ravening hunger was conveyed to me through
its field.

Once we were on the wall I settled near Hale Enbo and
said, "My friend, the enemy is there as surely as we are here.
You are trapped in flesh, for now, and I understand quite well
why it was necessary that that be so. The being yonder has not
noticed you, any more than it has the sand or the Sdnnn. You
are invisible to him while you remain so.

"That being true, the effort of moving through that maze
in search of it will tire you, deplete your energies, preoccupy
your mind. I, on the other hand, can move, undetected,
without effort, borne in any direction by the direction of my
will. That, I think, is my function in this plan. I am the

seeker. You are the slayer. The Sdnnn will be . . . what they are destined to be.''

He was silent for a time. Then he said, "I hate to admit it, Thheeer, but you seem to be right. I'll be able to see through your mind, as you search. Even if you should be . . . absorbed . . . by the thing, I'll know where to go to find it. But take care. I value you.''

Almost, between the two of us existed the perfect fusion that only Oti know. As I drifted toward the nearest of the rounded openings, I felt his concern even more strongly than I felt my own regret. Not in this form, I thought, would I meet him again.

Unthinkable aeons of bombardment by sun and wind had set up kinetic energies in the substance that formed the building in which I felt the presence of the alien. My senses were not suitable for detecting its nature, but the stuff was obdurate. Time hadn't touched it. It had absorbed gravitic impulses, and I was buffeted with interacting forces as I slipped through the long tube that led deep into its interior.

I emerged into a large space that retained the impression of many strong entities. I hung there for a time, feeling for my goal. But it was not within this building, as I had thought. I was near—very near, but in one that lay buried beside this. Once I had gone out of the first structure and examined the sand lying above that which I had sought, I knew how I must approach the problem. No opening existed into the place. An Oti can osmose through matter without trouble or danger, if it exists in a medium hospitable to his life-form. But not if encased in a force-bubble.

Upon this desert the humidity that was one of my two great enemies was no great danger, but the gravity of Sennlik was. I must decide whether the pull was enough to extinguish me before I could accomplish my goal.

Only one effort could be made, I knew. This was, I had no doubt, the exact place we had searched for. I must have time, once outside my bubble, to penetrate the sand and the stone of the roof and to give Enbo an exact pinpointing for the spot to which he must come.

He would be faced with terrific labor in trying to find a way

inside, too. Struck with a thought, I sent a call afar into the
desert and then returned to my problem. I measured, as well
as I could, the force that played against the outside of the
bubble. Strong, indeed, but less than that of many worlds. If
I could move quickly, I could accomplish my function.

I floated above the rounded roof. Now it gleamed with
weak energies that were overlaid with that miasma of blackness that radiated from its source as light radiates from a sun.
I settled onto it and began the formula that freed me from the
bubble. Enbo protested wildly; I sent a wave of reassurance
and esteem. Then I was free, and with one motion I slid
through the almost-stone of the roof and was inside the
building.

As I emerged into the huge central chamber, I felt the
presence of three entry-holes in the walls. I sent their locations outward to Enbo, knowing that he would grasp and
retain them. Then a greater presence distracted me. Under the
stone that should have been the foundation of the structure I
could feel a rippling and throbbing and restless play of forces.
I felt the floor with all my senses. There was an opening in its
center. The thing lay below, and I moved toward it.

I was now collapsing inward, my energies driven together
by the gravity. I could feel the light gases that contained my
sparks drifting away into the thicker air of Sennlik. Weaker
and weaker, I went toward that terrible entity that lay waiting, wrapped in its own darkness that was to a normal lack of
light as a sun is to my spark.

I hung there, dying. I felt Hale Enbo weeping for me.
There was no need. My knowledge would go to the Oti, for
Enbo's mind had fused with mine. He held it all. As for the
self that was I—it held neither fear nor regret as the blackness
absorbed the last of my lightnings.

XLIV.

Hale Enbo

I stood on the wall, feeling Thheeer die. So closely were we linked in that final moment that it surprised me to find myself opening my eyes, alive within my own flesh. Beside me Lrrr and Lthhh looked at me with big dark eyes. I knew that they, too, through their own link with the Oti, had felt him go.

Early dawn was streaking their glassy bodies with light. It gradually outlined the lumpish buildings of the city, moving up the sky to reveal the rippled sand between the rounded walls. The three of us looked down without speaking. Then we leaped onto the gritty surface and moved toward the house where Thheeer had found our enemy.

The curve of sand hiding the roof rose upward like a fungus. Thheeer had proven that there was no opening. We stood about, just looking at the mass of sand that must be moved.

"We have an energy weapon," said Lrrr at last. "It could melt through the material—but it might arouse the enemy inside. It is a very *strong* weapon."

As I considered this I heard a sound that grew in intensity. I sprang onto a roof and looked away toward the east. There, backlit by the sun, was one of the Sheeash. It was moving toward us at a fantastic rate. By the time I moved back beside the Sdnnn, they could see it too. Together we stood and waited.

Thheeer had called into the desert, I recalled, but I had been so concerned with his suicidal plan that I hadn't thought about it. Now I realized that he had, even at that final crucial

point in his life, been thinking of ways to make our task
easier. The Sheeash as an unequalled mover of sand!

As it neared I motioned to the Sdnnn. We all took shelter
behind a large building some distance from our goal. I
watched as long as I could manage to shield my eyes from the
storms of grit stirred up as the Sheeash approached. It was
more like a tornado, now, than it had been when we first saw
it. An ear-piercing shriek wedded to a thrumming roar
seemed to be its voice. The tensions in the whirling air were
enough to stop the breath in my throat.

It came directly to the roof where Thheeer had been when
he called it. When it reached the spot it grew very tall and
thin, stretching itself upward as if to surmount the sky. Its
voice roared and shrieked, and it came to me that the creature
knew that Thheeer had gone and was grieving for him, even
though it had known nothing of emotion.

It stood there on one slender toe of whirling force, crying
its incomprehensible message into the air. Then it began to
sink deeper and deeper into the sand, carrying away up its
spout the debris it removed. At that point my abused eyes
could see no more, and I took shelter with the Sdnnn.

When the uproar diminished, I risked a peep around the
wall. The tall shape was moving away, crying westward
across the dunes. Where it had been there was a well in the
sand, centered by the structure we needed to enter. Our friend
the Oti had arranged that a task that might have taken us
weeks that we couldn't spare be accomplished in minutes.
And I still believe that the Sheeash was crying.

We were now ready, for good or ill, to move ahead with
the mission. We had felt our friend's going, and it left us
steeled to do likewise, if that was necessary. We went down
into that well of sand, slipping and tumbling in the loose
footing, to come against the wall of that strange house. There
were two holes within reach. One was barely large enough
for me. The other was very small. The Sdnnn could never
manage to enter there even with my help.

We stood there staring at one another. Then I said, "It
seems that this is intended to be my work. It may be that I,
like Thheeer, will not come out of this place alive. If that

happens, you will bear witness of what was done here, together with warnings to all the worlds to keep watch. And remember that when all is done here, for good or for ill, the Khi will be near. Call out to them . . . they will come.''

I laid an arm about each of their smooth necks, and we stood quiet for a moment. Then I slapped them on their glassy flanks and said, ''Go outside the wall. Well outside. There will be forces loosed inside this place that may well shake this ancient city flat.''

With that, I climbed into the entry hole and wedged myself so that I wouldn't slide too swiftly down it. Most of the house must have been below ground level, even before the sand had covered it; I moved down at a sharp angle through what seemed to be solid stone, for a very long way before I found myself falling through still another hole into pitch darkness.

I hit with a thud, but the noise didn't bother me. That entity below had, I thought, no senses of the kind my sort possessed. A sound would be nothing to it. Only the disturbance caused by expending energies to fold space or to rearrange atoms would register upon it, I felt sure. For that reason I clung to my Primate form, stumbling across the space of that room, which radiated a terrible feel of ancientness through its darkness.

The air was thick—I must have puffed up ages of sandy dust in alighting. Coughing, almost retching, I pulled myself up short, waiting until some had settled. Then I moved carefully. I knew that the opening was in the center of the floor, but I had no idea of my own orientation with regard to it. Whether I had alighted near a wall or in the middle of the room I didn't know.

The time had come for light, dangerous though that might be. I closed my eyes (don't ask me why—I couldn't see anything at all) and concentrated on the strange power that the Khi had reawakened in me. Only a bit—the veriest wink—did I use. When I was done, the stone of the room glowed with soft radiance. Then I stood there with all my defenses up, hardly more than a stone myself, for a long moment.

I felt it. Beneath me there came a silent stirring of forces

that seemed to make the very atoms of the walls quiver. That
old, old room that no eye, most likely, had ever beheld was
filled with an unquiet that shivered new showers of dust down
from the rough textured walls. The curving shape of it,
inward-leaning and disturbing to rectangle-oriented eyes,
seemed to writhe slowly as distant objects do in the heat of a
desert noon.

There was no heat here, however. I found myself cold—
colder than I had ever been in the Ice Caves of Sennlik.
Colder than ever in all my life. My teeth chattered until my
skull rattled. In one glimmering of insight I learned something of the cosmos that had spawned the intruder . . . utter
cold. Utter dark. Neither side of me liked it at all.

There in that chamber, at the heart of a low house in a city
so old that no living thing remembered its building, I regarded the ending of all that I knew. I thought of Big Sandy,
gritty and drought-ridden and dear, pulled from its sun-
warmed ways and cast into cold blackness that had no place
in it for life. No matter that my cousins were there . . . that
touched me only shallowly. I realized that that big, rough,
gruff planet was dear to me, in and of itself.

I recalled the water-worlds I had explored for the Ginli.
They would become hells of ice, and all the teeming greens
and swarming lives would perish.

I remembered Khi-Ash. Almost, in a way, the planet of my
birth, it was the home of Khi-Sang and her fellows. Its joyous
woodlands, aflame with reds shading into golds and browns
and magentas, would go into darkness that knew no end. The
green-furred Varlian would flicker through the branches no
longer. The many evolving life-forms that I had come to
know would end.

"I will save the world of the Oti," I said aloud to Thheeer,
and I was sure that he heard me. "I will save this one, and that
of the Ginli and Old Earth itself. I will not leave our dimension to this thing that has no understanding of living things. If
it destroys this shape that I wear, together with every facet of
myself and leaves nothing where Hale Enbo once existed,
nevertheless I will take it with me wherever it sends me."

Being as cold, now, as it was possible to become, I forgot

about it and proceeded toward the trapdoor in the floor . . . though that homely term does little to describe the twisted oval of its shape or the unwholesome curl of vapor that rose above it. There was a smell, too. No human nose had ever encountered it before, so there was no term to describe it, but it raised my hackles.

Understand that my flesh wanted no part of this. My knees shook so that it was hard to place my feet. My skin was bunched so tightly that I could barely navigate. My damnable teeth would not stop clacking together, do what I would.

Standing over the hole, I realized that I was as near to my enemy as was needful. The time for creeping up secretly was over. I must come out of my camouflaging body and face that thing, spirit to spirit. If, indeed, it had anything so normal as a spirit.

XLV.

Hale Enbo (Ex Corpore)

You seldom realize silence. Now, in that strange place, I knew the sort of stillness that must exist in the centers of dead worlds. Still it was not emptiness—it was . . . waitingness? . . . no! Attention! Bodiless, breathless, emotionless attention.

I must already have moved out from my body enough that my true self could broadcast its energies unhampered. Shocked, I finished the transition abruptly and folded my empty shell outward, away from the city, to await the outcome of this battle. Then I hung, disembodied, in the dimly glowing room and looked through the stone of the floor.

Below me, I could see the latticework of molecular tensions that formed the stuff where my feet had stood. Shifting my focus, I looked deeper into what was no longer darkness but a vortex of energies that held no colors, no real shapes, but awesome power. That vortex looked back at me. Not with eyes that see material things, but with devouring intelligence and greedy acquisitiveness. I was force, myself, and thus subject to its appetite.

It stirred, and I saw the molecules begin to disappear, melting into the enemy as sugar dissolves into water. The stone house was absorbed about us, the walls growing thinner until it took no effort to look out through them and see the sun, now overhead, with the alien city standing about. We were in the middle of the sandwell, surrounded by crooked shapes that seemed to bend forward like spectators at some sports match.

I watched. No other course suggested itself. The ability to

fold myself—and other things—away through space and
even through time was of no use here. To what alternative
time or place might I fold us? I knew too little of it to try
shaping its physical aspect.

It was something to see. When the last vestige of the house
was gone, and the girth of the thing had grown to fill the space
where it had been, it began expanding toward the wall of
sand. It melted into it as if it were a laser. Instead of vaporiz-
ing, however, the sand simply disappeared quietly into the
growing shape that was enemy.

Now I was contained within it, and an inkling of my
function occurred to me. I must endure. I must not be
absorbed. I must hold my own energies inviolate amid that
maelstrom of sucking hunger. For the time that was enough.

In the midst of that dark thing, my perceptions were
obscured. I extended my vision in order that I might see the
entire city from above, and I got a shock. Coming over the
wall toward the pulsing and growing alien were two glimmer-
ings of reflected sunlight. My two faithful Sdnnn were coming to my aid.

The thought of the courage that it took for those two,
reared in the secure sameness of the caverns and unaccustomed to any stress or danger, to approach that ravening
vortex of power . . . it makes me shiver, still. I was moved
to warn them back, but something told me that this, now, was
their function. I saw them come to the edge of the sand-well
and wait for the dissolving-away of the verge.

I spoke to them, within their minds. They were
astonished—they thought that I had been destroyed. We
warmed together at our nearness, and our three spirits held a
tiny antithesis of the giant thing that now held us all.

The enigmatic creature, disturbed at last, began to digest
Sennlik. It began with the old city, and from a point overhead
my vision watched a circle of destruction grow wider and
wider. The nearest of the tall buildings drooped tiredly into
the maw of the alien and was gone. In my present state of
being, I could feel the aura of otherness that the buildings
exuded. What unguessable form of life had set them here,

and for what inscrutable purpose? I felt a pang at their loss.

With every atom it ingested the being grew stronger. Soon I was forced to withdraw the energy required for watching and to concentrate it about the three of us. The suits of the Sdnnn protected them from the physical dangers, I thought, but their minds were at the mercy of the terrors inherent in that fragment of an inimical universe.

The chill was all-enveloping. Even without nerves to convey it or flesh to feel, I was frozen. Worse was the depression that was also a part of that aura. With all the assurance that the Khi had taught me, all the power that I knew I might command, I was swept by tides of black despair. They washed through me like seas through sands, and I knew that my companions must be suffering far more than I.

I joined myself to them. Then I reached far out across Sennlik and folded a segment of warm and gritty desert about us. Though the Sdnnn, of course, could not feel the warmth and would have melted if they could, still they took comfort in the normality of that bubble of desert surrounding them.

We were comforted, and the creature was tormented. I felt it quiver through all its textures. Its energies recoiled, groping about the edges of the thing that now existed within its interior.

Is there black lightning? I would swear that something that can only be described as such flickered about us. We were quiet, there in the clouds as it moiled and twisted around us and pried and battered at the force that held that bit of desert in place.

The thing grew frantic. I had found that I could hold against it if I concentrated all my will upon that. The resistance in its very center seemed to fill it with infuriated frustration. I felt its energies beat about us, and I knew that it had abandoned its attack upon the city while it dealt with the threat within.

Now the battle was joined. I knew that the Sdnnn had served their purpose, guiding me, by their needs, to do the necessary thing to unsettle our enemy. But their danger was about to be multiplied enormously. I folded them away, back to the riverside where the webs of the Khi had glowed, where my own cast-aside body waited.

With the decks cleared for action, I let the desert go and hung suspended inside the blackness, one stubborn spark of life that defied the alien to absorb me. It greeted the departure of the desert as victory—until it discovered that I still existed, individual and undigested, as I had before.

And now I felt the presence of the Khi. Though they could not aid me directly, their nearness lent me confidence. I expanded, forcing the stuff of the creature outward. It reacted violently. It had never, I think, felt resistance of any kind before. As if it were in pain, it writhed and squirmed about me, trying to break through the shield of my will.

As were those bureaucrats in the caverns below, it was a thing locked into a single set of rules. Unless circumstances were covered in its hypothetical and cryptic "book," it was at a loss to cope with them. I expanded inside it, thrusting its blackness outward into a tenuous fog. It forgot hunger in desperation.

Black lightnings played about me, but they were only energies that I, as the enemy had done before, could use to bolster my own. We whirled, there in the sand-pit, rising higher and higher until we rivalled the Sheeash. I forced the thing out until it began to disconnect, segment from segment.

Then I hurled it back together in one swift move, folding it inward . . . and inward . . . and inward, as I had seen my mother fold linens, back on Big Sandy. Now it struggled to expand again, but I had assumed control. Down and down I folded it, compressing it into smaller and smaller compass until it was a black blot that squirmed in the air before me.

Khi-Sang came into focus beside me. I turned to her. "Has it life?" I asked.

She looked long at the thing, deep into it. Then she said, "Of a kind, Hale Enbo. Not our kind or that of any we know. But a kind of life, indeed."

I thought of Thheeer, of the Sdnnn. I thought of the Hril, holding our cosmos in the cup of their thought. "If I could kill it, I would not," I said. "Where does it belong?"

She cocked her glowing head, her not-quite-visible face turned slightly as if she were listening. Then she said, "Fold it thus, then fold it so . . ." and I saw the ways to do it . . . "and the Hril will see that it finds its home again."

I would have nodded, if I had had a head. Then I moved outward and surrounded the enemy with myself, wrapping it into a bundle of essential Hale Enbo, much as Thheeer had been wrapped in his force-bubble. Khi-Sang shone with approval and winked out, though I knew her to be nearby.

I adjusted energies; I rearranged tenuous matter; I regulated the flux of force that connected me with my victim. According to the instructions she had given me, I placed myself and the dark entity in a state totally unlike any other. Sennlik shimmered away as morning mist shimmers away in the sunlight. My awareness of my location, of all the lives on Sennlik evaporated, and I knew that I had been removed from that world—that part of the galaxy—perhaps even that galaxy.

I was near a sun, awash in a sea of brilliant light. There was no other star, no planet. Not even a meteor. There were no gases of the sorts that permeate our spaces. No life marked itself onto my internal grid. I hung, alone except for the detestable being cocooned inside myself, in the midst of bright nothingness.

I drew my senses inward, centered them about that invisible and intangible something that was the ultimate I. If my duty was to wait, then I would wait. In my present state I had no nerves, which was just as well. For company I had the black and writhing being. In that emptiness full of splendor, it looked like an opening into the realm of night.

It was, indeed, a complete lack of light. It existed, seemingly, in a state of ignorance concerning the existence of a complete spectrum of energies. Those that it had used in battling with me had been entirely other, drawn from some source so alien that I now was amazed that I had been able to turn them to my purposes.

It was squirming, frustrated. Cautiously, I opened a channel along that sensation. And looked into a universe of chaos so foreign to all that I had ever known or learned or been that my mind's foundations were shaken. I looked through a tunnel into ultimate negation of all that I was, that the Khi and the Hril dreamed for the universe I knew.

In the fullness of victory, safe in the hands of the Hril, I lost any orientation I had retained. The cosmos spun about me, and I screamed aloud, though voice and mouth were aeons of space away.

XLVI.

Lthhh, the Sdnnn

We were afraid—extremely so. Though our whole lives had been spent in longing to see the surface of our world, to experience all the perils and adventures that must exist there, Lrrr and I knew, when faced with the actuality, that we had also learned fear.

As long as Hale Enbo remained with us, that was subdued, a mere whisper in the backs of our minds. Even when he brought me from the caverns in such a strange fashion I was only a little afraid. The presence of Lrrr, who was formed in the same pool and at the same time as I, gave me courage that I might not have known alone.

Still the thought that some incomprehensible alien was about to consume our planet and all of our people with it was—unsettling. We set out with Hale Enbo and the Oti, ready to do whatever we could manage, but we felt, deep inside, that we were less suited to such endeavors than any other kind of being we could imagine. We have, as all know, no natural weapons. Our energy weapons, Enbo assured us, would only fuel the enemy's strength.

Strangely, it was the Oti who made it plain to us that not always is one's task an obvious thing. Sometimes, he told us, it is enough that you simply exist in a given spot at the proper time. That, we felt, was something we could manage.

Our shock was great when we realized the existence of the Sheeash. Though Lrrr had met one before, he, too, was staggered again when we saw another. No rumor of such beings on our world had even filtered down to any we knew. That added to our fears. How, indeed, could our kind consider themselves the masters of Sennlik when we were so ignorant of all that existed on its surface?

As we shuffled forward, legs aching with the unaccustomed weight of the devices Hale Enbo had made for us to keep our hooves from sinking into the sand, we thought of the questions that we must ask our superiors, if we ever were able to return below. That brought out even more terror. The thought of facing Hrrrak, the master of teachers, with objections to the validity of all that he had taught to newly formed Sdnnn through all his life was enough to make us turn pink.

Then Lrrr thought of something else . . . worse. "We must go to Hrrrll, the master bureaucrat. He must add to the directives all that we have learned here, so that others of our kind may know. Now that it is obvious that we can survive on the surface in force-suits, others will surely venture upward. Not all are so close-minded as Hrrrak and Hrrrll."

Shuddering at the thought, I agreed. I could envision those two, enraged at being questioned and, worse yet, taught by their inferiors. They were of the variety of Sdnnn that Hale Enbo calls spider-shaped. The sight of the red anger suffusing their many limbs is enough to strike horror into any Sdnnn alive. In contrast, the prospect of being devoured by some dark entity from another kind of cosmos began to seem positively inviting. So, having frightened ourselves into enthusiasm for the task at hand, we went along more cheerfully.

However, our arrival at the sand-clogged city brought us back to ourselves. We are not a people who must build shelters. Though we know that less-fortunate kinds must do so, we had never seen a city. On another world, where it would be a natural thing to expect, it would have been an interesting novelty. This city stood on the surface of our own world, and no Sdnnn had ever dreamed that it was there!

It breathed terrible age. Our caverns are, of course, as old as our world, but they are living parts of the bones of the planet, changing slowly with the changing of time. These built things were made of some stonelike substance that was not and never had been alive, as we felt the stone and ice and liquids of our environs to be. It was more terrifying, even, than the Sheeash, to see this alien place.

We stood on the wall with Hale Enbo, watching Thheeer
float among the buildings. Though Enbo could see through
the Oti's senses, Lrrr and I could only stand there and worry.
In our short acquaintance with that queer being, we had
learned that one's friends need not be encased in matter to be
esteemed. We had a strange feeling that Thheeer would not
return to us from that ill-seeming place.

A long time passed. We could see on Enbo's face a tension
that spoke of worry. When Thheeer's bubble paused long
above a sand-humped roof our companion spoke aloud to
him. We knew that the Oti was about to risk some dangerous
action. Straining to see, we watched as he let the force-
bubble roll away from himself. Even in the sunlight, we
could see his lightnings played against that dark stone.

We knew that he could survive for only the shortest of
times without his bubble. It was with grief that we saw him
sink through the stone and disappear. When Hale Enbo drew
a long breath and sat upon the wall, we, too, felt dimly the
passing of our friend.

Then the Sheeash came across the desert. The air grew
thick with sand, as we stood regarding the impossible task of
moving all the stuff from the building we sought. We hurried
for shelter, and when we came out again the Sheeash had dug
away all the age-old accumulation from about the structure
that Thheeer had found. Our frustration at being unable to
enter it was great, but we knew that our Primate friend was
correct.

When he sent us away from the city we went in a divided
mental state. Thankful to leave the danger behind, we were
still unhappy at being sent away like untaught young from the
scene of the work our friend was attempting. We didn't go
far, only to the top of a dune that gave us a good view of the
city.

Enbo went away into the hole. For a long time we could see
and sense nothing. Then we saw to our horror that the
building was growing *thinner*. We could see, dimly at first,
the houses on its other side coming into view. But nowhere
could we see Hale Enbo, though we both felt his presence
there.

A huge black thing came into view as the last of the house disappeared. It was growing alarmingly, and it seemed to be consuming the sand about it and eating into the stone house nearest it. And Enbo was there, somewhere, in the middle of it.

Lrrr looked into my eyes. I bobbed my head. Neither of us would have had the courage to go, alone, into that dark mass. Together we had just barely enough to see us to the edge of the hole where it whirled. Then we felt Enbo strongly, and he spoke inside our heads, as the Oti had used to do.

Then we learned what fear truly was. Though the thing could not attack our bodies because of the suits, it was enough to shatter our minds and spirits. It was filled with terrible things that had no counterparts among our kind. Hungers and compulsions shook us to our very hooves, though we could neither understand nor fulfill them. We looked into the heart of all that despises life. We knew that we were lost.

Though he seemed to have no body, our companion was very strong now. He formed about us a portion of the desert. We could see the heat shimmer on the sun-brightened sand, though the being about us held all sight of the sun from our position. We could hear the patter of blown sand against our suits, and the homely sound distracted our thoughts from the horrors of the dark outside that bit of desert.

So we stood, comforted and strengthened, enduring while the thing moved all around us as if our presence caused it pain. It grew darker, still, and strange black energies struck against the walls that held our desert in and the thing out. Then Hale Enbo spoke into our minds the fact that because of our presence he now knew how to battle this enemy. With that he did something odd with space, and we found ourselves beside the river that we had left so many days before.

The sun was setting. The trees across the river were dark against the reddish light, and it was a moment before our eyes grew accustomed to the dimness. When we looked about we saw that Hale Enbo's body lay beneath two of the trees where the Khi patterns had been. He lay awkwardly, as if he'd been flung and forgotten. We felt that his true self had been too busy to see to the comfort of his physical self.

We straightened it carefully, laying the head on a clump of grass and putting the arms neatly at the sides. We had no feeling that our friend lay here—this was his equipment, set aside for the moment. So we tended his possession for him and waited beside it.

The sun was now down, though gold still glowed high in the sky. Freed of our task, we could savor this upper world, as night brought the stars out.

They blazed in the sky, worlds and peoples among them that I would never know, though some might find their ways into our caverns someday. I looked up and saw stars, down and saw grass, outward and saw starlit sands. It was enough, I felt, and Lrrr agreed, that even if our friend lost his battle and all we knew must end, we have lived more fully than any other Sdnnn ever ventured to.

Day followed the night, then another sunset. Then Hale Enbo's body opened its mouth and screamed.

XLVII.

Hale Enbo (Ex Corpore)

I saw again the dimension of the Hril that had been shown to me long ago. The inevitable and mathematically satisfying shapes of not-quite-plants and surely-not-buildings hung before my eyes in seeming solidity. Analogs that my mind created in order that I might interpret them comprehensibly.

The conical shapes that were in some sense the Hril moved along their paths. One moved toward me. Its great eye swallowed me up, and the thing that I held captive was swallowed, too. And then I hung in a warmth of concern and order that slowed the wild swingings of the universe until they settled into the old patterns. Once again I knew the answers to all the impossible questions asked by every race that has evolved past the animal. I knew. I understood. I gloried in the fantastic beauty of it. But there was sadness, too, for I knew that it would be lost to me when I returned to my own place.

Still, the thing that was the purpose of the Hril was done. I was myself again, and the thing of darkness was removed from me into the care of the Hril. As the diamond light faded, I felt the wrenching that denotes being folded through space.

I existed in another place entirely. I saw it as if through a force-shield, and it was soon apparent that the shield was necessary. Chaos ruled the realm about me. Extend my sensing as I would, I could find nothing alive, nothing patterned and ordered like the cyclings and fluxes that my own universe knew. Yet interwoven with that roiling darkness were energies like that which I had conquered, unalive but there.

239

I could discern, amid the teeming nihilism, an activity that was alien to it. I focused upon that, drawing myself nearer to it by the force of my will. Wonder filled me.

Khi-Sang was there, her golden shape shining like a sun amid the chaotic darkness. She held in her hands the shape that I had removed from Sennlik. As I watched, she moved her hands, and the thing in them expanded.

She grew to match its increasing mass, her hands retaining their control over it. When she had filled the entire area that I watched, and the thing was heaving and struggling within her grip, she flung it from her into the black hell that had spawned it.

She spoke four syllables. I heard them, even through the tumult that filled the space. They moved from her like golden birds and printed themselves across the face of the black spaces. Shiningly alien to all that existed there, they stood out like a warning sign between the world of life and the world of negation.

A voice inside me said, "Mark well the shapes of those who dwell here. They must not escape again into the ways of life."

I understood. The warning was posted, the guards set. The lesson had been taught. But should any of the entities here attempt to disregard them, I would be called again to do battle. Those energy-forms etched themselves into my senses.

Khi-Sang turned to me, her not-quite-visible face glowing gently. She reached her hand, and it linked us immaterially across the space between. "Let us go back," she said, her voice ringing through the inarticulate uproar.

Her words ran like fire across the billowing darkness, edging its clouds with brightness. I felt the presence of the Hril about us, even as we folded space and were elsewhere.

XLVIII.

Hale Enbo

I woke into flesh. Stiff and lethargic, I stirred my muscles, moved my protesting bones.

The Sdnnn, on either side of me, turned their long necks and looked down at me, their big dark eyes anxious. "You cried out," said Lrrr. "We were concerned, for you had not yet returned to your body. Is all well?"

I surmised that the two had suffered agonies of worry in the time of their waiting. I groaned to a sitting position and leaned against a tree. "All is very well," I answered. "The thing is back in its own place, and if it can learn, it must have done so. The Khi have set a warning against its return, yet if it or any of its kind should try to come again I know what to do to stop them."

They nodded solemnly. Then Lthhh asked, rather shyly, "Are you hungry? We saved your foodstuff from your pack for you."

This, more than anything, touched me. Beings that do not need regular meals have a tendency to forget that others do need them. Yet these two, out of their element, out of their sphere of knowledge, out, indeed, of their depths, had remembered that Hale Enbo is always hungry.

Though when in my expanded state I don't really need food and drink and rest, still I am completely capable of enjoying all three (and several more). Grinning from ear to ear, I reached for the pack Lrrr handed me. Dried fruits never tasted so delicious. Lthhh hurried to the stream and filled the water carrier that I'd conjured up for crossing the desert. That drink had a freshness that water seldom had before.

When I had finished, I stood. "My friends," I said, the Sdnnn rolling off my tongue with ease, "are you ready to go home?"

They danced on their pointed hooves, leaving the heart-shaped prints in the soil beneath them. "We are, indeed. We have seen and done and been more than our kind have ever before attempted. Now we must go back and teach our teachers."

I laughed. The scarlet-lined figure of the VIP whom I had so infuriated rose in my imagination. It would be redder, still, when these two brash youngsters finished their tale, I thought.

Without ado, I folded us down into the Caves of Sennlik, where the chill squinched my brown skin into goose pimples at once, and the sweat of the desert lay clammy in my clothing. I had reckoned precisely. We winked into being in the office of that very VIP, the one my companions called Hrrrll.

Without speaking to the startled Sdnnn, I linked with the big computer that crowded the office, feeding into it the entire history of the adventure just ended, as well as the complete memories of the Sheeash, as Thheeer had given them to me. Then, leaving Lthhh and Lrrr to tell their own tales in their own ways, I folded myself to the office of the Epfelen.

He was napping, of course, on the ceiling with his youngest. When I woke him he slithered down the wall as quickly as one of his sort could move, shook himself out into furry rotundity, and settled into his deep chair. "My dear fellow, I'm delighted to see you," he rumbled. "I'd never dreamed that this dreary hole could be as interesting as it has been since your unexpected departure." He looked gravely at the ceiling, and the eye that I could see slowly closed in a wink.

"You must tell me the whole story. Those idiots will wring all the juice out of it, reduce it to dusty facts and figures, then issue a report. I want to hear it with all its fur on." Here he was interrupted by Grynn, who heard the word story and came scrambling down to take his place in his father's lap.

"Grynn!" I said, and the young one bounced with delight that I remembered him.

"Sherbet?" it rumbled. Heff said, "Maybe later. Now be quiet, or some quick-frozen bureaucrat will come barging in and do us out of our tale."

I settled into the pleasant warmth of the Epfelens' quarters and told Heff and Grynn the story, leaving out nothing at all. When I was done, they both sighed (very bass sighs) and Heff said, "We've picnicked up there a dozen times. . . . Camped out there, too. *We* never got to see a Sheeash. *We* never found a city older than it has a right to be. Some people have all the luck. Why we've never met one of the Khi, though they seem to be showing themselves more and more."

"That I can remedy," I said. Khi-Sang, Khi-Rehm, and Khi-Lohm glimmered into being near the air curtain that shielded the door from the outer chill.

Both Epfelen grew big-eyed and very polite. But I had more reason than one for summoning the three. "Would you check on Lrrr and Lthhh?" I asked. "I've a feeling the Master of Bureaucrats isn't believing a word they say. They'll be pleased to see you, I'm certain. There is no possibility that even a VIP can cast doubt on the word of the Khi."

They shone their golden smiles on the Epfelen and winked out.

"Whoosh!" said Heff. "You're full of surprises, Hale Enbo. I never thought I'd have *three* of 'em blink into my own office, say how-d'ye-do and blink right out again. I think it's time for some sherbet to cool our nerves. Eh?"

Grynn and I agreed with enthusiasm, and the robot was sent for. While we wrapped ourselves around lime sherbet, Heff gave a graphic description of the tumult that had followed my escape.

"You won't believe it, but it was days before they thought to check on the Oti (poor chap). You see, nobody could ever go into his rooms, and as long as all the telltales said his gases and electrical impulses were being fed into the place at the proper times, nobody thought to look. When Hrlll found out

that he was gone too, you'd have thought an earthquake had
struck the place.

"Everyone who had had anything to do with you was
called on the carpet . . . even Grynn and me! Of course they
had to tread lightly with us, but they trampled on the Sdnnn
pretty harshly.

"When Lrrr didn't return down the shaft and later parties
found no trace of any of you . . . well, it was something to
see. They knew that Lthhh had been as close to you as Lrrr,
and they were in the process of grilling him when you popped
in, grabbed him, and popped out again. What went before
was nothing. It was foaming fits, after that." He chuckled his
fruity chuckle and I grinned along with him.

Then I sobered. "It's very funny, and everything turned
out well for everyone except Thheeer. He was . . . well, we
were pretty close. It's a pity he had to be the one to suffer."

"Hum! Ho! Here, my boy, the Oti don't exactly suffer—
or die either. Not in the sense of cease-to-exist. When their
energies are snuffed the selves are rerouted. He'll pop up
again—maybe as a Varlian or a Fssa or even an Epfelen. You
and I may not meet him again, but that mind of his won't be
wasted, you can be sure." Heff looked at me benevolently. I
smiled back.

"You've eased my mind," I said. "And speaking of
minds, can you make sure that all the stuff I put into the
computer will be shared with the Oti? Thheeer fused with me
so that if he didn't return all his new knowledge wouldn't be
lost to his kind."

Heff nodded. "Can do. Anything else?"

I rose from the chair and patted Grynn's furry head. "Not a
thing, chum. Now it's time to go. I don't intend to be put back
into the hostage quarters, even though I could come right out
again, now. By the bye, if you hear a certain amount of . . .
uproar . . . after I leave, don't worry. I've a debt to pay for
an old friend."

His dark eyes widened, then narrowed, while a snort of
laughter gusted from him. "You're not . . . ?" he gasped.

"Every last one," I replied, and folded myself away.

As I folded I invisibly and nonphysically punched every

button in the entire complex of the Caves of Sennlik. The resulting chaos followed me as I moved by short hops through the caverns, marveling a last time at the blue ice and the blue light and the sudden cessation of the blue voice.

I peeped into Hrrrll's office as I passed. The VIP was scarlet from tentacle-tip to spiderleg-tip. His office had gone mad, with alarms buzzing, bells ringing, screechers screeching. The big computer was hiccupping gently. The Khi were there, glimmering with amusement.

Lrrr and Lthhh, after a short start, looked at one another.

I left Sennlik with a sense of accomplishment. I had taught two of the Sdnnn to laugh.

XLIX.

Khi-Sang

He has gone again, our friend Hale Enbo. Back into that light-hearted young self that we envy so much. Who else, among all the billions of lives in the cosmos, would so choose for a second time? Yet it is no less than we expected of him.

We stand before the diamond wall. Beyond it the Hril go about their lives, making and unmaking among their dreams and thoughts. They seem happy, as well they should. I can admit now that when they proposed choosing a Primate as the instrument for saving their worlds from destruction we of the Khi thought that their long lives were ending in madness. Which only proves that we ourselves aren't nearly so old or so wise as we like to think.

The blue stone-child still radiates energies from its perch in the blue world. I would like to return there with its father, one day, to think happy thoughts toward it. When will that be?

Even we cannot know. I think that the Hril do not know. Only Hale Enbo will know when he considers himself grown up enough to be immortal and all-powerful.

As for us, there is much to do among the dimensions. And we of the Khi are immune to time.

BEST-SELLING
Science Fiction
and
Fantasy

MORE SCIENCE FICTION! ADVENTURE

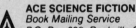